DANGEROUS
GAMES

DANGEROUS GAMES

a novel

KEITH MORRIS

Covenant Communications, Inc.
Covenant

Cover design © 2004 by Covenant Communications, Inc.
Cover images: running silhouette © Comstock Images/Getty Images;
    Salt Lake City Olympic City by Jessica A. Warner.

Published by Covenant Communications, Inc.
American Fork, Utah

This is a work of fiction. The characters, names, incidents, places, and dialogue are products of the author's imagination, and are not to be construed as real.

Printed in Canada
First Printing: June 2004

10 09 08 07 06 05 04   10 9 8 7 6 5 4 3 2 1

ISBN 1-59156-528-6

PROLOGUE

Somewhere over the Sea of Japan
The B-29 *Morning Glory*
Altitude: 22,000 feet
Sunday, March 18, 1951, 0130 hours

The world is so calm up here, Captain Sykes thought to himself. He usually found the blackness of night comforting when he was flying. If he couldn't see anything out there, then he knew no one could see his beloved plane. Radar, of course, could and probably would spot him. That didn't bother him though. He wasn't going where the enemy expected. The argument could be made that where he was going, the people weren't even the enemy.

Yet.

The world may have been calm, but Captain Paul Sykes, USAF, wasn't. He was jumpy, and thankfully the constant shake of the plane hid the almost uncontrollable twitching of his hands. He'd managed to hide his nervousness from his copilot, Lieutenant Pike, but he couldn't hide it from himself. He couldn't escape it. Well, he thought, that's not all I won't be able to escape.

"Cap?" It was his navigator, Lieutenant Campbell.

"What is it, Campbell?" At flight school, Sykes had been the last one in his class to get the hang of speaking into his mask. But the sound of *Morning Glory* was deafening, and if you wanted to communicate, you did it.

This was his plane. He'd named it. Before he joined the air force, Sykes had once seen a B-29 taking off in the early morning hours, and it had blocked out the sun. It was a sight to behold. At the time he saw it, it was the largest bomber in the world. He knew then he wanted to be a pilot, and the name for his future plane came to him: *Morning Glory.*

"We're nearing North Korean air space."

"Thanks. You worried?" Sykes asked.

"Naw," Campbell's southern accent was as foreign to Paul Sykes as the Japanese he heard around Yakuza Air Base. "I don't 'spect any trouble from the NKs just now."

No, Sykes thought. "Hope it stays that way."

The *Morning Glory* was speeding at 220 miles per hour toward a rendezvous with fate. Captain Sykes hoped it wouldn't be a one-way mission. He hoped that maybe, just maybe, they'd be welcomed home as heroes. That was what that colonel had said.

"What was his name?" Sykes mumbled. Colonel . . . Green. Yes, that was it, Colonel Green. Green had promised Sykes that he and his crew would be like the cavalry coming to the rescue.

"Don't you want to be a hero, Captain? You would be like the Seventh Cavalry riding to the rescue on the plains. A hero." Green had paused for effect. "Your name, the pilot's name, will be remembered throughout history. School children will learn about your flight, your mission, and they will know your name. Don't you want that?"

"Yes, sir." Riding to the rescue, Captain Paul Edward Sykes and the rest of the cavalry, saving the day. Being a real hero! Sykes smiled, "Yes, sir, I do."

"Very good, Captain. That's why I chose you for this mission."

When Colonel Green told him what the mission was, it was crystal clear why no one else on his flight team had been involved with the briefing. Yes, crystal clear.

It suddenly occurred to Sykes, that he, a captain in the U.S. Air Force, had been briefed by an army colonel. Why hadn't he noticed that then? That was odd. Outside the chain of command. Sykes assumed his COs knew about and approved the mission.

Maybe they hadn't.

Sykes now doubted that Green was even really *in* the army, let alone a colonel. Green said he was from General MacArthur's personal staff, and the mission *was* a reality. Maybe he was army after all. Sykes followed Green's orders not to brief his crew on the mission. In fact, Green ordered him to lie to his men, men he trusted with his life. And they trusted him with theirs. He did lie. They weren't headed for the reservoir above the Yalu River. They were going much farther than that. Would they still trust him?

Now, at 22,000 feet and headed for Manchuria, it was no longer crystal clear. In fact it was a murky haze, and Sykes's smile was long gone.

Sykes looked over at Pike. He looked nervous too, and *he* didn't even know the real mission.

"Hey, Pike, you're a history nut, right?"

"What, Captain?"

Stupid intercom! "You like history?" Sykes asked again.

"Yeah, sure, Cap."

"You know anything about the Seventh Cav?"

"What? Cap, we got a mission and stuff. Couldn't we talk . . . ?"

"No." Sykes was impatient now. "Just tell me. Okay?"

"All right. Very famous unit. Started out as horse cavalry. Fought in the Civil War and later in the Plains Wars against the Sioux. You ever heard of Little Big Horn?"

Pike thought he was so smart. "Of course I've heard . . ." Sykes stopped speaking. The Seventh Cav—that was Custer's unit. Why would Green compare them to the Seventh Cav? Custer and *all* of his men got wiped out. Destroyed.

Sykes had no intention of dying like Custer.

Pike was still talking. ". . . Totally mechanized now though. Haven't had horses for close to four decades now. I think they're out of Fort Hood. But it could be Fort Benning. I'm not really sure . . ."

Sykes tuned him out again. Custer may have died, but *Morning Glory* wasn't a horse; the Chinese weren't Sitting Bull, Red Cloud, or two thousand Sioux warriors; and they weren't going to fight a battle on ground. In fact, there wouldn't even be a battle—just a cloud in the sky and death on the ground. His smile returned, a grim monument on his face, invisible under the mask. He wasn't going to die. This time the Seventh Cav would not be the victim.

"Hey, Pike. What was the name of that plane that bombed Japan?"

"Plane, Cap? Thousands bombed Japan. Boy, you sure must be nervous. Just a minute ago you asked me about . . ."

Sykes ignored him. No, there weren't thousands, there was only one. *The* plane that bombed Japan. His brow furrowed in thought, and his eyes grew wide in surprise and recognition. *Enola Gay*. It too was a B-29, and the *Enola Gay* had carried a payload similar to the *Morning Glory*'s. Even six years after its historic mission, he could still remember the name. He wondered how long people would remember the *Morning Glory*. Colonel Green said it would go down in history. Even if his name was forgotten, lost to history, if his plane was remembered, then he would be too. Yes, they were the cavalry coming to the rescue of the wagon train.

"Listen up, everybody." Sykes knew he had to tell his crew, his friends. Besides, soon, when they flew beyond the Yalu River, they would want an explanation. "Pay attention. We have new orders. We are not going to the Yalu River."

Everyone started talking at once. "We're what? Cap?"

"Sir?"

"Where?"

Sykes went on. "Listen up! Quiet! No, we are not going where you thought, and our mission has changed. We are going to hit the forward deployment base of the Communist Chinese Third Shock Army, sixty-five miles inside Manchuria."

There was a short pause, then Sykes's headset exploded with noise. "Hit China?"

"Why, Cap?"

"Are we at war with the Chinese now?"

Through it all, Sykes could make out the voice of his copilot. "I don't get it, Cap. What good is one plane, even a B-29 Super

Fortress, going to do against a base of that magnitude? I mean, will the Chinese even know we're there?"

Yes, they would know. But only for an instant. "Everyone calm down and relax. This is just another run. We have our mission, and our mission is to drop a hydrogen bomb."

The silence was heavy, and then it began again. The noise exploded in his headset, and he took it off. But he still heard someone ask, "Isn't this wrong?"

Wrong? How could it be wrong? Everyone knew the Chinese were openly helping the North Koreans. The marines were killing Chinese troops on the ground anyway. How many marines had been slaughtered by the Chinese around the Chosin Reservoir? They had killed marines as they tried to escape over the frozen land. It lasted for weeks, the chase south back from the Manchurian border. It was a total humiliation. The marines made it back as best as they could, and still the Chinese came killing the marines. The Chinese were already in the war. No, it wasn't wrong.

It was about time.

The Japanese bombed Pearl Harbor on the Sabbath; no one was prepared for it. It was a devastating, stunning attack, an honestly brilliant bit of military planning. Most of America thought of it as a sneak attack, and Sykes did too. But as a bomber pilot, a modern-day warrior trained to rain destruction on his country's enemies, he couldn't help but acknowledge the genius of the attack on Pearl Harbor.

He was thirteen years old when Pearl Harbor was attacked. Almost thirteen. That war had ended before he could enlist. Now, this was his war, his chance to fight for his country. He was young, unmarried, an officer in the United States Air Force, and in command of his own plane. Destruction and devastation obeyed his commands. He smiled.

Sykes didn't pretend to know when, or even if, the Chinese had a Sabbath day, and he didn't really care. This was also a brilliant bit of planning, as bold as Pearl Harbor, but with far greater consequences. He was supremely confident that they would be successful. He knew too that they, and the *Morning Glory*, would go down in history as heroes. Victors of a war with communist China that would never be fought because of their actions.

The *Morning Glory* flew on unseen by anyone. But Captain Paul Sykes and his crew would fail in their mission. They were never forgotten by their families.

They were forgotten by history.

chapter 1

The face of Carol, the anchorwoman for KSL, filled the screen. The caption beneath her read *Breaking News in Utah County*. She had a serious look on her face, so I decided to listen.

I was on a treadmill at the new Deseret Health and Fitness Club. It was after work, and while I normally don't consider gym time as good time, I figured it couldn't hurt me either. It reminded me of jogging at Quantico. That's in Virginia, and it's where I lived for a while. Reminded me of it except here there are big mountains and it's not humid.

Anyway, I slowed to a walk and turned up the volume on the TV in front of me. I could hear Carol the Anchorwoman now.

"Recapping the breaking news out of Utah County, a body was discovered in the charred remains of a warehouse in Springville. The fire burned through the night. It wasn't until late morning that investigators were able to search the rubble. The Utah County Sheriff's Office announced the discovery of the body just a short time ago, and have identified the man as Jason P. Russell, a local sculptor. They are still trying to ascertain whether foul play was involved. Now, Mark at the KSL national news desk has another breaking story. Mark?"

The camera switched to Mark at the national news desk. "Thank you, Carol. It was just three months ago today that an unidentified terrorist group detonated a crude biological weapon in Torino, Italy, site of the 2006 Winter Olympic Games. While thankfully the death count was lower than expected because of the small size and crude construction of the weapon, it unfortunately doused the city with deadly strains of anthrax and Ebola. With the Olympics now just six months away, the World Health Organization officially announced today that they will keep the tourism ban in effect and that the clean-up efforts have not been sufficient to keep the games in Torino."

Taped footage showed what Mark described, then the camera was back on Mark. "As you know, other cities have been preparing to serve as emergency host of the games. The Norwegian government has offered the use of facilities at Lillehammer, host of the 1994 winter games. Lake Placid, New York, host in 1980, and Nagano, Japan, 1998, have also offered to host the games in the wake of the horrible bombing."

I thought that was nice of them.

"The IOC announced its decision today. It recognized the hospitality of Norway, Japan, and Lake Placid, but decided against them." He was smiling now. Beaming. I noticed that the vast majority of TVs in the cardio area were all tuned to KSL. Small groups of people were gathered around the TVs. Mark paused, smiled again, and said, "The IOC has chosen *Salt Lake City* as the emergency host of the 2006 Winter Olympic Games!"

All the people at the gym broke out in cheers.

All except for me.

I got a pain in my gut that didn't come from the jogging.

Six Months Later
Thursday, February 2, 2006

Working part-time security for the LDS Church doesn't pay much, which is why I was at my other job. Not that I don't like my part-time job; I do. It's the best job in the world, aside from the money. Anyway. It was a cold day. Business was slow. I had decided against going back to work for someone else, besides the Church. So I'd opened my own business. It's called Grant Consulting and Investigations. I'm Grant. I consult and investigate. I thought about calling my business Grant, Private Investigator Services. You know, Grant, PI. But I don't drive a Ferrari, and Utah is not Hawaii. Oh, and I look nothing like Tom Selleck.

Well, maybe just a little.

Really.

It was late. The sun had been down for hours. Northern Utah was being hit by a snowstorm. Three inches had already fallen, and the word was there would be more. I hate snow. Maybe I should move to Hawaii.

My office is in a small street-level complex. A strip mall, I guess. There is no sign above my door or in the strip mall's neon parking lot sign. Small letters on the front door proclaim what I do and who I am. I don't want external signs. People who need my help and experience will find me. My office is the business, not some flashy sign.

I have a large mahogany desk. I love my desk, the color, the sheen. It cost me a fortune, but it was worth every penny. It's spacious and it affords me more than enough room. I also love the captain's chair I sit in when I'm at my beautiful desk. It's black and leather. A laptop computer sits on my desk, which I guess makes it a desktop computer. There are no pictures on my desk or on the wall. I don't know anyone that I would have pictures of anyway. Not my ex-wife. No children. My parents are deceased. My father spent some time in the U.S. Diplomatic Corps. They were good people.

I have an older brother. I was the "oops" child; I wasn't planned on. My brother and I are almost seven years apart in age. We're friends and love each other and all that. He and his family live in New Hampshire. He went there for law school and stayed. I think he is a divorce lawyer. Divorce lawyers cost more than being married, so I'm sure he makes good money. I hear it's a growth business. Anyway, we keep in touch. Pictures of my parents and my brother and his family are at my home. I have some friends, and I have lost some friends. I don't need pictures to remember them.

The ones that are gone are never forgotten.

I was tired but wasn't ready to go home yet. The small bell attached to the front door jingled and jarred me from my thoughts. I stared. Someone I had not seen in a long time walked through my door. Six foot one, and blond. Blue eyes. Athletic. Probably popular in high school. Mr. Student Body President/ Captain of the Football Team walked into my office. I knew him from the FBI. He was good at his job. Actually, I'd seen him last week on the basketball court, but a week can be a long time. It all depends on your perspective and who the person is. I don't hesitate to say that we are not buddies, because we're not. But I knew he wouldn't be here unless he needed something. I didn't get up and he didn't sit down. Just stood there.

"Hello, Grant," he said.

"Hello, Cook," I said. There was a forced politeness to our words. "How is the Bureau, Cook?"

"Better than the day you left."

I doubt that. "Really." I am somewhat of a minor legend. I specialized in violent crimes and in solving the unsolvable. I stopped that serial killer in Sacramento when no one else could. I left the FBI before I was forty, and everyone thought I was crazy. I joined the Bureau when I was twenty-four, and I left when I was thirty-six. I grew to not like it. I loved the work; I just didn't like the FBI. Maybe I'm just a minor legend in my own mind.

He nodded, slowly and deliberately.

We stared at each other for a full ten seconds.

"Why are you here, Cook? It's late and I don't like having the FBI around after dark. It's bad for business."

"From what I've heard, you have no business to hurt."

He was right.

So what.

"I don't need career advice from the likes of you, Cook. Leave."

"It might help. Don't pretend you aren't glad to see me, Grant. I was thinking I owe you for that cheap foul on the court last week. And why should I leave?"

I could think of plenty of reasons, but only shared my two favorites with him. "Well, number one, this is personal property, and you were not invited in. You are not pursuing a suspect, and you're not investigating a crime. So your unwelcome, unjustified presence in, on, or around my private property violates my constitutional rights. And number two, maybe I just don't like having you around. Pick one."

He looked at me, and I at him. He smiled.

"What do you want, Agent Cook?"

His response must have been painful. "I need your help. I need one of the best, and that's still you."

One thing I've learned is to *never* believe a compliment that comes from the FBI. But I was instantly interested. I know I am one of the best, and I don't need anyone from the FBI to remind me of it. "What's happened?"

"There's been a murder."

"Where?"

"Spanish Fork. South Utah County. Been there, Grant?"

No. "Sure. Why are the feds concerned with a murder in Spanish Fork, Utah? They have a police department. There's probably a sheriff too. Let them handle it."

"I can't tell you why right now."

Let me translate that. In Bureauspeak he was telling me that I was no longer in the FBI, and he wouldn't tell me unless I had a need to know. Obviously he didn't think I had a need to know. I hate this stuff. That's one reason why I left in the first place.

"If you want my help, you better reconsider."

Cook was quiet for a heartbeat, then made a decision. "I can't tell you everything, but I'll tell you what I can. In recent months we have come across the trail of a man, a terrorist, we would dearly love to catch. He has eluded us, Scotland Yard, Interpol, and the rest of the world's law enforcement for twenty-plus years now. The opportunity to stop him is why I'm here."

"It's not . . . ?" 9-11 was a few short years ago and still a fresh memory.

"No, it's not Al-Qaeda. This guy's Korean. North Korean. One of Pyong Yang's favorite men. We don't even know his real name, and he goes by numerous aliases. We do know he lived in South Korea until his early twenties, approximately."

"Approximately?"

"Yes, Grant. Approximately. FBI. NSA. CIA. MI-6. Interpol. No one has a decent picture of him. The South Koreans have a few high school pictures of him. Which are useless after more than twenty years and who knows how many plastic surgeries. We know he attended the KGB American School in Moscow in the late eighties, before the Wall came down. Undoubtedly he's been trained by the Chinese intelligence branches as well. We think this guy was one of the masterminds behind that attack on the South Korean president in 1983. It was successful too. That's it."

I smiled. "You suspect he was involved with a murder in Spanish Fork?"

"Maybe."

"But why?"

"I'm not prepared to detail our basis for this to you right now. Maybe later. I need your help."

"You misunderstand me, Cook. Why me? If this involves any federal crime, even some stupid misdemeanor, you have authority to take over any investigation. You know that, Cook." Cook and I are good at this. We pretend to not like each other, but each knows that we respect one another. Like I said, we're not buddies. I wouldn't go to a bar with him to share a beer. We don't drink. But we are not enemies, either. Otherwise, I wouldn't play basketball with him.

He gave me an exasperated look. One that said, Please just trust me.

I don't trust. Except for partners and close friends. It's kept me alive in a career that sometimes comes to an unfortunate and sudden end.

"We were caught off guard by the Olympics coming back here, and we're spread pretty thin. The director knows you, and so do I. We thought you wouldn't mind helping."

"Really?" That was a better explanation than that "you're one of the best" line.

"Really. Look, we can't prove anything. There's an outside chance this terrorist is involved in the murder. If he is, it could be a diversion for something bigger. Maybe it's just your everyday homicide. We don't have time to find out. And if we got involved right now, it would just complicate things."

"You mean it would put your target on alert."

"You're getting ahead of me, Grant—"

"He would know you were looking for him, and most likely this would have one of two effects. He would either go into hiding or become even more brazen and possibly kill more people. And if I get caught in the middle and end up dead, it's no skin off the FBI's nose."

"Something like that," he admitted.

"You knew I spent some time in Korea, didn't you?"

"Yeah. Did you ever learn the language?"

"No. And my posting with the Bureau in Korea only lasted about a year."

"I know. But you made some good contacts there, and you may need to go back to Korea. You can ask some unofficial questions that we can't. Will you help?"

I thought about it. I'd already decided to help, but I wanted Cook to stew for a few minutes. "What do I get out of it?"

His right arm reached out to me. He was holding something, giving it to me. It was my FBI identification. "You will have very limited arrest powers. Raise your right hand, Grant."

I did. Cook went on. "By order of the director, Federal Bureau of Investigation, and for the duration of this assignment only, you are hereby granted all the rights and privileges associated with the FBI credentials. I suppose that ID may be effective in opening some doors." I took it from him. "Just don't upset the local cops, okay?"

"I want computer access too. Same security clearance."

"Why?"

"Because I might need access to the FBI database and all the rest of it, Cook. Done?"

Cook nodded. "I'll take care of it tonight. I'll e-mail a tech at Quantico. Good enough?"

"Good enough," I said.

Cook went on, filling me in about what happened in Spanish Fork. The killing had occurred sometime between 6:00 and 8:00 p.m. He'd arranged for the body to remain where it was found until 7:00 a.m. tomorrow morning, or until I could see it. The local ME was not happy about that, but she had agreed to the request. It had been a violent death, and they suspected the victim had been tortured.

"Okay, I will. But, Cook, I need to know how the FBI picked up the trail of this terrorist. I can't go into a situation like this blind."

"All right, but this is top secret information. We have reason to believe that over the past two years someone has been feeding information to the man that we want to catch and stop."

I was not prepared for his answer. "Wait just a second, Cook. You mean inside information was leaked. FBI information? A traitor?"

"Yes. A traitor. Most likely in the FBI." Cook held his hand up. "We don't know who the double agent is. So don't bother asking."

"Is the traitor connected with the Korean terrorist?"

"I told you, we simply don't know. Could be in our Istanbul office. Could be in our Toronto office. Maybe here. Don't ask for more, 'cause I honestly can't help you. And no, before you ask, CIA and MI-6 have confirmed the Korean terrorist is not connected with the group that hit Italy."

Okay. "Where was the body found?"

"Some place called the Relief Mine. Ever heard of it, Grant?"

"No. Should I have?"

"I don't know. Maybe you should read up on your Church history. Keep in touch, Grant." He turned to leave.

"Wait a minute, Cook. I'm leaving the country in five days."

"Why?"

"My day job. Going to northern Asia. In fact, I think we're going to South Korea. Maybe I'll run into this North Korean terrorist. We could have lunch or something."

He looked grim. "Watch your back, Grant. Odds are he'll know who you are soon enough."

So there really was a problem with someone leaking information to the bad guys. "It may be hard to do any investigating when I'm gone."

Cook didn't like this. "Just fill me in before you leave. I assume you know the number." He left my office.

I was suddenly tired. More tired than I'd been in a long time. The FBI was sucking me back in. I could almost hear the sucking sound.

I hate that sound.

Friday, February 3, 2006, 2:46 a.m.

I had the dream again. My last partner in the FBI was Dan Begay. Full-blooded Navajo. We were like brothers. He was the first LDS partner I had in the FBI. He grew up with an LDS family in some small southern Utah town. He called them his "white family."

We were at a bank robbery in Denver, Colorado. We just stumbled onto it. We stopped to help the few policemen that were on the scene. Dan told me to wait, but I jumped out and he followed suit. Shots rang out just as we exited our car. He was hit in the chest and went down. I held him, telling him he would be all right, while I watched his life slip away. Why do we feel compelled to lie like that? I could see he was dying, but still I lied to him. I actually confessed that to my bishop. Confessed that I lied to Dan while I watched him die.

Dan died in my arms again. I know we dream in black and white, but the colors seem so vivid now. The blue of the sky, the metallic dark blue of our car, the colorful flashing strobe lights, the white of his shirt, the earthy red of his skin, the brighter red spreading from his wound.

I tried to save him.

Someone called for an ambulance.

But I knew it was too late.

He was my last partner.

And I failed him.

CHAPTER 2

Like many security organizations, Latter-day Saint Security Service (LDSSS) has code names that readily and easily identify the subject of our protection. They are not used to disrespect the protectee, but so we may identify him without actually using his name. These code names usually come from the subject's personal interests or for something he or she is known to have done. The United States Secret Service uses a completely random computerized assignment of code names. We don't. This subject had, in his youth, worked for the Union Pacific Railroad, so his chosen code name was Conductor.

Normally, members of the Quorum of the Seventy don't have security details assigned exclusively to them, not even members of the presidency of the Seventy like Conductor. My team at LDSSS normally was assigned to the prophet; there were smaller teams assigned to other high-profile leaders in the First Presidency and the Twelve. But for the past six months, Conductor had been high-profile security, and he was my primary responsibility.

Conductor had been one of the main representatives of the Church to the Olympic Games in 2002. After his assignment during the 2002 Games, he'd been called to be the area president in the Asia North Area. When the games came back to Salt Lake

City with such short notice, the Church needed his experience and Conductor was called back. Only he wasn't released from his calling in the Asia North Area. For the past few months he'd been flying back and forth between his area and Salt Lake City, juggling both assignments.

Waiting for Conductor gave me a chance to think. The night before I'd had that dream again; it was starting to mess with my head. I can never change how it ends. My partner always dies, and I'm always powerless to stop it from happening. For a long time, I hadn't had the dream—heck, it wasn't a dream, it was a nightmare. It had started again last week. Except now there was a twist. My partner still dies. I'm still holding him, telling him, "It will be okay. It's not serious." My eyes still stare at the growing red stain on his shirt as I tell him it will be okay. But now, it's crazy to even think this, but I get the feeling he's trying to tell me something. Something important. I dread sleeping now.

"Brother Grant, the president will see you now."

I looked up from the January 2006 *Ensign* I was glancing at. "Thank you, Sister Wilkins." The receptionist was nice and cordial for 6:00 a.m.

Much nicer than I am at 6:00 a.m.

The Church Office Building is in downtown Salt Lake City. It is a large building—almost tall enough to be classified a "skyscraper." I wonder how high a building has to be before it is a skyscraper. Maybe the Church Office Building is a skyscraper.

Just west of the Church Office Building is Temple Square, which was originally laid out by Brigham Young when the Saints first arrived in the Salt Lake Valley in 1847. His plans allocated forty acres, in what would become downtown Salt Lake, for the establishment and construction of Temple Square. The forty was eventually dropped to ten, the size it is today. The centerpiece of the square is the Salt Lake Temple, but this was not the first structure on the site. That distinction goes to the Tabernacle, finished in 1868. It sits directly west of the granite temple. To the south of the Tabernacle is the Assembly Hall. A high wall separates the property from the rest of the city, and an interior wall (inside the square) separates the temple from the rest of the square.

It is open year round, and LDSSS is constantly watching and monitoring it. More people visit Temple Square annually than Niagara Falls, even if you don't count conference weekends. Visitors enter and exit through gates on the north and south or through the new Main Street Plaza entrance. There is a visitors' center at both the north and south entrances. LDSSS has ways to get around Temple Square that are not known to or used by the public.

Underground tunnels connect the Church Office Building, Temple Square, the Joseph Smith Memorial Building (which is on the same block as the Church Office Building, south of it), and the Conference Center (north of Temple Square). My fellow agents and I are responsible to watch all Church property in downtown Salt Lake. Not just Temple Square.

A worldwide organization is run from the Church Office Building. Presidents, kings, queens, and prime ministers have all stopped here on their way through the Wasatch Front. Conductor's office is on the first floor. The lobby was pretty much deserted, aside from myself and the other security person, Sister Wilkins. From the looks of it, she was unarmed.

Looks are sometimes deceiving.

I got up and walked toward the first-floor office. Immediately behind Sister Wilkins's desk is a large, ornate wrought-iron fence. It is approximately twenty-five feet long and is shaped in a semi-circle. On either side of the fence there is an arch. It is situated such that everyone entering or exiting through the first-floor lobby must pass through it. Passing under the arch allows cameras, partially obscured by the fence itself, to track all who pass beneath. No one outside security knows when, or if, the closed-circuit TVs on the other end are being watched in real time. They are, however, being constantly recorded by digital recorders.

I had been in Conductor's office many times before. I feel comfortable around Conductor, and we have a good friendship. He never makes me or any other team member feel unwanted or feel as if we are in his way. Because of the nature of our work, we get to see him when the people are gone and he is left alone. Being with him as much as we are has only strengthened my conviction of his calling as a General Authority.

Despite the familiarity he and I share, for some reason, this time I was nervous. Maybe it had something to do with this being a Friday, and six in the morning. Oh, and the reason I was here. I was up against the clock, and it was ticking. I really wanted to get out to Spanish Fork as quick as possible, or at least before 7:00 a.m.

The office I walked into is spacious. There is one large window in the north wall, but at this early hour little light comes through it. Brown and burgundy are the dominant colors. Conductor sat behind a large, deep-colored walnut desk. He got up and walked toward me.

Hanging on the wall behind his desk is a painting of Joseph Smith. On the side table on the east wall there is a glass statue of the Nauvoo Temple, as it looked in the 1840s. I have never been to Nauvoo. Maybe I will go someday. I want to see the new temple. Above the representation of the temple hangs a painting of George Washington kneeling in prayer in front of his horse. On the opposite wall hangs a large painting of the Savior in a red robe.

Conductor is not a big man. He is five foot five and weighs approximately 165 pounds. His hair, what's left of it, is gray. He's not bald but is nearly so. He was born and reared in central California. His physical stature may not be imposing, but his eyes can be when he feels the need. He has great energy. Conductor has been a leader in the Church most of his adult life, first at the local level and since 1962 as a General Authority. He is eighty-eight years old.

We shook hands, and he was smiling, but he could tell something was bothering me.

"Peter, how good it is to see you."

Only three people ever called me Peter: my ex-wife during our divorce, the prophet, and Conductor. I don't mind when the latter two call me that. But I normally prefer Pete or Grant.

"Thank you, sir."

"Please, Peter, sit down." He motioned to a pair of dark brown leather chairs near his desk. I sat in one, and he in the other. He was fully awake, but I wasn't, and I stifled a yawn. He noticed anyway.

"I know it's early."

"I didn't sleep well." I once told Conductor about Dan Begay. It helped.

"The dream again, Peter?" he gently asked.

"Yes." I leaned forward, my hands covering my face, and I took a deep breath, my voice somewhat muffled. "When will it stop? When will the guilt go away?"

"You know the answer to that already."

"I know."

"Have you sought a blessing?"

"Yes. More than once. The blessings help. Probably the only thing that allows me some rest. But . . . the guilt." Speaking with Conductor about it was like speaking with my grandfather or the ultimate bishop. I found myself wanting to tell him, to share with him how I felt. I knew he would understand. But I didn't have time for this. I kept my composure. "I'm not here for this, and you are far too busy."

His eyes sparkled in the early morning light. "So, what brings you here so early on a Friday morning, Peter? Before you answer, it is being reported on KSL radio that the president of the United States will attend the Olympic opening ceremonies. Did you know that?"

I should have. Thanks a lot, Cook. What if this terrorist I was tracking was after the president? That could be important information. I assumed there would be some official visit. He came the last time the Olympics were here. "I did not. But that is nice to know. Is he planning on visiting here?" If he did, we would have to coordinate security with the Secret Service. A twenty-minute visit from the president of the United States requires almost two weeks of preparation.

"He might. I'm sure we will be told if he plans to."

"Of course," I said.

"Now, Peter, I don't need your team to be ready until nine thirty this morning; you didn't forget about traveling down to BYU today? Utah County is safe enough."

Utah County? I hadn't forgotten about Conductor's trip down to BYU, but Cook's visit last night was preoccupying my thoughts. Conductor was speaking at a pre-Olympic celebration at the Marriott Center. There was no indication that he was in danger. LDSSS has a good relationship with the Salt Lake FBI office, and I was confident that if they had any information about some wacko or terrorist coming after a General Authority, they would have passed such information to us. They have before.

Besides, I told myself, he's going to Utah County. It's an inside joke with Church security that the safest place a subject can be is Utah County. In the Beehive State, Utah County is known as a bastion of very faithful Mormons. They go to BYU and have babies. The belief is that nothing bad happens there. Obviously that belief is erroneous. But some misinformed people spitefully call it Happy Valley. Well, I've been there many times, and it is happy.

"Watch out for stray strollers, sir." It came out before I knew it.

"That wasn't funny, Peter." He smiled though, just barely. "Now, tell me why you are here."

"Something has come up, and I will have to meet you at BYU this morning, sir."

"What are you talking about?" His eyes were searching mine.

"The FBI has asked for my help. They asked last night. I told them yes."

"I see. Is this about what happened in Spanish Fork?" he asked.

My shock and amazement at his guess registered on my face. "Yes. How did you know?"

He smiled at me. A warm, fatherly smile. "The man found at the Relief Mine, John Taylor, was a stake president. He still would be if . . ." He trailed off, paused momentarily. "I met him once or twice and knew his father quite well. Do you know where the Relief Mine is?"

"No. I need directions."

He got up and walked around his desk to his phone. He buzzed Sister Wilkins. "Please bring me the file. Mr. Grant will need it."

It was quiet in his office. We didn't speak. A minute later Sister Wilkins walked in and handed a manila folder to Conductor.

"Thank you," he said. She turned and left quickly.

He gave it to me.

"Read," he said.

I did.

It was a dossier that contained some brief biographical information about the man whose body was found at the mine. I finished after a few minutes and looked up. "Hopefully this will be helpful."

"I heard about the tragedy late last night. Something stinks about this, Peter. It takes a great weight off my heart to know the FBI has asked you to help."

It's hard to argue with that.

"I will do my best."

"I expect nothing less." Conductor sounded serious.

"Where is the Relief Mine?" I asked.

"It's near the mouth of Spanish Fork Canyon. I actually know the detective you'll be working with. Give me five minutes, and I'll arrange for you to meet a Detective Anderson at the scene. There are detailed directions to the mine in the file. You'd better hurry."

"I have one request."

He looked at me, and I could feel the power in his eyes. "What, Peter?"

"When you talk to Detective Anderson, tell him I'll be a little late."

Conductor smiled at me and nodded his head.

"Peter, whatever happened there, as far as you are concerned, needs to be wrapped up soon. We leave for Korea on the seventh, and I want you with me."

"I told the FBI that."

"Fine. Every hour counts now. Go."

I left.

CHAPTER 3

Near the Mouth of Spanish Fork Canyon
Forty-five Minutes Later

I actually made good time to Spanish Fork. Spanish Fork is a small city in the southern end of Utah County, and it is a straight shot on I-15. The northbound lanes were already pretty congested with cars heading for Salt Lake. Luckily, I was southbound.

The Bureau taught me to use time wisely, so I tried to recall all that I knew about the Relief Mine. It didn't take long. It was a mine of some sort, and at one time it had something to do with relief. That was all I knew. I knew nothing.

The only thing worse than driving alone is doing it in silence. I like Billy Joel, so I put in a tape. I sang along to stay awake and get my mind working.

"Sing us a song, you're the piano man."

I don't sing well.

At all.

I found the correct exit and took it. I was going in a southwest direction now. I've lived in California, Virginia, Colorado, South Korea, and Illinois. They are all beautiful, but they don't compare to the Wasatch Front. The mountains shoot up some six thousand feet from the valley floor at an incredibly steep angle. Because Utah sits on a plateau of approximately four thousand feet, the mountains are more than ten thousand feet above sea level. The Relief Mine was on a mountain bench. That much I did know.

"Amazing," I said aloud, gazing at the mountains as often as driving would allow.

I almost missed my next turn. I passed a golf course to my right. The clubhouse was empty and the course covered in snow. After a few minutes I was surrounded by dairy farms. I don't like cows. I just don't. Maybe it's the smell. Don't get me wrong. I like a good beefsteak just as much as the next guy, and I love milk. I just don't like cows.

The next turn, to the left, was harder to find, but after passing it twice and retracing my path, I found it. Some four hundred yards later it bent to the left again and took me parallel to the mountains. It was an old road, a narrow reminder that cars and roads are wider now. It was, I guessed, also a dead end. No other road in or out. I stopped, got out, and looked around. The nearest farmhouse was about two miles away. I'd passed a recently built house about a mile back, but I couldn't see it now. The road followed the rolling topography of the mountain bench.

Thirteen hours. The sun set around 5:20 p.m. A car in this area would need headlights slightly before that. Around 5:10 or so. Had someone seen the killer or killers driving away? I got back in my car and continued down the road. Over the next rise, I saw what I was looking for: many, many police cars. I turned Billy off.

I was stopped by a young officer blocking the road. "Afraid you'll have turn around. You can't go on," he said.

I held up my identification. "Special Agent Grant, FBI. I need to see Detective Anderson." I snapped my wallet closed. Technically I was back on the "team," at least temporarily. Agent Cook had purposefully been unclear about how much of an agent I was now. But I did have my credentials back, so I decided to use them. Plus I had taken the oath again. I looked at the young man; his badge said SFPD. "*Now*, officer." When needed, I can be intimidating. I needed now. He backed away.

"Up with the rest of 'em." He pointed up a dirt road that began where the pavement ended.

"Thank you."

I followed the road up its steep embankment to a small area where it leveled off. From here I could see what had to be the mine itself up the mountain, or at least the man-made structure that housed the mine's entrance. It was a three-level white building. It looked like a triple-tiered wedding cake, cut through the middle. The bottom floor was the largest. The next two sat on top of it and were smaller. The front facade and sides were angular, but there was no back to any of the levels because they seemed to be swallowed by the mountainside. I probably would have to walk some of the way, and I didn't like the looks of the walk: too steep.

The dirt road led to a bridge with a large, heavy-looking gate. It was open, and I pulled through. On either side was a sign that read:

PRIVATE PROPERTY
NO TRESPASSING BY ORDER OF THE RELIEF MINE CO.

Apparently someone had trespassed, and President Taylor was dead. Maybe he'd been a trespasser too.

The road turned to gravel and climbed the mountain at a very steep angle. Around sixty-five vertical yards later, I'd come to another miniplateau. I saw more police cars and officers. I could see a small house on this plateau. It was off-white with a dark red trim. Its lights were on.

I got out and approached one of the officers. "I'm looking for a Detective Anderson." I'd gotten past the road sentinel, so this officer assumed it was okay for me to be there. Never assume anything.

"Up there," he said. "You'll have to leave your car here though."

Oh goody. "Thanks," I said without enthusiasm.

Five minutes later, I reached the wedding-cake building on foot. I'd passed a few officers on the way up, and one looked really queasy. His buddy helping him down didn't look like he was in much better shape. I stood and looked at the building's exterior. It was large enough to be seen from the road. Maybe from the freeway, if you knew where to look.

"Why hadn't I seen it from the road?" I asked aloud.

"The snow," a woman's voice responded.

I turned to see who'd overheard my question and answered it. I noticed her eyes first. It was one of those moments. A stop-you-in-your-tracks kind of moment. Life-defining moment. You just meet someone and you could swear you know that person. *Have* known that person your whole life. I think I started to blush. "Excuse me?"

"The snow. You couldn't see the building from the road because of the snow. It's white, and so is the building." She must've thought I didn't understand her. "The snow acts as a natural camouflage."

I knew that. I'd become accustomed to snow and hadn't noticed it was even there.

"Thanks," I said. "I'm looking for a Detective Anderson. If you could just tell me where I can find him, I'll be on my way."

"Him? You must be mistaken. I am Detective Anderson, and you're late, Mr. Grant."

Huh?

"Sorry. Of course you are. Where's the body?" I recovered quickly, but my jaw was probably still hanging open when she said, "This way."

Never assume anything.

I took the opportunity to look at Anderson. She was wearing dark slacks and some casual walking boots. She was also wearing a dark green jacket with *SFPD* plastered across the back. It was heavier than a windbreaker, but not by much. Her hair was medium length, long enough for a ponytail if she wanted to wear it like that. She was shorter than me, but not by much. She looked athletic. She wasn't wearing much makeup and in my opinion didn't need much anyway.

I could see a few people walking in and out of the building's main floor. One was the crime scene recorder.

"Hey, Anderson, back for more?" the man with the Sony camcorder said.

"Whatever, Ned. You finished yet?" She was all business. Very professional. She carried herself like a pro around the crime scene.

She knew her job. I found myself liking her attitude. And her hair. Auburn. Probably smells great too, I thought.

We walked to the front of the building, where the only visible door had been obviously forced open. Whoever forced it wasn't too particular either.

"Not too often you see an entire door almost blown to smithereens," I remarked.

"No," she replied. "And it's not all that often, thankfully, that you see this."

She stepped to the left so I could see, and I knew what had made those two officers queasy. Lying on the floor of what looked like an office was a body, male. Presumably President Taylor. It was already in the early stages of decay. From what I could see, it looked like a painful death: one nasty cut across his larynx. Deep brown stains covered his body. And I could tell, from experience, that the body had suffered other traumas.

"Has the medical examiner been here yet?" I asked, kneeling down and examining the body. I peered at the cause of the brown stains, just below the chin. This doesn't help the victim, but it does me. He had been around six foot tall and of average build. Still, it would have taken a few men to control him. I was guessing that he'd come here voluntarily. Just a gut feeling.

"Yes. Come and gone," she answered. "Grant?"

"What?" I was in deep thought and hadn't heard her. "Has the ME been here yet?"

She gave me an exasperated look. "Yes. Come and gone. Let's step outside, and I'll fill you in."

Okay.

I followed her outside. Tough guy that I am, ex-FBI and all that, I was glad to be outside.

She jumped right in. "The ME says that death occurred between five and seven last evening."

The FBI's information was accurate.

She continued. "Cause of death was the laceration across his throat."

Really.

"But the ME says he would've died anyway, even without the laceration. He'd been beaten severely about the head, his left eye was put out, and he'd suffered other major traumas."

"What does that mean?" I asked.

She handed me the report and continued. "According to the ME, the blood on the pants dried before they, whoever they are, took the final action. Also, his wrists show signs of being secured, probably by rope. She'll have a more complete report for us Monday."

Us?

What are we, partners?

"They wanted information," I said.

"Yes, they did. They tortured and then killed him."

"Do you think they got that information?" I looked at her, searching her face. She had some freckles, not too many. She didn't have dimples, at least not "supermodel" dimples. Her eyes were a deep blue. Almost a crystal blue. I'd never seen eyes like hers before. Deep blue and . . .

"Did you hear me, Grant?"

"No. I was thinking about something important."

"Important? What could be more . . . ? Anyway, I said yes, I do believe the killer or killers got the information they wanted. But was that information complete, and will they kill again? I think it's possible."

"Agreed." I need to work on my listening skills.

Two men dressed in white lab coats, carrying a litter with a large bag on it, walked by us into the office. The back of their lab coats read *Utah County Medical Examiner's Office.*

"I thought you said the ME had been here."

She stared at me with a look that said I was dumb.

"She has been. But I requested that she let the body lie there until you got a chance to see it. She agreed and told those two assistants," Anderson motioned to the two who had just gone inside, "to stay behind and pick up the remains only after you had seen them. You should feel honored; the ME normally doesn't do things this way. I must have asked extra nicely or something. Okay?"

I felt stupid. "Yeah, okay. And Anderson." She may have asked nicely, but I knew someone else had asked the ME to do the same thing.

"What, Grant?" She didn't sound too happy with me.

"Thank you. I was hoping to see it before it was picked up." I saw no reason not to be polite with my new partner.

She smiled.

"What about the house?" I motioned to the small house below.

"What about it, Grant?"

"Maybe someone saw something."

"Nope. That's the caretaker's house. He is in Missouri. Been gone on vacation for almost two weeks now. Someplace called Branson. No one was here last night."

Someone was. They left Taylor behind.

"This place was picked. The killers knew no one would be watching this old mine, and they decided to use it."

"Seems reasonable," Anderson said. "But why?"

I didn't answer.

Because I didn't know.

"Can we go in?" I asked.

"In where?"

"Into the mine," I said. "Maybe there is something inside we should see." Then again, maybe not, but it wouldn't hurt to look.

She didn't protest.

We walked back into the main office and avoided the ME crew. A hallway branched off to the right. We followed it. It was poorly lit. The overhead fixtures were old and inadequate. The further we went, the more narrow the hall was. The hallway progressively grew darker. It veered sharply to the left, almost to the point of being circular, and then it ended.

A small black door blocked our way. There was no sign on it, and the knob looked very old and rusty.

"Shall we?" I grabbed the knob and gave it a steady twist. It sounded almost unearthly, but the door opened. Blackness filled the tunnel beyond. The door frame covered up a rough-hewn entrance to the mine. It was large enough to walk through two at a time. I could see nothing beyond what little light the hallway threw into the tunnel. It was cold in the tunnel; we both felt the chill.

"You see anything, Anderson? Besides your breath?"

The blackness was so thick it almost looked alive.

"No. Just a sec." She was looking for something in her pocket. I didn't watch her too closely. I kept staring at the tunnel, hoping I could see something, anything. "Let's go," she said.

I thought she meant back the way we came, but she grabbed my arm. "So we don't get separated," she said, and headed for the tunnel. She didn't need an excuse to grab my arm. A small beam of light pierced the darkness.

"I found my penlight."

"Good work, Anderson. Always prepared. Were you a Boy Scout?"

"Shut up, Grant. And I notice your lack of preparation, so you must not have been a Scout."

Touché.

"Are there mountain lions around here?" I asked.

"Mountain lions? I seriously doubt there is a cougar in the mine."

I hoped she was right. The last thing I wanted was to run into a 120-pound cougar. In the darkness of a mine shaft. With only a penlight. Oh, I was armed and so was Anderson. But it isn't a good idea to start shooting in the dark at close quarters.

We were walking slowly. "What's the difference, Anderson?"

"Difference of what?"

"Mountain lions and cougars."

"Be quiet, Grant."

Okay. I bet she doesn't know.

The tunnel went straight for some thirty or forty feet. It bent to the right at about forty-five degrees. She kept the light on the ground in front of us. It was dusty and misty.

"Someone has been in here. Recently," I said.

The floor was dusty, and clear sets of shoe prints were visible.

"I see them too."

Anderson swung the beam of light up and inspected the ceiling. Rough-cut timbers spanned the small width and were connected every ten feet to similar beams that ran down into the granite floor. Then I almost fell over an edge. If she hadn't been holding my arm, I would have fallen. It's always a good idea to let the person holding the light walk in front.

Next time I will.

"Light the floor up," I said.

The floor just ended. I was ready to turn back, and would have, but I thought I saw something against the wall.

"Over there, Anderson."

"Over where, Grant? I can't see where you're pointing."

Oh yeah. "To the right, along the floor against the wall. Move it slow . . . I saw something." On the other side of the ledge, but against the tunnel wall, was a ladder. "Hold it steady." I meant the flashlight. I got down on my stomach and reached out for the ladder. The dust was bad, and I fought off the urge to sneeze.

"Be careful, Grant."

I got a hold of it, and dragged it against the ledge so we could climb down. It was an old, rickety, wooden ladder. The wood was cold. Frozen probably. I was lucky I didn't get a splinter.

"Think it's safe, Grant?"

"One way to find out."

I started down. It wasn't a chauvinist thing. I was the one that saw the ladder. I went down five rungs and couldn't see anything below me. I could almost feel the darkness. It was eerie, like thousands of fingers were pulling me down into nothing. My hands were cold now. I had to concentrate on gripping the ice-cold wood.

"Anderson, flash your light down here."

"I am, Grant. It's not powerful enough."

I climbed back to the top. "Give me the light."

She handed it to me. I put it in my mouth, and I went back down. One rung . . . two . . . three . . . four . . .

I stopped at the fifth rung again. I grabbed the light and pointed it down so I could see below.

I saw ground. One more rung down, and the tunnel continued. I skipped the last rung, and called up to Anderson, "Come on down."

She did.

I blew into my hands to warm them up and could hear Anderson doing the same thing. I grabbed her hand this time, strictly for warmth, and we went on. I held on to the light and used it as best I could. I thought the upper tunnel was dusty, but this was worse. This time, there were no shoe prints in the dust, just a lot of dust in the dust. The air was stale and thin.

Anderson said, "No one has been down here in a long time. The air is almost hard to breathe. Can you feel it, Grant?"

"Yes." It felt like each intake of breath coated our lungs with dust.

"To continue, or not to continue, that—"

"Don't say it, Grant."

I chuckled. "You don't like Shakespeare?"

"I like his plays fine. I just don't want to hear you slaughter them."

Fair enough.

"We have a small light, no one knows we're down here, the air is thin, the dust horrible, it's below freezing, and if we go on, we could get lost. We should go back." I have this thing about getting lost under the earth.

I don't like it.

"But what if it's here?"

"What if what is here, Anderson?" I couldn't see her face, so I flashed the beam of light on her. Her face was dusty.

Dusty but pretty.

"Gold."

"Gold? Treasure? If there is something in this mine, we won't find it. Come on, let's go back." I tugged on her hand, but she didn't move.

"Grant, legend has it that this was a Nephite treasure vault. They say there is more gold in this mountain than all the gold the conquistadors took from the Aztecs and Incas." She was walking ahead, pulling my hand. "What if we found it? Can there really be that much gold in this mountain? Think about it. What if . . ."

I cut her off.

"What if we get lost in here and die a slow painful death? I don't like the sound of that. Gold is worthless to a dead man. Come on." I pulled her to me. "Let's go." Together we stood there, and for a split second I was tempted to ponder "what if" too . . . What if I was still married? What if I go bald? What if I have bad breath? Who cares. The temptation was gone. "We are going back. Nephite treasure or not, we are not going any further." I tugged again, and she followed me.

We retraced our steps but didn't bother putting the ladder back where I'd found it. We were almost out.

"Just what do you think you're doing, Detective Anderson? Who is this man?" We could see someone at the beginning of the tunnel. Whoever it was didn't sound too happy. It was a man's voice, and he was shining a powerful flashlight right at us. He kept moving it to our eyes, blinding us. We stopped moving. Finally he moved it away from our faces, and we started moving again, our eyes slowly adjusting to the brighter light outside the tunnel. When they did, I saw a short man with glasses standing in the doorway. His hair looked red. He reminded me of some twisted version of Ralph the Mouth from *Happy Days*. Whoever he was, he was acting irritated.

Anderson's clothes were dusty, and her hair was browner now because of the dust. My clothes were dirty from the dust and from crawling on my stomach.

The short man with glasses spoke again. "You have no business down here. The Utah County Sheriff's Department already searched down here." That solved who had left the shoe prints in the dust.

I could feel the anger build in Anderson. "Did you find anything?" she asked.

"No. Whoever the killers are, they didn't come down here. It was dumb of them too. They could've dumped the body in the mine, and I doubt it ever would have been found."

"Next time keep me informed, Detective. This is city property, and I expect you to make reasonable efforts to keep me involved." Anderson knew how to protect her turf.

He was right, though, about the killers. I was thinking the same thing but wanted to see the mine itself, to make sure. Why hadn't they? It made more sense to dump the body in the mine. But killers rarely make sense.

"Detective Anderson, who is this man? Civilians are not allowed at a crime scene. You know that."

She let go of my hand and started back toward the office and the outside. Detectives and police officers are happy people in general. The ones that are good know how to protect their sources of joy and happiness. If they don't, they don't last long. The same was true in the FBI. Whatever perversions and evil you'd encounter, you couldn't allow them to break you. Many law enforcement agents lose spouses and families because they allow the evil to nearly destroy them. I did. But I got out alive.

Whatever source of joy and happiness Anderson had, I could tell it was nearly used up today, and it wasn't even eight thirty yet. Whoever this man was, he wasn't causing joy or happiness. But I gave him the benefit of the doubt.

We were outside now. She looked at me, patted her jacket and pants, knocking dust off, and took a breath. "Special Agent Grant, this is Detective Millhouse."

I smiled. I was running my hands through my dirty hair and offered one to Millhouse. He hesitated, and we shook hands. "Nice to meet you," I said.

"Millhouse is with the Utah County sheriff. For this case, it was decided to share responsibility for the investigation. Pressure from the top," she explained.

Millhouse wiped his hand on his pant leg. "That's right. Spread the glory around." He wasn't happy to see me. "Why is the FBI here?"

"Sorry, Detective Millhouse. That's privileged information. 'Need-to-know' basis. You don't need to know." I smiled. "And it's only glorious if the case is solved."

"Oh, I will solve, I mean, *we* will solve it, right, Anderson?" She forced a smile.

"Hey," he continued, "why don't we get together and compare notes? You know, have a big brainstorming session? I would love to know what you think about this case, Agent Grant."

I bet you would. "Maybe. And it's Special Agent Grant. I'll give you a call."

"Call me? For what, a date?" His voice rose in pitch, like an adolescent girl's. "'You'll never call me!' You know how many girls said that to me in high school and college?"

"One?" I smiled again.

Anderson chuckled.

He gave me a weird look. "That wasn't funny. Let me see your ID."

"Don't have it on me." I turned and walked away.

Anderson followed me. "Sorry about that. He's a little over-bearing."

A little?

"You have nothing to apologize for. Guys like him give law enforcement a bad name." Not to mention men in general.

We walked in silence down to the cars.

"Grant?"

"What?" I looked at her and realized two things: one, I enjoyed being with her, and two, we really were partners. At least for the duration of this mess. I'm leery of partners. The last two partners I had left me with bad memories. Dan Begay was one. My partner before Dan. I thought we were buddies too, but we weren't. He liked my wife. He—

"Did you hear me, Grant?"

"No."

"Did the FBI force you to retire because you couldn't hear anymore?"

"No. I'm a deep thinker. What did you say?"

"I need a ride."

"Why?"

"I rode out with a patrolman and sent him back." She added, "I was waiting for you."

"Hope you like Billy Joel. Get in," I said.

"You don't sing along, do you?"

"No."

What a dumb question.

We drove over the bridge and past the young officer doing such a good job keeping unauthorized persons away.

"Well, Detective Anderson, is there someplace good to eat breakfast in Spanish Fork, Utah? I need something to eat."

"We have a Denny's."

"Not great, but good enough. Direct me, and talk."

"About?"

"About a murdered stake president."

"Spanish Fork PD dispatch received an anonymous tip that there was a body up at the Relief Mine."

"What time?"

She was staring out the window. "Nine thirty last night. It's isolated up there, no passing traffic. The body was in the structure. No way it was seen by chance or accident. The killers called the tip in."

"Yes. Or it means that the anonymous caller is just connected with the killer."

"But," she interrupted, "if so, why call the cops? Doesn't it make more sense to keep it quiet, for as long as possible?"

"Yes it does, but not always. Maybe the killer, or killers, need the publicity."

"Publicity? I don't understand."

"Okay." I only did because I'd spent a good part of my life bringing killers down. "Maybe they think the attention the murder will attract will act as a free and clear warning to someone else."

"Turn right. Then you think they will kill again?"

"Not necessarily. But they could. There is one more possibility. The most disturbing of all. They don't care that we know. Serial killers . . ."

"Turn right at the stop sign."

". . . rely on secrecy because they lead a double life. They aren't readily identifiable by just looking at them. Strip away their secrecy, their protection, and then the monster emerges. Very scary. They are difficult to find, and for every Ted Bundy or John Gacy that you capture there are probably five more roaming free. And killing. The problem is they look as normal as you and I."

"Go forward till the next stop sign and turn left. Then go forward again. And you don't look normal." She smiled.

"How long?" I asked. I found myself liking her smile.

"Long enough."

Okay.

Anyway.

"Serial killers," I continued, "crave the attention. They need it. They have power by causing fear in others, and they love the power." Not unlike terrorists, I reminded myself. "But that is also their Achilles' heel. They keep killing to satisfy their need for power. It sounds sick, but the more they kill, the easier it is to find them."

"You're right, it does sound sick."

"But what if the killers don't need or crave the attention? What if they don't care that we know about this murder? Remember Son of Sam?"

"I know Yosemite Sam. Brothers?"

"No."

We were in Spanish Fork proper now, and the businesses along the street were just opening.

"It's across the street, Grant."

"It is? I don't see a Denny's sign, Detective Anderson." We stopped at a traffic light. "Anyway, Son of Sam was a serial killer in New York City who taunted the police, daring them to catch him. They did. Thing is, his own insatiable ego made it easier. But what if we have killers that don't need to kill again and don't care that the cops know about it? They even go so far as to *call it in*?"

The light turned green.

I pulled into a parking lot and stopped the car.

"I thought we were going to Denny's, Anderson."

"This is the closest thing to it in Spanish Fork. The food's better here anyway."

We were parked in front of something called Trail's End Café. I didn't see the trail end, but we went in.

We were seated quickly. For early morning, it was busy in the café.

She stood. "Be back in a minute. Order me whatever you get, plus a glass of skim milk. I'm hungry too."

I watched her walk to the women's bathroom, and I ordered then waited alone for our food. I closed my eyes and tried to think. But the constant hum and activity in the café made it nearly impossible.

"You sleepy too, Grant?" Anderson was back.

I opened my eyes. "No. After breakfast, what's your plan?"

"Solve the case. What about you?"

"I have some business at BYU."

She smiled. "How long will we be there?"

There it was again, that "we."

"You don't need to tag along, Anderson."

Her smile disappeared. "I am not your tagalong, Grant. And it's *Detective* Anderson. I know what you do for a job, and another pair of trained eyes can't hurt. Plus after that we can head over to Springville High and speak to the vice principal. He knew our victim. I made an appointment to see him today at 3:00 p.m., while you were snoozing this morning. Okay?"

"Okay," I said.

Our food arrived: buttermilk pancakes, OJ—skim milk for Anderson—and bacon. We ate in silence and in no real hurry. I didn't have to be at BYU until 10:30 a.m.

After paying for breakfast, keeping the receipt for reimbursement from the FBI, we headed for Provo and the BYU campus. It's a good school, with a good enough sports program, and it was there I earned my bachelor's degree in police science. It was a very long time ago, and my course of study doesn't really exist anymore. Now it's called "criminal justice."

Whatever that is.

Provo is the largest city in Utah County and the home of BYU. Since BYU is overcrowded, so is Provo. Too many people trying to squeeze into a confined space. This was readily evident from the amount of traffic taking the same I-15 exit I was. Traffic, and I, were backed up onto the freeway. Provo had changed a great deal since my days in college. A lot of what I remembered was gone, replaced by strip malls and new housing developments.

We took the Provo Center Street exit. It would have probably been faster to take the University Avenue exit, but I was running through nostalgic memories and wanted to drive east on Center. It took fifteen minutes to get off the freeway because of the early morning traffic. I hate traffic. I don't hate people; I just hate it when they drive and are in my way. Maybe I should move to North Dakota or Idaho. When I was at BYU, there was an excellent eatery on the corner of Freedom Boulevard and Center Street. But not anymore. A nightclub was there now. Four good years at the Y. Made a lot of friends and still keep in touch with some. Life in the FBI didn't make that easy, but I tried. I continued along Center, eventually turned left on Ninth East, and finished my drive down memory lane. Anderson took the time to call in and advise Spanish Fork PD of her whereabouts and what she was doing.

"If you need me, call my cell." She hung up.

I met up with my team, five of us in all, in the BYU president's office. Ken Jones, ex–Secret Service; Mark Jones (no relation), former FBI; Harry Makia, twenty-two years Los Angeles PD; and Scott Bartlett, also from the FBI. We all trusted and liked each other. I was closest to Bartlett. We knew some of the same people in the FBI and even worked in the same field office in Sacramento. Never as partners, but we knew each other. He's the number two guy, and if I can't be with Conductor, Scott's in charge. When—if I ever marry again, Scott will be my best man.

Greetings were made all around. Conductor was speaking at a morning devotional, and he and the school president were discussing the school and its students. No one seemed to notice my new partner, and I quickly and quietly briefed my team about the presence of Detective Anderson. No one, that is, except Conductor. He greeted her by name and shook her hand. He knew her.

We escorted our subject to the Marriott Center. It is one of the largest indoor stadiums at any college in the country. Seats nearly 23,000 people. It was already packed by the time we arrived. The devotional lasted about an hour and a half. In all there were two or three speakers. I'm not really sure. It's not my job to listen to the talks. It is my job to take Conductor's safety seriously. That may seem like a no-brainer at BYU. A General Authority of the Church at the Church's flagship school. But it was just some years ago that a president of the Church stood at a pulpit at BYU and was rushed by a man claiming to have a bomb. No fingers were pointed and no one lost their job, but from that day, even at BYU, the security of Church leaders is taken very seriously.

Conductor stayed as long as he could after the devotional ended and greeted as many of the thousands of students as he could. It was nearly 2:00 p.m. when he felt it was time to leave. I took him aside and we spoke for a moment. We separated and I walked to Anderson.

"What did you ask him?" She turned and walked with me.

"I told him about our appointment. He told me he was going to drop by the MTC, with security in tow. Bartlett will be in charge. He's good. Oh, and that I should check in the day before we leave next week."

We kept walking.

"What's next week, Grant?"

"A trip to parts of Asia. And no, you can't come."

Silence spoke for us as we walked. I found myself liking to be around Detective Anderson. She made me feel . . . comfortable. Like I'd known her a very long time. She was walking next to me and I caught her looking at me. Was I walking taller? Straighter? Yeah, I like being around her.

We found my car where I'd left it and drove to Springville High. There were some students milling around the school. I thought about making a wisecrack about kids and going home after school, just because it meant you were away from school. But I decided that Anderson wouldn't appreciate it, so I kept it to myself. We parked in the mostly deserted faculty parking lot and headed for the office.

"Grant, let me do the talking, okay?"

"No prob. I'll follow your lead." I really had no problem with that. I preferred to listen to what was said.

The office door was unlocked, and we walked in. It was a large office, with three rooms connected to it by doors. Only one door was open. There was no support staff, so Anderson spoke up.

"Hello? Anyone here?"

A voice rang out from the open-door room. "Yes. Just a moment." The voice was gruff.

We waited quietly. Anderson was smiling at me, her hands clasped behind her back. Soon enough a large man walked out to greet us. He towered over Anderson and me. I guessed he was six foot six and easily 320 pounds. But he moved with grace. His extended right hand was equally large.

"Hi. I'm Vice Principal Rooney." I shook his hand. "You must be Agent Grant and Detective Anderson. Please come into my office." He turned and we followed.

He moved behind a desk that was too small for him and motioned to some chairs opposite. "Please, sit."

We did. I looked around his office. A bachelor's degree in communications from BYU and a master's degree in administration from the U hung on his wall. A picture of him in a BYU white-and-blue football uniform also hung on the wall. He saw where I was looking.

"Played O-line for the Y back in '86 to '88. Blocked for Covey when he was QB. You follow BYU football, Agent Grant?"

I shook my head.

Anderson said, "I do. Too bad you missed playing with Detmer."

They chitchatted about BYU football, and I listened. He was a nice man. Didn't hesitate to offer his opinion when he felt he had the facts to support it. Anderson moved effortlessly to the reason for our visit.

"How long had you known Mr. Taylor?"

Mr. Rooney smiled, probably at a memory, "Almost ten years. He was the principal that hired me. About three years ago, I was named his vice principal . . ."

The big man in front of us paused. His massive shoulders slumped forward, and his head bowed under the emotion he felt.

"Mr. Rooney, can you think of anyone that didn't like Mr. Taylor?"

He was quiet, thinking. He shook his head. "No. Not enough to want him dead. Not like that. No."

She pressed him. "Anyone at all?"

"I wish I could say yes, but I can't. He worked here more than twenty years. Respected in the community, loved at church. He was a caring man. Why did this happen to him?" He made a fist with his right hand and hammered down on the desk. "Wish I could help, but no one disliked John Taylor."

"It's okay, Mr. Rooney. We need your honesty, and I thank you for it. When did you see him last?"

This went on for another ten minutes or so. Anderson gathered some basic information about John Taylor's life at the school. She would check it later against other resources to confirm what we were hearing. Information is always good to have. And simple police work could very well lead us to a break in the case. Details.

Never enough details.

Anderson was standing, shaking hands with Mr. Rooney. I quickly stood and did the same. He walked us to my car, then turned and left.

"Well, that didn't turn up much, did it, Grant?"

"Yes, it did." I got in and unlocked Anderson's door.

"What?" She sat in her seat, waiting for my answer.

I pulled out of the school and headed for the freeway. "We learned that digging through this victim's private life probably isn't going to turn up anything that will lead us to his killers. What it is about the victim is not buried; it's staring us in the face. And because it's already in the open, it will be that much harder to recognize."

She thought for a minute. "Sounds reasonable. But for now, I need to go back to the station house and go over the reports of the officers that interviewed the victim's family. They should have the prelims filed tonight."

"Sure." I pulled onto the freeway, driving to Spanish Fork again.

My thoughts were consumed with the late John Taylor. And with Detective Anderson. I glanced quickly at her left hand to make sure. No ring or tan line where a ring should be.

Then my cell phone rang.

"This is Grant . . . Hello, Cook . . . What? Are you sure? Yes, I can tomorrow. It'll probably take most of the day, right? . . . Things are going well here . . . Any news on our friend that tells the family secrets? . . . No, just hoping . . . Yes, he could be connected to this . . . Yeah, sure, Cook, tomorrow 8:00 a.m., the federal building." I ended the call.

"Who was that?" Anderson played well at not listening, but how could she not when she was sitting next to me?

"A friend from the FBI. I have some business tomorrow. Turns out the president of the United States is going to visit Church headquarters during the second week of the Olympics. I have to coordinate some stuff with the feds."

"Lucky you."

"You probably have tomorrow full too, don't you, Detective Anderson?"

She nodded. "I'll spend most of the day checking into our victim's life."

"Good. Listen, how about we meet on Sunday and go over some of it?"

"No can do," she replied flatly.

"Why?"

"Because it's Sunday. I always go to my meetings on Sunday when I can, and this Sunday I have off. You know what a cop's schedule is like."

"We're investigating a murder," I pointed out. And that terrorist thing too, I thought.

"I know what we're doing. You can come to my ward, if you want, and we'll compare notes after, okay?"

"What time?" I asked.

"Eleven."

"Can your husband get up that early?" I am so sly.

"Nope. Not married. Never been."

"Where is your building?" I asked.

She told me. I took the Spanish Fork exit and headed down Main Street. Traffic was light, and I made green lights all the way to the station. I pulled into the station parking lot, and she exited my car.

"See you Sunday, 11:00 a.m."

"Okay. Work hard tomorrow, Detective." I pulled away and headed back to I-15. Headed to Salt Lake. Back to my little house in the Avenues.

chapter 4

Saturday pretty much went as planned. I thought about John Taylor and Anderson. I was nervous about church. I kept telling myself it wasn't a date. I pretty much convinced myself of it. I worked with Agent Cook and Agent Bremer of the Secret Service, coordinating the U.S. president's visit to Church headquarters. It went smooth and took most of the day. During a break for lunch, Cook and I discussed my case in Spanish Fork. But we both knew it was much too early to expect results. Still, all cops—feds, state troopers, county, and city—like to discuss their cases, always looking for that missing element, that missing angle.

By the end of lunch, it was still missing.

I slept okay Saturday night, even though I had the dream again. I woke up early Sunday morning. My ward started at 9:00 a.m. I made it on time and enjoyed sacrament meeting. Afterward, I was walking out when I overheard a young returned missionary being congratulated by his buddies. Turns out he got engaged.

"Way to go, Rick!" one said.

"Congrats, man. Will I be your best man?" another asked.

"You really only knew her two weeks before you got engaged?" the first one asked.

The soon-to-be-groom said, "When I saw her on campus, I just knew . . ."

I dodged around the group surrounding him and made it down the hallway and out to my car.

No traffic on Sunday morning. Or very little of it on I-15. I drove down to Spanish Fork, telling myself I wasn't nervous.

I made it in time, barely, for the 11:00 a.m. meeting, and Anderson was waiting for me in the west foyer, like she said she would.

She looked great. She was wearing a black skirt and a dark burgundy sweater. Her hair was curled a little, and she had some makeup on. I just stared at her.

"I said hello, Grant. And nice tie."

Uh. "Hello, Anderson." I made sure to wear my best tie.

And suit too.

"I saved us some seats." I followed her into the chapel. The opening hymn was "A Poor Wayfaring Man of Grief." It's not an easy song to sing, but Anderson made it sound great. Er, I mean the congregation did. This was Joseph Smith's favorite hymn. The day before the martyrdom he asked his friend and fellow prisoner John Taylor to sing it for him. He did. Remembering this cleared my mind. Focused my spirit the way only a sacrament meeting hymn can. My John Taylor hadn't been in Carthage Jail with the prophet. But I could hear his voice, or what I believed was his voice, singing that hymn. He wasn't alone on the other side. I wasn't alone here. Then and there I knew we'd find his killers.

I just didn't know when or how.

The service ended and we started to file out. We had to pass by a line of older sisters on the back row. They saw me, and they saw Anderson.

"How nice you look today, Sister Anderson. I love what you've done with your hair."

"Such a lovely outfit, don't you think, Phyllis?"

"Yes, it is, June. You look lovely today, Sister Anderson."

I knew all of this was said for my benefit.

We were almost past the gauntlet. "Sister Anderson, aren't you going to introduce us to your friend?"

"We saw you two sitting together."

"What a lovely couple you make."

"Doesn't she look lovely, Brother . . . I'm afraid I don't know your name."

"Brother Grant. And yes, she looks very nice."

We filed past them. I was smiling. Anderson wasn't.

"Sorry about that, Grant."

"Why? I quite enjoyed it." I laughed. "How could you not like that?"

"I grew up in this ward. I guess they saw you and assumed . . ." We made eye contact. Her eyes were deep. Blue. We stopped walking and paused for a brief time, lost in the moment. Then a Sunbeam rammed into my leg on the way to Primary and the moment was gone.

"Come on." I grabbed her hand and led her out of the building.

"Wait." She broke free. "I need my coat." I waited for her in the cold of February and didn't notice it a bit.

"Meet me at the station. I'll be there in ten minutes," Anderson said as she walked by me.

I drove to the station and waited.

Twelve minutes later, Anderson pulled up. She got in my car, a leather briefcase slung over her shoulder.

She'd changed her clothes. Nice slacks, a different color sweater, and running shoes.

She wiggled her feet. "More comfy than two-inch heels."

If you say so.

"Drive and talk, Grant."

"What about?"

"John Taylor. Who killed him?"

"I don't know. You tell me, Anderson."

"Well, I was thinking about it last night. I was pretty near asleep when it came to me."

"What?"

"We're assuming he was the first."

"First what?"

"Killing."

I stopped the car. Stopped in the street.

I should've seen that possibility, but I hadn't. A sudden sense of urgency and fear filled me. Something big was going down, and I was standing too near the center. I needed a new perspective, to step further back and look at it. If a terrorist was loose in small-town Utah, would he kill only once?

"Where is the freeway?"

"Straight ahead, that way." She pointed west. "What's the matter, Grant?"

"Maybe nothing. Hopefully nothing. If Taylor was the second killing, then we need to find the first and discover their connection." I loosened my tie. Helps me think better.

"Knock it off, Grant. You're freaking me out. Why would you be concerned with looking for an earlier victim?"

"I don't know. But I am. Something tells me I'm missing something, something important. Isn't that enough? Something more than my gut. Call it instincts. Sometimes I think it's just pure inspiration. When it is, you don't ignore it. We have to find that connection soon. Very soon. I need to think. Enjoy the scenery for a while, okay?"

She looked at me and said, "All right."

The silence helped me think. But thinking about it only made me anxious. What I needed was information. I can work with that. Use it to find that connection. So I put in Billy Joel again. I didn't sing along.

"I'm done thinking," I said.

"That didn't take long."

"No, it didn't. What do you know about that mine?"

"It's been there for a long time," she said.

"How long?"

"It was built in the late nineteenth century. I grew up in Spanish Fork and heard all sorts of stories about it. The legend of the Nephite gold. Stuff like that."

"Any of 'em true?"

"Not many." She took a deep breath. "It was started by a man named John Koyle. He was a local bishop and respected by many people in Spanish Fork. I don't remember the exact date, but it was begun sometime in 1894. According to Koyle, the mine led to a vast amount of ancient Nephite treasure. He claimed that he had been told in some visions, by two of the Three Nephites, to begin the mine. To help finance it and to keep it going after his death, he sold shares in the mine. My grandfather purchased some stock in it."

"Where was the third one?" I asked.

"The what? Oh, I don't know." Anderson had a good mind.

"Was any treasure ever discovered?" I asked.

"Not that I know of. If there is gold in that mountain, then they have done an excellent job of keeping it quiet."

"Tell me, Anderson, why is it called the Relief Mine?"

"Again, there are lots of stories for that. The most plausible one is Koyle believed that one day the Church would go bankrupt and that the treasure from the mine would offer it relief from its financial worries. So it was called the Relief Mine. Get it?"

"I do. Do you think there is a connection between this mine and the victim?"

"It's possible. But I don't see how. Why would anyone kill over an empty mine? We need to check that out. Maybe he was a disgruntled stockholder."

"Yes, we need to check it out. One more thing, Anderson."

"What?"

"See that manila folder on the seat there?"

"Yes."

"Read," I said.

She did.

Salt Lake City
Parking Garage near Temple Square

"You active in the Church?"

"You were just at church with me. I go as much as I can. Cops have crazy schedules. Why?"

We were in an underground parking garage. "Because you're about to see a whole new side of Temple Square." I turned the car off. "Let's go."

"Go? Go where? We're in a parking garage." She didn't look real happy.

"Follow me." I took a few steps and noticed she hadn't moved. I turned around. "I said, follow me."

"Not yet. What if I don't want to see a whole new side of Temple Square? What if I don't trust you?"

"Look, we're not the FBI or National Security Agency. They both pay more and have better bennies. We don't require blood samples or waivers of personal dignity. We are Church security. We protect the prophet and the General Authorities. We specialize in information. We need information. So here we are."

She still looked unsure.

I took a deep breath. "I promise you that you are safe here. You have nothing to fear. Partner to partner, it's okay. Let's go."

"Why do you trust me?" She still hadn't moved.

"My gut says you're good for it."

"I thought inspiration was better."

"It is."

This time when I walked away, she followed.

The main elevators and stairwells are on the west side of the building. That's the way most people exit the garage. We went to the north wall, where there are two doors. The left one read:

MAINTENANCE PERSONNEL ONLY
ACCESS RESTRICTED

The right one read:

SECURED DOOR
AUTHORIZED USE ONLY
UNAUTHORIZED USE IS RESTRICTED

Anderson remarked, "Looks like the sign on the women's bath-room at our station house."

"Which one?" I asked.

"Take your pick," she said.

"No, you pick. Which door?"

She took a step back and then forward, eyeing the doors closely. "It's a trick. The door marked 'maintenance' is it."

"Really? Why?" She was right, but I wanted to hear her reasoning.

"It just makes sense. Misdirection is an old trick that's been used for years. Plus it looks heavier, bigger I mean. More imposing."

"Yes, it is. Let's go. Is anyone watching us?" I asked.

She looked around, staring at the nearly empty parking garage. "No. I don't see anyone."

"Good." I pressed my hand against the word *access* on the maintenance door and held it there for three seconds. The door slid open to the left. "Stay close."

We passed through into a white, well-lit hallway that descended at a gentle angle.

Anderson asked, "How do you know just anybody can't open that outer door?"

Good question. "Three reasons."

"Tell me."

"First, you have to know exactly where to push. Second, the door is monitored at all times by closed-circuit cameras. Third, you have to know how much consistent pressure to apply and for how long."

"Has anyone ever breached it?"

"No, Anderson, no one has. We're not in Fort Knox or a bank. Not a lot of people are trying to break in."

After fifty feet the hall banked hard to the right and ended at a door. About five feet up, on the left wall, was a slot that required an electronic key card.

I took mine out of my wallet and slid it in.

Parallel to the card reader a panel folded down, and I put my right hand on it. There was a brief light, and then the door slid open.

We stepped inside. I pushed a button on an interior panel, and we started moving down.

"So, it's really an elevator?"

"Hadn't noticed. You sure you're a detective?" I was having fun. "Are you packing?"

"Aren't you?"

"Yes. Glock, .40 caliber. You?" It was from the FBI. It was standard issue now. The FBI wanted something with more stopping power than a 9mm but with less kick than a .45 or a 10mm. So they got together with some gun makers and the .40 cal was invented. When I was a rookie agent, we carried Colt .38 revolvers. It wasn't a joyful experience to have six-shooters when the bad guys had semi- and fully automatic weapons. It took a while, but eventually the Bureau authorized its agents to carry meaner weapons. I, for one, was a happier man that day.

"Did you hear me?"

"Huh? No. What did you say?" I really need to work on my listening skills.

"I carry a Smith and Wesson 9mm semiautomatic. One in the pipe and ten in the clip. Mine carries more than yours," she added.

Wonderful.

"That all?"

"No. I've got a .25 semiauto strapped to my left ankle."

"Really?" I was impressed. I've got a .25 on my right ankle.

The elevator stopped and the doors parted. We stepped into a brightly lit room. The room held seven desks. I was lucky; one of them is mine. It's not a huge room, but it is big enough for our purposes.

"Welcome to Security Level Four," I said.

"Thanks."

"But you can call it Rockwell. We do."

"Rockwell?" Anderson was puzzled.

"Orrin Porter Rockwell. The first Church security agent. Joseph Smith's personal bodyguard. Brigham Young's most trusted scout and tracker," I explained. "Don't you know your Church history?"

She gave me a blank stare that said to shut up.

I didn't. "Down that way," I pointed down a hallway to our right, "are some offices, a quiet room, and a few rooms with cots. Sometimes we pull all-nighters."

"So do I, and I don't have a place to sleep at the station."

"I don't work for the city of Spanish Fork, Detective Anderson. That's my workstation over there." I pointed across the room to my desk. Aside from my computer and a few other things, it was empty.

The room was almost void of agents, and the few that were there were busy. It was Sunday, but security services don't completely take days off. They took little notice of Anderson. Or me.

We walked to my desk, and the lack of anything personal suddenly struck me as strange. Maybe sad. More sad than strange. I flipped a switch and then heard the gentle hum of the computer. I motioned to a chair opposite my desk. "Bring it over," I said. Anderson scooted it behind so she see could see my computer screen.

"No pictures, Grant?"

"No."

"Any kids?"

"No."

"Wife?"

"My wife left me for my partner six years ago. I took it kinda hard. I mean one day, everything is fine, and the next I find out they've been having an affair."

"Why?"

"Why what, Anderson?"

"Why did she do it? I assume you weren't beating or abusing her."

"You assume correctly. Why?" We stared at each other, and I realized in that moment that I would tell her anything she asked me. That had never happened to me before. Like that returned missionary who goes to college and one day he sees the woman he will be sealed to for time and all eternity. Doesn't know her name. But he *knows*. She *knows*. It was my turn to be freaked out. "I don't know." I closed my eyes, reliving a memory that I didn't like to visit. I opened my eyes and Anderson was close to me.

"What did you do, Grant?"

"Do? I didn't do anything. I remember falling to my knees, anger and disbelief washing over me . . . At first, I blamed myself. I figured that I must have done something wrong. I somehow caused her to look for comfort in the arms of another man. After a few years, I came to understand that she was never happy with me. Not from the beginning. I guess me being an FBI agent just pushed her past the limit."

"You grew apart?"

"No. We were never really on the same page. To grow apart, you have to begin together. We never were. I like to believe that at some point we were really in love. But looking back—and I have for six years—we never were. I think that one day she got bored with being my wife and made up her mind to leave me. But she couldn't just leave; she had to hurt me. I don't know why."

"I'm sorry, Grant."

"Don't be. It's okay. I'm okay with it now."

"Really?"

"Mostly," I said.

"I didn't mean to pry."

"You're not. You're my partner, and partners can't pry. I don't know why I told you all that though. The funny thing is, she dumped that guy two years after they became a 'couple.'" I found that very funny, and therapeutic in a way. I even smiled.

"Any more personal questions, Anderson?"

"What was his name?"

"Who?"

"The partner who betrayed you."

"I can't remember. Anything else?"

"What was his name, Grant?"

Talk about pushy. I like that.

"I think his last name was Anderson. Do you have an older brother?"

"Yes. But he's not in the FBI. Never was."

"Anything else, Anderson?"

"Not that I can think of right now. Give me some time."

Okay. "To answer your original question. I don't have any pictures on my desk because there is no one I want to see every day."

I felt awkward and stupid at the same time. I think my palms were sweaty. Like I did when I was sixteen and wanted to go out with Cindy Sorensen. I tried for months to work up enough gumption to ask her out but never did. She was really cute. Her hair was—

"Did you hear me, Grant?"

No. But I took a guess. "All the information that I had on President Taylor was in that folder you read. You spent all day yesterday checking into his life. Let's review. Go ahead." I guessed right.

Anderson cleared her throat and opened her briefcase. She pulled out her own manila folder that was thicker than the one I had. Much thicker. "Born John Andrew Taylor, July 17, 1941, in Manti, Utah. Worked on his dad's farm."

"What did they farm?"

"Does it matter?"

"Yes," I said. No, it doesn't really matter. I just like to know things about the victim of a crime. If you get to know the victim, it may help you later in an investigation.

"Fruits. They had orchards."

"Sounds peachy." I am so clever.

"He graduated from BYU in 1966. Married Ann Kimberly Weber, May 30, 1966, in the Salt Lake Temple. Earned a master's degree from the University of Utah, 1970."

"Anything odd there?" I interrupted.

"No. Aside from graduating from both BYU and the U, nothing odd. But both degrees were in art history. Being an art nut isn't odd, is it?"

Maybe.

"What did he do for a living?" I asked.

"Taught at Springville High School for twenty-five years. Was the principal for almost ten years. He planned to retire after this school year. By all accounts he was well liked. Kept in touch with many of his former students for years after they graduated."

"Again, anything odd?"

"No." She flipped a few more pages. "This was just an ordinary guy. Lived a clean life. Well liked. No known enemies. At least, no enemies who would do to him what someone did."

"Agreed." But somewhere in his life was the clue we needed.

The key to a thorough investigation is asking the right questions. When you don't know what to ask for, you ask as many as you can.

"Who did he leave behind?"

"A wife, Ann Taylor. She's fifty-eight. Detective Lewis, Spanish Fork PD, informed her the morning his body was found. She took it pretty hard and didn't provide any useful leads. Our phone logs show she called to report him missing the night before at around 11:30 p.m."

I nodded. "Kids?"

"Three. Two boys. Donnie, age thirty-one, and Michael, age twenty-four. The daughter's name is Rachel, age twenty-seven. Donnie lives in Wichita, Kansas, and is divorced. No kids. Michael lives in Seattle and is happily married. He has two kids. Rachel had triplets when she was twenty-two. Her husband owns a hardware store in Manti. She's been in Manti ever since she got married," Anderson continued.

"Both parents are deceased. Father in 1984, mother in 1988. Both are buried in Manti."

"Brothers? Sisters?"

"One brother, younger. Name's Jared, and he lives in northern California. Nothing much on him beyond that. Two sisters, one older, deceased, and a younger one in Manti still. Younger's name is Rebecca. She's married with children. According to this, she and Rachel, her niece, live near each other. The older's name was Thelma. She died in 1994. She's also buried in Manti."

Maybe they should leave Manti.

"In the FBI I heard of cases where one brother contracts to have one of his siblings killed. I'll admit that this was probably a contract killing, but I think investigating his brother or sister would be a dead end," I said, then added, "No pun intended."

Anderson made a face, then thought for a minute. "I agree with what you're saying, but why do you think it's a professional kill? Local punks may have thought he saw them stealing or something. It starts small enough, and before you know it, it gets out of hand and BANG!" She clapped her hands together.

"For starters, he was tortured. Why torture an ordinary man?"

"Wait, how do you know he was tortured? The ME said we wouldn't know for sure until tomorrow afternoon at the earliest."

"The fingernails on both pinkie fingers had been removed. Forcibly. I noticed it when I examined the body. Didn't you see that?" I asked.

"No. This is my first homicide. I did notice his hands were bloody though. You know, Grant, I thought I was ready for it. I mean, I am ready. But it's not too often that we have a case like this."

No, it's not. I continued, "He wasn't wealthy or famous. He didn't have military connections or know anything top secret. He had no ambition beyond his job and life. He was tortured for information. They got that information and then killed him for just that. Knowledge. He died because he knew something he wasn't supposed to."

Anderson jumped in. "So he may not have even realized what it was he knew, or maybe he actually knew nothing at all. In any event, dead men don't tell tales, or blow the whistle." So far I agreed with everything she said.

"The anonymous phone call still intrigues me," I said. "It sticks out like a sore thumb. If our assumption is correct, and the killer, or killers, did place that call, what does that tell us about them?"

"They're arrogant. The police knowing about the killing doesn't affect their plans. They very easily could've dumped the body somewhere in the mine but didn't." Anderson was right. If the body had been dumped deep enough in the mine, it could have been weeks, months, or years before it was found. Or maybe never at all. The police knowing about the death of Taylor did not bother the killers.

"Or a timetable? Their timetable?" I suggested.

"Timetable for what?" she asked.

"I don't know. Maybe the killing is giving us something to do, to keep the local police busy."

"You mean a diversion?"

"Quite possibly." I paused. "But these are only guesses. Educated guesses, but still guesses. We need to keep our minds open to all possibilities."

"Of course. But our guesses fit the facts as we know them."

"Yes, they do," I admitted. Plus those guesses jived with what Cook told me, though I couldn't tell that to Anderson. "But our facts may not be complete."

We thought for a few minutes, both of us contemplating what our guesses could possibly be pointing to, if anything.

"Did you take art in high school?" Something was poking me in the back of the brain.

"No. You?"

"No. I've got the artistic ability of a dead frog. Were there any popular teachers in your high school?"

"Sure."

"Ever see them? Since graduation?" I asked.

"No. Not unless it's unavoidable. Why?"

"How did he keep in touch with his students?"

"Uh . . . doesn't really say that. Only says that he did."

"How would you, if you were a teacher or a principal, keep in touch with a large number of your former students?" I had an idea.

"Letters, e-mail, phone calls, things like that."

"Yes, that's right. But what I mean is, where would you go to see a large number of former students, all at once? Remember, he was the art teacher; he was well liked and was popular with his students." I got up and walked around my desk. "Maybe he had his own little cult of personality? He was hip, the 'cool teacher.'"

"Where are you going with this? And Grant . . ."

"What?"

"No one is *hip* anymore."

I am.

"I bet he was the kind of teacher that was invited to almost all the class reunions. Didn't the really popular teachers at your school attend the reunions?"

Anderson thought for a second. "Sounds morbid. What if he was invited?"

"Well, if he was, maybe a former student is involved. Maybe this student and our victim had a conversation or promised to meet later."

"The student was the killer?"

"Or maybe our killers were afraid that the student and teacher exchanged information. Maybe the student was killed as well. Maybe the first killing, if there was a first killing, was the student."

"So what does that do for us?"

"We need to check for any mysterious deaths, unexplained deaths, involving any of his former students in the last seven or eight months. Probably a former art student."

"Why seven months?"

"Most reunions are held in the summer—"

She cut me off. "Let's do it another way."

"Okay. How?"

"Let's start with Utah County and see how many unexplained or suspicious deaths involve his former students. That way, we check faster and further back than just seven or eight months."

She was right.

"But how do we get access to all that information? I'm not even sure the other cities in the county would cooperate," I said.

"Let me make some phone calls," she volunteered.

"Wait. I think we can do it from here." I sat at my desk again.

I typed my password, 1701-D, and waited.

"1701-D is your password?" Anderson started to laugh.

"Yes. Don't laugh. Do you know what it means?" I asked.

"No. But it's stupid. Why not one of your kids' names, or your wife's?"

"I don't have kids, and my wife left me, remember? Good enough?" I sounded testy, but I didn't mean to.

"Good enough. I'm sorry."

I sighed. "Look, it's okay. It was a long time ago, and I'm over it. Mostly."

"But why 1701-D?" she persisted.

I lowered my voice. "It's personal."

She whispered back. "I'm your partner. The old ladies in my ward like you. We have no secrets."

"Okay, I'll tell you. But you have to promise to keep it quiet. You promise?"

"Yes. I promise."

I told her. "I like *Star Trek*. The starship *Enterprise*. It's the ship's registration number from *Star Trek: The Next Generation*."

She was giving me a weird look, and I think she scooted her chair back some. I hastily added, "I'm not some freak or something. I just like it. I don't wear pointy ears or go to the conventions. Not that there's anything wrong with that. They're people too. Besides, what's your password?"

"That's privileged information."

Apparently we do have secrets.

I still had some too.

I got online and went to the FBI home page. I clicked on the "secured" link and waited. A smaller screen popped up and requested my user name and password. Anderson looked at me, and then at the screen.

"Let me guess," she said. "The password is *Enterprise* and the user name is *Kirk*." She smiled. I like her smile.

"You think you're so smart. The user name is not *Kirk*."

"But I'm right about the password, huh?"

"Maybe."

"What's your code word, Grant?"

I typed it in. But dots replaced the letters as I typed.

"Come on, Grant. What is it?" She poked me in my ribs, and I jerked away. "Tell me, Grant."

"You know I can't tell. I won't tell you that." I changed the subject. "Do you like Tolkien?"

"What the heck is that?"

"Not what, who. Did you ever read Tolkien?"

"No. What is he? An author?" she said.

"Yes. You should read the books," I told her.

"Did he write *Star Trek*?"

Write *Star Trek*? *Everyone* knows Gene Roddenberry created *Star Trek*. At least they should. "No, J. R. R. Tolkien did not write *Star Trek*. If I remember, I'll buy you a few books he did write. We can read them together. Maybe see the movie version too."

"Sure."

Did we just make a date? My palms weren't sweaty, and I hadn't stuttered and stumbled through it. So no, it was not a date. The information I'd given her was low-level stuff; nothing important or confidential was accessible with the passwords I'd given her.

I typed some more words at the appropriate places and waited. Still, I felt vulnerable. I had never told anyone before about my *Star Trek* passwords. Not even my ex-wife. Now I had. What she knew now wasn't really that important. What was important was that I'd shared those words with her. And why? Because I liked Anderson's smile? Because she had a nice singing voice? Maybe it was because I liked her smile *and* her hair. Oh, and her eyes too. A nice blue. I like blue.

"Did you hear me?"

"No."

"I asked you where you got the access for this program from?" She was staring at my computer screen. On the monitor were the words:

STATE OF UTAH
DEPARTMENT OF SAFETY

"My grandma."

"That's some grandma."

"Sure is. You should try her oatmeal cookies."

chapter 5

I took Anderson home Sunday night. It was a nice drive. The sky was clear, the night chilly. We talked about my life in the FBI, my days as a missionary. She mentioned an old boyfriend. She thought she loved him, but it turned out they wanted different things. She wanted to marry in the temple, and he didn't really care. She said it hurt, but they split up.

"Anyway, that was years back."

"How old are you, Anderson?"

"Thirty-one."

"I'm thirty-seven."

"You're ancient." But she said it with a smile.

I dropped her at the police station and agreed to meet her there Monday afternoon.

Which I did.

Our research had painted a portrait of a well-liked, well-respected man. But he was also dead. Our research had also revealed two mysterious deaths of Taylor's former students in the past eight months. Which explains why on Monday we were in the basement of the Utah County Health Department looking at dead people. The room was white and sterile and cold. I know it's cold for medical reasons; it helps preserve specimens and samples or something. But knowing this didn't make me feel any warmer.

The medical examiner was a middle-aged woman. She was thin—almost too thin if you ask me. She had big hazel eyes, and she wasn't wearing glasses. At least she wasn't now. Her name tag read *Dr. Sherman*. Dr. Sherman wasn't wearing any makeup, and her hair was pulled back tight. Dr. Sherman went directly to the point, and I noted she was using sanitized equipment. Keeping things super clean did little to help her patients, but it did help ensure her work was not contaminated. She seemed a perfect match for this basement.

She was talking to Anderson. "Death occurred around 6:00 p.m."

"From?"

"Could've been a lot of things, like loss of blood or a punctured lung, if not for the deep cut across the larynx."

"Were you able to determine what kind of blade was used?" Anderson asked.

"Something sharp, but not new. Maybe a hunting knife of some sort. Something with approximately an eight-inch blade. If we ever find it, we could probably match it to him." Dr. Sherman motioned her head in the direction of what used to be President Taylor.

And hopefully match it to the killer, I said to no one.

"What about his other wounds?" I said aloud.

"His left eye was put out by something hot. A poker or something like it. Not very nice. There's something strange though."

"What?"

"Here. Look." She pulled down the sheet covering his body. "See that?"

"No. What am I looking for, Doc? Can you see it, Anderson?"

"No." She sounded weak.

"Look at his right armpit. See that wound? My guess is it was done with the same weapon that put his eye out."

"But," Anderson pointed out, "the responding officers said nothing about his shirt being off when they found the body."

"That's because it wasn't. His clothes are in a bag you can pick up before you leave, but I can assure you that his shirt doesn't have a hole in it that corresponds with this wound. It would've been a very painful wound. It's almost four inches deep. It caused the right lung to collapse."

"Sounds painful," I remarked. "Anything else?"

"Yes, the fingernails on each small finger have been forcibly removed from their bed. Most likely by a small pair of pliers."

"Can you tell how early?" Anderson asked.

"No. Not exactly. Not yet anyway. But there was a lot of blood on both hands. Probably ten minutes or so before he was killed. Whoever did this, they were trying to look professional. But aside from the wound under the arm, it was sloppy," Dr. Sherman said.

"Doc, have you seen anything like this before?"

"Well, you see, Agent Grant, I interned in Washington, D.C., and I saw a lot of things. I—"

I cut her off. "Excuse me. What I meant was, have you seen anything like this around here?"

"No. But I am very busy. My staff is small, and overworked." She brushed a stray hair away from her face. "We can check my files." She walked away from the body, and we followed her out of the basement morgue.

Her office was down a short hallway. It wasn't very big, but it was warmer than the constant chill of the autopsy room. It wasn't as clean though. The desk was small and overflowing with paperwork. I could see the remains of a mostly eaten plain bagel and an empty jar of orange juice nearest her chair. The computer was the only item on her desk that looked liked it was used often.

"Please, sit." She motioned to two rickety wooden chairs.

Anderson sat. I stood.

"I wonder if you could check your notes for two specific cases." Before Dr. Sherman could respond, Anderson continued, "We have tried to narrow the parameters of the search a little."

"How?"

"We're looking for murders in the last eight months. Beyond that, can't tell you how or why." I looked at Anderson. "Give her the names."

"Justin K. Barlow and Jason P. Russell. Both are from Springville."

One of the most important things about an investigation is to make sure that you never "coach" or "lead" a witness or someone you want information from. Sometimes it's an easy thing to avoid. Sometimes it isn't. But I wasn't interested in a bunch of medical terms. I wanted details. Ideally, I wanted a similar underarm wound found on someone else. I decided to tell her what I was looking for.

"Doc, all we need to know is what the deaths were ruled and any notes or info you may have saved regarding each. Okay?"

"Sure, Agent Grant. Give me a minute."

She was quiet for a minute, and we all listened to the sound of her computer humming to life. "Spell it," she said.

"Spell what?" Anderson asked.

"The *names*, Detective. I'm a horrible speller."

She did.

"Let's see. Barlow, Justin K. Died October 31, last year. Cause of death, multiple gunshot wounds to the upper chest. Ruled a homicide."

Anderson was taking notes. She took good notes. She listened carefully and wrote quickly. She was very thorough, and when she had more experience she would be a very good detective. I started looking around, in, and out of Dr. Sherman's office.

I noticed a custodial engineer go down the hallway. In high school they were called janitors. Now it seemed everyone wanted to be an engineer. I don't. Too much math. He had black hair. And he was short.

"Nothing strange here. No fingernails missing. No other damage. The head was left alone. No wound to the right armpit. Or the left one. A fairly routine autopsy," Sherman remarked.

"Fairly?" I asked.

"Yes. It seems that a premed student vomited while it was performed. I wonder if he still wants to be a doctor?" She almost snickered.

"What about any others?" I asked.

"Hmm . . . Russell, Jason P. Died in a fire. His shop blew up July 28."

Alarm bells went off in my head. "Tell me more."

"Okay. It was ruled a suspicious death. Possible foul play."

"Why?" Anderson jumped in.

"Don't know. Probably because the cause of the fire was never determined. But that's just a guess. No wounds to the head or eyes. It was all over the news. Maybe you saw a report on it. Wait, there is a notation about a wound to the right armpit."

The bells were louder now. "Did you do the autopsy, Doc?" I asked.

"No. Dr. Williams did."

"We need to talk to him," I said.

"You can't, Agent Grant. He died last month from a massive MCI."

"MCI?" I was puzzled.

"Myocardial infarction."

I gave her a quizzical look.

"A heart attack, Agent Grant."

I knew that.

Sherman went on. "That's why we're understaffed now. He was a good doctor. Very careful. You don't know of any good doctors looking for a job, do you?"

"No. But if we come across any, we'll be sure to send 'em your way, Doc."

Dr. Sherman looked at us. "I need to get back to work."

"Thanks, Doc." I put my hand out. "Thanks for all your help."

I turned and walked out of the room, and bumped into the janitor. I knocked his garbage can off its cart.

"Whoa! Excuse me." I picked up the can and put it back on the cart. It was empty anyway. I looked at the custodial engineer. He was Asian. I asked, "You okay?"

"Yes. Thank you. I just empty it."

"You hurt?" I looked at him. Something was wrong.

"No. Thank you."

"Yeah. Lucky you."

We stared at each other. Something was wrong. I heard

Anderson's voice and poked my head back in the room. "Come on, Anderson, let's go."

When I turned around, the custodial engineer was gone.

The important thing was that we had found our first murder victim: Russell, Jason P.

"Russell, Jason P., who are you? Who killed you?" I asked aloud.

"What, Grant?"

"Nothing, Anderson. Can you access Springville PD info from Spanish Fork police headquarters?"

"Yes. All general info is on a common database. Now that we know where to look, we can use it. Let's go."

We did.

Hindsight is twenty-twenty, and if I'd known then what I know now, I would have shot that garbage man on the spot. And saved myself, Anderson, and Sherman a lot of trouble. It would have saved Sherman's life. But I was too excited by the discovery of information to pay any attention to an Asian janitor with an empty garbage can.

Like I said, hindsight is twenty-twenty.

Police Headquarters
Spanish Fork, Utah
Monday, February 6, 2006, 5:20 p.m.

We didn't talk much on the way over. I was in the mood for Billy Joel, not conversation. Besides, it's easier for me to think when I'm not talking. We made it to Spanish Fork police headquarters in about thirty-five minutes.

"Nice desk, Anderson." Her desk was immaculate. But I did notice that she had a picture of an older couple near one of the desk edges. I guessed it was her parents. I also noticed the lack of a boyfriend picture.

"Thanks, Grant. Do you want me to mess it up so you'll feel more comfortable?"

Whatever. I didn't answer.

"Have a seat, Agent Grant."

I sat in a chair opposite from her. "Look, you don't have to call me that. Just 'Grant.' Okay?"

"Okay." She turned her computer on. "So, we have our first victim."

"Let's not get too far ahead," I said. "They could be unrelated."

"I know. But come on, Grant. This has to be it."

"No, Anderson, it doesn't *have* to be. But, unofficially, I agree with you. We have our first victim. Officially, we have a lead we need to follow up on."

She nodded her head in acknowledgment but didn't look up from her computer. I could hear her fingers assaulting the keyboard.

"You type well, Anderson."

"Be quiet, Grant."

I looked more closely at the room around me. We were on the second floor of a three-story brown brick building. I surmised that this was a new building. It didn't have the normal clutter of a police station. Don't get me wrong; I don't mean filth. It just didn't look like other police stations. Except for the newer ones.

"New building, huh, Anderson?"

Sarcasm dripped from her mouth. "You must've been a great agent for the FBI."

I was.

It wasn't very crowded in the room we were in.

"How many detectives are there in Spanish Fork?"

"Three. Not counting me. One is on vacation. That would be Simmons. Over there is Detective Lewis." She pointed to somewhere behind me. "He's kinda touchy about his height."

I turned in my seat. I don't know why he was touchy. He looked perfectly normal for a short man.

"Did you hear me, Grant?"

"What?"

"I said, don't make fun of his height. Got it?"

"Got it. Don't make fun of the short one."

She continued. "That desk over there belongs to Detective Sorenson."

"How did you get so lucky to work with me?" I asked.

"I was the only one here."

Lucky you.

"Here we go. Russell, Jason P. Died in a shop fire July 28 of last year. The time frame matches ours."

"Yes. It does."

"Cause of the fire was never determined. But it was suspected arson. It apparently began with some solvent that Jason kept on hand."

"What kind of shop was it?"

She read a little further before responding. "He was an artist."

"What kind?"

She looked at me. "Sculptor."

"Anything good?"

"Nothing you would know, Grant."

How does she know? I might.

"Does it say anything about the wound in the right armpit?" I asked.

"Just that it was suspicious. Cause unknown. Officially the case is still open. We can speak to the primary detective in Springville."

"We don't need to." My mind was racing. "Jason Russell isn't the key. What was done to him is. He was tortured for information, just like President Taylor was. But we know Jason Russell told them something."

"How do we know that?"

"Because President Taylor was murdered. Jason Russell told them that he'd spoken to someone. He told President Taylor something, and it got Taylor killed. But what was it?"

"That's a lot of supposition, Grant. And who would care what Jason Russell possibly told a third person? Was it worth killing for? He was an artist in *Springville, Utah*. Why kill him?"

Good question.

"I don't know, Anderson. All I do know is the killer thought the information was important enough to protect. Jason Russell told John Taylor something, and that something ended up getting him killed."

"Right. Grant, I have to ask you something. Before we search further."

"What?"

"Why are you here? It's been bugging me from the beginning. Why is an ex-FBI man working on a murder case in small-town Utah?"

I'd been waiting for that question. I was glad to hear it had bothered her from the beginning. It bugged me too, but I knew why it bugged me. I'm not a big fan of international terrorists. I didn't answer her.

We looked at each other, searching. "The Olympics are coming here, Grant. Again. This makes Salt Lake City a prime target for every terrorist nut in the world. An average man is found murdered, and the FBI sends you down. Why? Is there a connection?"

Despite my growing affinity for Anderson's company—is that what it was?—I couldn't tell her all I knew. As much as I hate the need-to-know policy, it exists for good reasons.

"Why I am here has nothing to do with rogue terrorist cells or their activity." North Korea is a rogue country, not a rogue terrorist cell. "Don't ask me how I know because I can't tell you. Trust me. Please." I pleaded with my eyes. I knew that she did trust me and that I trusted her too. Even though I don't like to trust anyone. We were partners, and partners trust. They have to. Anderson turned away from me and typed on her keyboard for a minute or so. She didn't look at me; she just typed like I wasn't there. I couldn't tell if she was mad at me or not. I wasn't sure if she should be or not.

"How do you know Conductor?" I asked. She stopped typing, her hands resting on the keyboard. Her nails weren't painted or polished.

"Who?"

I told her who.

"Oh, he and my grandfather knew each other as kids. They went to school together. He was just always around. As much he could be. He was like a third grandpa. He was at my high school graduation. He called me early Friday morning and asked that I look after you. Told me what you look like so I could spot you."

I wonder how he described me. I was about to ask but she looked at her watch.

"It's after six, Grant. You'd better get back to Salt Lake. Traffic will be horrible."

"Okay. See you at seven thirty. Where do you live?"

"Why?"

"So I can meet you, Anderson. You know, pick you up."

I mean, we are partners.

"Oh. Right. Thirty-five West 300 North right here in Spanish Fork. It's a three-story Victorian, right off Main Street. It's been in my family for three generations."

"Cool. What about your parents?"

"Don't worry about waking my parents. My folks live in Mesa, Arizona, and my brother lives in Omaha, Nebraska. Any more questions about my family?"

"Not now. See you at seven thirty, Detective Anderson."

I stood and left.

Spanish Fork police headquarters is on Main Street too. I almost turned right, in search of Anderson's house. It might be handy to know where my new partner lived. But I'm retired FBI, not a stalker, so I turned left instead.

Main Street took me to the freeway, and I headed north for Salt Lake and my small house. What a crazy day it had been. One murder had become two, and we had plenty of ideas and theories, but no real evidence to link any of it. Except for a wound found in the right armpit of both victims.

I would put in a call to some friends with the Bureau when I got home and ask for some help, I thought. Maybe those types of wounds are associated with particular groups of people. Like the old KGB. Probably a dead end, but I would ask anyway.

I knew for sure that one old friend in particular would help me. I thought about calling Agent Cook, but I was pretty sure I was too busy to call him. So I didn't.

I was passing Springville. On the east bench of the mountains I could see the huge white Y. It was lit up for some reason. Homecoming? I was in BYU territory. I think Church schools are a good idea. I keep waiting for the BYU—Rome campus to open. I had a good time at BYU. I learned a lot at and from the Y. It really is a good school and the FBI, NSA, CIA all love it. It's a campus full of clean, dedicated, returned-missionary, honest young men and women who believe in honoring the government. At least that's the crowd I hung out with. The Young Republicans have a big chapter on campus too, but I don't see how the two are related.

I was hungry. The grumbling of my stomach interrupted my thoughts. I took the Provo Center Street exit off the freeway and went in search of a place to eat.

chapter 6

I drove on, heading east on Center Street. At the corner of University Avenue and Center Street, I found a restaurant, Los Hermanos. But I wasn't in the mood for Mexican food, and it looked crowded. I didn't stop.

I turned onto University Avenue, and a half block down I found what I was looking for. I parked on the opposite side of the street from the restaurant, in front of an abandoned theater.

I crossed the street, at great personal risk, and walked into A Touch of Seoul. It had been a few years since I'd been in Korea. And to tell the truth, I spent most of my time at the U.S. embassy in Seoul or at the U.S. consulate building in Pusan. I was busy, and the only Koreans I really ever spent time with were my counterparts in the Korean intelligence branches. I didn't learn much about the country is what I'm trying to say. Oh, I drove the streets, ate their candy and snack food, and drank their versions of Coke and Pepsi. But that was pretty much it. And the language is as similar to English as Egyptian. It's not something you learn in high school.

Conductor was going there soon, and that meant I was going back. I figured on trying some food before I went. Food that didn't come in a candy wrapper or box. Food I made a habit of avoiding while I was there. It's easier than it sounds when you have access to the embassy cafeteria and grocery. Maybe I could recommend a dish that Conductor should try.

It wasn't very crowded, and I was seated quickly. The table was clean, mostly, and the restaurant smelled good. Hopefully that was an indication of good food. I speak English, and I can curse a little in Spanish. But no Korean. My waitress spoke some English, more than I did in Spanish. Despite her broken English and my utter ignorance of Korean, I managed to order something.

She was nice and didn't seem too concerned with my staring at her. Did I know her? Not possible. She looked like a Korean woman because she was Korean. And she was pretty, but I had never seen her before. But there was something about her voice, the way she talked. I stopped staring when she walked out of my line of sight. I kept thinking though. Maybe I had seen someone that looked like her? That must be it, I thought, but who? In any event, my dinner was ordered, I didn't really know what I was getting, and it didn't matter because I was hungry. On the north wall was a television tuned to KSL.

My waitress brought me a Coke. At least I hoped it was. It was kind of flat, but I was thirsty so I gulped it down. A few minutes later she brought out my food, and I ordered another Coke. The food smelled and looked horrible. I suddenly remembered why I always ate in the cafeteria or in restaurants that catered to Westerners.

"Excuse me, miss, but what is this?"

My waitress gave me a funny look and said, "*Kimchi chigea. Kimchi* soup. Very good."

"Oh, okay. Thanks." That helped a lot.

I know exactly what *that* is.

She put a bowl of steamed rice and three smaller dishes on my table. One had in it what looked like the stuff I had in my soup. So I guessed it was *kimchi*. Pieces of red and orange cabbage. The second had bean sprouts, and the third dish had what looked like yellow turnips in it. I have a rule I live by. I learned it from my father, and it has served me well throughout my life. It is a simple rule: Don't eat anything yellow unless it is a potato chip. See, it's a simple rule and surprisingly easy to follow. I didn't try the turnips. My waitress left me alone to ponder the wonder that is *kimchi* soup.

I took a few bites and found it was actually pretty good. The taste far exceeded the look. I would have to recommend this to Conductor.

I decided to slow down and think. My food was hot. What did we know about these killings? I was positive that the two were connected. Each man was murdered by the same people, for the same reason. But what was the reason?

A few bites later I thought I was going to die. Whatever *kimchi* is, I decided I didn't like it when it wasn't in the soup. But I would still recommend it to Conductor. Maybe he would like it. I pushed the bowl away from me and tried to think.

I gave up after a few seconds. I was getting a headache and nausea from my first experience with South Korean cuisine.

The TV was on. KSL's anchorwoman, Carol, was talking to a reporter. The reporter was standing in front of a building that looked vaguely familiar. I walked over to the TV and read the caption explaining where the reporter was. It read *Utah County Health Department Building*. I turned the volume up.

Carol the Anchorwoman was speaking, "Shelly, do the police have any leads? Or possible suspects?"

Shelly, the reporter, responded, "No, Carol, they don't. My sources tell me that it is too early to expect that. They stress that this does appear to be just a random killing and are asking that the citizens remain calm."

That's cop talk for, "We don't know nothin' so leave us alone so we can do our job. And when we do learn something, we might share it with you."

Carol the Anchorwoman said, "Thank you, Shelly. That's Shelly Ostler, live from outside the Utah County Health Department Building." The split screen went away, and with it Shelly Ostler. Anchorwoman Carol continued. "Recapping our top story, the chief medical examiner for Utah County has been found dead in her Provo office. Foul play is suspected, although police are not saying very much at this point." Carol the Anchorwoman smiled.

"I'm sorry, Doc." She didn't deserve to be another victim of this mess. My mind began to whirl.

You know in the movies when the good guy finally has "that" moment: the flashbacks fly fast and furious, suddenly a piece of the puzzle fits, and the camera zooms in from far away right up to his face? That moment when he realizes something that he should have seen coming but didn't? I had a moment like that. I prefer to think of it as personal revelation. In any event, I *knew*. I knew Anderson was in danger, knew whoever killed the ME would try to hurt her. Kill her. I wasn't going to lose this partner, not if I could help it.

Besides, I try not to argue with personal revelation.

It wasn't the waitress I'd seen before. The janitor! The waitress's voice, the way she spoke. She reminded me of *him*. The one with the empty garbage can. It hadn't just been empty; the can had been clean. He was Korean. *The* Korean the FBI wanted.

I dropped a twenty on the counter and ran out.

Detective Anderson.

I wasn't going to lose her too.

Why did I leave?

I could've stayed in Spanish Fork.

They have motels there.

Maybe.

I reached my car and threw it into gear. Spanish Fork was about twelve minutes away. Twenty with traffic. It hadn't snowed for a few days, so the freeway was clear of snow and ice.

My heart was racing. I struggled to get my emotions under control and drive at the same time.

I did.

Barely.

* * *

Spanish Fork, Utah
35 West 300 North

Detective Elizabeth Anderson was near exhaustion. It had been a long day, and it wasn't even "late" yet. The dash clock in her '91 Honda Accord read 5:50 p.m. Grant had been gone nearly forty minutes, and she was still smiling. He made her laugh.

She shook her head. She had to be exhausted, or mad, to be thinking about him. He was infuriating. So smug, almost arrogant. Almost? No, she thought, he *is* arrogant. But still, she smiled. She liked his sarcasm. He thought he was so sly. And he was embarrassed to admit he liked *Star Trek*. He was a big teddy bear. An older, divorced, sarcastic, arrogant, know-it-all teddy bear. No, she thought, he acts like he knows it all but isn't afraid to admit when he doesn't. That was one quality that separated Grant from guys like Detective Millhouse. *That* guy had asked her out once, and she had politely but firmly refused.

She deepened her voice, "So, Anderson, is 11:00 a.m. church too early for your husband?" He thought he was so sly. And the older sisters in her ward were probably already planning the wedding reception. She didn't mind telling Grant she wasn't married. She knew he wasn't.

Her house was only a five-minute drive from the station, but traffic was heavy for Spanish Fork, and some dork had already cut her off.

"Nothing like driving to keep one awake," she remarked.

She turned onto Third North, went almost a third of a block, and turned into her driveway. The house really was too big for her. The three-level Victorian had been built around the turn of the century by her paternal great-grandfather. She'd spent many hours playing games inside as a child with her brother and knew it like the back of her hand. It was in need of some minor repairs and a paint job. Elizabeth Anderson was too busy to do either and couldn't afford to pay someone to do it. Cops don't make a lot of money. And she'd seen some "home repairs" done by fellow officers.

She would save up.

Or wait until she had a husband. Heck, she'd settle for a boyfriend. But she didn't have either. She dated when she could, but it wasn't that often. She was busy. Too busy to worry about chasing after a man. Besides, if she did have a husband or boyfriend, he probably would be too lazy to do it anyway. Most men are. Maybe after all this was over, she would get Grant to do it. "I wonder how handy he is?" she said out loud. Probably not very.

She didn't have any other houses directly next to hers. To the east was the business district, to the west a credit union, to the north an empty auto repair garage, and to the south, behind her house, was a vacant lot. Between her house and the credit union stood an old wall. Her grandfather hadn't liked the family who lived where the credit union now stood, and he'd built the six-foot wall that separated the properties. It followed the property line and swept around the back of the house. As a little girl, Anderson had climbed it once, fallen, and broken her leg. She'd never climbed it again.

She lived in the middle of a city and was isolated at the same time. But she liked it that way. In the winter it seemed even more isolated because of the white blanket of snow and ice that covered the house and everything around it. The last storm was supposed to dump at least three inches. But for some reason southern Utah County had been spared the extra snow. She looked at her lawn and could see patches of her dead winter grass peeking through the snow.

She went in through the kitchen door at the back of the house.

She locked the door.

She was tired.

The stairs were at the front of the house, down a narrow hallway. She headed for the stairs. She put her 9mm Smith and Wesson on a stand near the phone and started up the stairs. Three quarters of the way up, there was a small landing. The stairs then pivoted to the right until they reached the second floor. It was here, on the landing, that she paused and knelt down. Her pants leg was already up, her hand reaching for the velcro strap that kept the small .25 on her ankle.

CRASH!

CRASH!

Detective Anderson spun around before she'd even heard the second crash. The first crash had come from her kitchen door, the second from her front door. She could see an arm, covered by a black sweatshirt, reaching through the broken pane on her front door, trying to unlock her door. She couldn't get to her weapon near the phone. She ran to the second floor. To the phone in her bedroom.

She was positive she hadn't been seen on the stairs and had a few seconds while the people coming for her had to search the first floor.

Detective Anderson did not panic. It was not her nature, and she was a police officer. Training kicked in, and she quickly evaluated her options. She picked up her cordless phone and dialed 911, walked to her closet, and took down her 12-gauge shotgun from the top shelf. It was loaded. It held six cartridges. Anderson knew that with a shotgun, in an enclosed space, she had a small edge. Unless her attackers had automatic weapons with them. Then it wouldn't matter what she did.

"Please state the nature of your emergency," said a voice in Anderson's ear.

"Listen up. Officer in distress. Code 257. Thirty-five West 300 North, Spanish Fork. I nee—"

The line went dead. They'd most likely torn it from the wall downstairs. But she got her call for help out before the phone went dead. She tossed the phone onto her bed and repeated the call on her cell. Then she left it on and tossed it on her bed.

She ran over to her dresser and pushed with all her strength. It moved—too slowly, she thought—till it sat in front of her bedroom door. Most people would think her room had only two ways out and that she'd just blocked one.

There was a third way out, but it was concealed, and it only led upstairs to the attic. The old doorway was concealed by an antique china hutch. It was good and heavy. It would take at least two or three men to move it and expose the old door. Only Anderson knew about the door and stairs behind it. She also knew that the flight of stairs in her bedroom behind the china hutch wouldn't support her weight, let alone multiple attackers. The stairs were original and in desperate need of replacement. For once she was glad she couldn't afford repairs.

The remaining exit was a connecting door to another bedroom.

* * *

I did have a radio in my car. In the glove box. I was speeding, and praying that a Utah Highway Patrolman would see me.

"Please try to stop me."

I didn't realize how cluttered my glove box was. "Where is the UHP?!" If they tried to pull me over, well, that would be one more cop going to the party at Anderson's.

I was finally able to reach my radio. I clicked it on and said, "This is Special Agent Peter Grant, Federal Bureau of Investigation. Any law enforcement officers hearing this: Officer in distress. I repeat, officer in distress. Detective Anderson, Spanish Fork PD, is in danger."

I suddenly felt lame. I couldn't remember her address. Heck, I didn't even *know* that she was at home. I threw the radio on the floor.

* * *

She was alone.

She had to stay alive.

A flight of stairs to the third floor was in her room, but she didn't take them. Anderson didn't want to fall to the first floor. She knew a different way to the third floor. She grabbed some extra shotgun shells and ran through the connecting door into a smaller room with three exits, counting the one she'd come through. She knew the house better than her attackers and was gambling that they didn't know about the third way out.

She could hear them on the stairs.

She figured ten minutes or less before help arrived.

A voice called out.

"Detective Anderson. We know you are here. We wish only to talk."

Sure you do, she thought. Maybe that's all you wanted with Jason Russell and President Taylor too. The voice sounded . . . different. An accent she wasn't familiar with.

The second floor branched two ways from the top of the stairs. She could hear them in her bedroom.

She heard the popping of a gun, but it was in the other room.

A body crashed through the hallway door and rolled into a kneeling position five feet in front of her. It fired. Anderson was smart. She was behind the sturdiest thing in the room, an old cast-iron tub. Her mother had used it as a flower bed on the back porch. Anderson never had time to water plants, and even plastic plants died under her care. So she'd never used it like her mother had. But she liked the tub and had emptied and moved it to the small bedroom upstairs. Where it was now. Now, she was using it as a shield. Three slugs hit the tub and stopped.

She fired her shotgun.

The attacker's head snapped back, and he crumpled to the ground.

Bullets sprayed the wall behind her. She could see a figure in the doorway to her bedroom and one blocking the hallway from view.

She yelled, "Grant, get the one in the hallway!" It was the only misdirection ploy she could come up with. It didn't need to be brilliant; it only needed to be enough to cause some hesitation and confusion for her attackers. Just to give her a few seconds.

Then she fired into her bedroom and ran for the closet.

A pain ripped her right shoulder and left leg.

She seemed unable to hold the shotgun in her right hand. Her hand wouldn't, couldn't squeeze anymore. She dropped the shotgun and crashed through the closet door.

* * *

Anderson had told me that her house was down the street from Spanish Fork police headquarters. I knew that was on Main Street. I ran the off-ramp's red light, narrowly avoiding a red Toyota Celica. The driver gave me an obscene gesture.

"Nice manners." I meant me.

I headed toward the mountains and Anderson's house.

I hoped.

I passed a shopping center and a gas station/quicky mart. I'd almost reached the police station. I was running out of space and time. Then I saw what I needed.

A police cruiser went flying past me, lights flashing and siren blaring.

I followed.

I just hoped it was going to the same place I was.

* * *

Anderson landed at the foot of a narrow flight of stairs. The closet door was a newer addition to the house, but there was no closet behind it. Just stairs. Stairs that were in only slightly better shape than the flight of stairs in her bedroom. They were very narrow and steep. Her attackers could only follow her up one at a time.

She just might survive as long as no one found and somehow traversed the stairs up from her bedroom. If so, with attackers in front and behind, she would be an easy kill.

She made her way up as fast as she could. Her left leg wasn't working very well, and her right arm was going numb. A surge of adrenaline propelled her up the stairs. She slumped down behind a low wall that acted as a railing at the top of the stairs and tried to yank her .25 from her right ankle. It took three tries, but she finally commanded her body to grip the gun. She put it in her left hand, the hand that could squeeze the trigger, and fought to control her breathing. She didn't care if they could hear her, but breathing hard meant her heart would pound and the sound would reverberate in her ears.

"Detective Anderson, please stop. This running and shooting is of no point. You have lost your gun. I have it in my hand. You have lost. I have questions to ask of you. Tell me, do you like living in the Spanish Fork? I know you are wounded. Please let us help."

Why don't you shut up? He knows I won't surrender. Why is he still talking? Why . . .

She jumped up and fired five quick rounds down the stairs. Two black-clad figures were on the stairs. She hit them both, and they fell backward down to the second floor.

She knew they probably weren't fatal shots. Her gun was a small caliber and didn't have the stopping power of her 9mm. She didn't have to kill them. She just had to stay alive as long as she could.

Then she heard them.

Sirens.

Her strength left her, and she had to lean against the wall just to breathe. Even that was hard. She fired two more rounds into the ceiling, screaming in pain, defiance, victory. She felt her gun arm go limp, and her gun dropped to the floor.

She couldn't lift it.

Even if she had to.

* * *

Mine was the second car there, right on the rear bumper of the police cruiser. The cop in front of me jumped out of his car as I did mine.

"Easy, officer." I flashed my ID. "Grant, FBI."

"Good. More are on the way." He meant police officers. "What's going on?"

"I don't know. Be alert." I pulled my Glock out.

We heard two shots from inside the house.

"You take the front; I'll go in back."

The driveway on the side of the house hadn't been plowed for a while. So, despite the lack of freshly fallen snow, the only path through the driveway was made by the tires of Anderson's Honda.

The tire ruts were icy. I almost fell a few times and had to slow down. I finally reached the end and rounded the last corner. I saw two figures trying to scale the back wall. One was having trouble with it. Whoever he was, he didn't make it over the wall. He acted injured.

"Stop! Police!" I'm not a cop, but it sometimes works. This time I was one for two. The injured guy stopped what he was doing. The other was over the wall and gone.

I ran up to my catch. He was dressed in black, including a black ski mask. I pushed him to the ground and put my knee in his back. His black outfit stood out nicely against the snow.

"What are you supposed to be? Scary?" I tore his ski mask off. It revealed a mess of black hair, a nose stud, and an earring.

He was smaller looking now, maybe 160 pounds. The mystery was gone and so was the fear he hoped his black getup would trigger. He wasn't the Asian I was looking for. Just some punk. A punk that had tried to kill, maybe had killed, Anderson.

My Anderson.

That made me mad.

"Shouldn't you be in school, junior? How about detention?"

"Screw you."

"No thanks, jerk. You don't drive a red Celica, do you?" I already didn't like this perp. Which was somewhat surprising. That usually takes at least fifteen minutes. Not tonight.

"Where are you hit?" I'm not devoid of compassion.

"In the leg."

Nice.

"Which one?" I was patting him down; I couldn't find a weapon.

"That one."

I swear, he was stupid. "Okay, you only have two choices. Left or right?"

"The right one." He was in real pain, and the back of his right leg was wet. With blood, I figured. He was also at ease with me. He'd dealt with cops a lot, obviously.

"You sure?"

"Yeah."

"Okay, get up. I'll help you walk back. You try to run away, and I will shoot you. Understand?"

"Yeah, cop. You gonna cuff me?"

"Later. Walk." I gave him a shove in front of me.

He almost fell down.

I didn't care.

"Is she dead? 'Cause I shot her." He sure was being talkative. I thought about advising him of his *Miranda* rights. You know, the right to remain silent and all that stuff. But I didn't initiate this recent bout of info sharing, so I didn't tell him his rights.

"Don't know. Why?"

"'Cause, pig, I got her. I bet she's dead."

I don't like being called a pig. After all, I'm not a cop.

But that's not why I kicked the idiot in the back of his right leg. Hard.

His scream was slightly high-pitched.

I grabbed him and threw him to the ground. "I want to know who contracted you and your boys to kill a police officer. I'm only asking once."

His breathing was shallower now, trying to compensate for the pain. "You think I'll tell you? Man, you must be a dumb cop."

I think he liked pain. I squeezed the back of his right leg, and he screamed again. "I said I was only asking once. Who?"

For a tough guy, he sure was whimpering a lot.

"You stupid—"

His own scream of pain put an end to his obscenities.

This time it was more of a wail.

"I don't like to be sworn at. What are you, punk, dumb or deaf?" My gun was out, pressed against the front of his head. "I want a name, and I want it now. Who?"

"You can't shoot me, man. I gave up. I stopped running. You stopped me. I give up!" He yelled the last part, probably hoping that someone else would show up and get me off him.

Or at least my gun off his head.

"You give up, huh? Tell someone who cares. I want to know, now!"

"All right . . . Okay . . . I can't give you a name . . ."

"Why not, punk?" I think the barrel end of my Glock was leaving a permanent impression on his forehead.

"He didn't tell us his name . . . All I know is that he's Korean."

Really? "How does a low-life scum like you know that he was Korean and not Chinese or Japanese or French or something else? You speak Korean? I doubt that. You look too dumb."

"My friend . . . José . . ." He was breathing quickly, shallow.

I didn't care.

". . . he called this guy Japanese . . . This guy . . . he flipped out . . . man, he lost it, almost killed my friend right in front of us . . . he told us he wasn't . . . said he was Korean . . . told us not to never forget it, or he'd kill us all . . . I swear . . . don't kill me . . . he said he was Korean . . . Korean . . ." He mumbled it a few more times, and then started crying, I think.

I didn't shoot him.

Never even considered it.

I helped him up, sort of.

CHAPTER 7

First thing I did when I got back to the front of Anderson's house was to drop off my limping sidekick. The street was full of police cars and officers. My little buddy had recovered from his crying episode and felt tough again. He was cursing up a storm, threatening to kill me, my mother, my dog, and finally my wife.

"I don't have a dog, stupid." I kneed the back of his right leg again, for good measure, and handed him over to a blue-clad patrolman.

"This young man confessed to first-degree burglary, assault with a deadly weapon, and attempted murder of a police officer," I said. The officer escorted my new friend to a waiting patrol car and cuffed him.

I never saw him again.

By now, there were cops everywhere. Police officers and blue and red flashing lights all over the place. If there'd been any more lights, it would have been a disco. There was also an ambulance. Its lights were flashing red. Then I saw her. She was alive. And I found hope. Anderson was being carried out the front door on a stretcher. I forgot about the lights and all the cops. She was coherent but in a lot of pain.

I walked to her.

"Hey, partner," I said, and squeezed her right hand. "You'll be okay." I wanted to say so much more. Wanted to tell her how I felt. But couldn't.

"Grant." She was having trouble speaking, and I leaned down to her. "You are not a doctor." She closed her eyes. A paramedic put an oxygen mask over her face.

"Where are you taking her?" I asked one of the paramedics.

"UVRMC." She was slid into the back of the ambulance, and it drove away.

I asked the nearest police officer, "What the heck is UVRMC?"

He looked at me like I was stupid, or from Salt Lake. I wasn't going to tell him he was at least half right. "They're taking her to Utah Valley Regional Medical Center. It's in Provo." He pointed north.

I know where Provo is.

SFPD could handle the scene. I jumped in my car and followed the ambulance. Anderson was still alive, and if I had a say, she would stay that way.

* * *

I followed the ambulance closely and pulled into the hospital just behind it. I was just behind the stretcher, and I followed it as far as I was allowed. It wasn't very far. Like Anderson said, I'm no doctor. A nurse stopped me outside a pair of double doors that read:

AUTHORIZED PERSONNEL ONLY
BEYOND THIS POINT

I felt authorized, but I obeyed the nurse. I went to the waiting area just a few feet away. All I could think about was Anderson and how stupid I'd been. She was wounded, and it was my fault. The nurse's voice roused me out of my bout of self-pity.

"Dr. Crockett, they are waiting for you. Thank you for responding so quickly."

I looked at Dr. Crockett. He was six foot six, Polynesian—I guessed Hawaiian—and was wearing a blue T-shirt and what looked like a skirt, or a floral print bedsheet of some sort, wrapped around his hips. A pair of flip-flops completed his off-duty medical garb. For Anderson's sake, I prayed Dr. Crockett was a better surgeon than dresser.

Dr. Crockett grunted hello to the nurse, said something about a pool and kids, and walked through the "authorized only" doors.

The next few moments of my life were consumed with wondering how *he* was authorized and I wasn't. I mean, at least I was wearing pants. After that, I went in search of someplace quiet. Hospitals usually have chapels or other designated quiet places. UVRMC has one near the emergency room, and I went inside. I didn't know what to do, so I prayed. I prayed for guidance, for comfort, for solace, patience, understanding, and humility, and I prayed for the doctors and nurses caring for my partner. But most of all I prayed for Anderson.

After about ten minutes of prayer, I went back to the waiting room. It was crowded with police brass from nearly all the surrounding cities and towns. My good pal Detective Millhouse showed up.

I stayed out of the way and avoided anyone with a badge. I managed not to be seen by Millhouse. Eventually, the number of cops dwindled, and even Millhouse was forced to leave. His superiors didn't like him standing around doing nothing.

No one bothered me.

About three hours later, Dr. Crockett came through the "authorized" doors and quietly talked to some of the remaining brass assembled outside. He wasn't wearing his skirt anymore. In his green scrubs, he actually looked like a doctor. I wormed my way close enough to overhear some of what the doctor said.

". . . bottom line, she will live and should recover fully. But for a while there, it was dicey. A 9mm jacketed slug caused some severe damage to the right shoulder. A half inch to the left, and it may have been fatal. The bullet shattered and ricocheted off the clavicle. The clavicle won't properly heal for at least four to five months. It also fractured the right scapula." He ran a hand through his thinning black hair.

"It did cause some nerve damage too. We won't know exactly how much until she tries to use her shoulder again. That won't be for about a month though. She probably won't like it being immobilized for that long, but a month of nonuse is better than never being able to use it again. I've worked on patients whose wounds were much more severe, and they recovered fully. I mean, 80 percent mobility and use of her shoulder is a success. She can expect an even higher recovery if she does what she is supposed to."

Dr. Crockett looked pretty tired. I bet Anderson did too. Crockett went on. "Her left calf was hit; that bullet was smaller, probably a .22 or a .25. Most likely a shotgun pellet. It nicked the tibia, but didn't fracture it. Probably painful, but not life threatening. She was lucky. It took some time to find all of the slug fragments, but in the end, I think I got them all. All told, she won't be back to work for probably six months or so, if she heals quickly."

The police brass acknowledged his words and slowly poured out. Two uniformed patrolmen stayed in the ER and most likely would be posted outside Anderson's room. Good.

I caught up to Dr. Crockett before he disappeared behind the magic doors.

"Dr. Crockett?" I asked.

"Yes?"

"My name is Peter Grant, and I am Detective Anderson's partner." We shook hands. "I just wanted to thank you for what you did. I mean, I know you did your best. Thank you."

"You're welcome, Mr. Grant. It was close. The wound to her shoulder was serious. She should recover. Now, if you'll excuse me . . ."

"Sure, Doc. Just one more thing." I didn't know how to ask delicately, so I asked it normally.

He looked at me for a minute. I was afraid he would say no.

"Follow me."

We walked through the authorized doors. I didn't feel any more authorized than before, and this side of the doors looked like the other side, but I wasn't complaining. We walked down a wide hallway. Nurses and doctors were everywhere, all doing their jobs. We made a few turns, and then we were outside her room.

Dr. Crockett said quietly, "She's on some pretty powerful painkillers right now, and she may not respond to you or me at all."

We went in. It was dark. I saw a bed and a large chair. On the wall opposite the bed, just over halfway up, was a small television. I thought I was prepared to see her, but I wasn't. She was on the bed, just lying there. She was reclined some, and her upper body was wrapped, or encased, in a white cast of some sort. Tubes ran in and out of her body. One was for an IV, and another ran into her nose.

She was fighting for her life, and she looked beautiful. I felt a pain in my chest. I thought I might be having a heart attack. But then I realized why I ached and why I would find the strength to carry on. She was right in front of me.

I approached the bed. Dr. Crockett stayed by the door.

I stood there and wished I could give her a blessing. I was glad I was worthy to, but I thought it probably wouldn't be appropriate. Still, a feeling of peace came into my heart. I knew her Heavenly Father loved her and was concerned for Detective Anderson. She wasn't just a number or a face to Him; she was his daughter, unique and special. I didn't understand how, but I knew everything would be all right.

Anderson didn't move. I'd hoped she would. Move her head, reach for my hand, blink her eyes, or anything, something. I just wanted Anderson to be Anderson. But she didn't move. I would have to be satisfied with her being alive right now. I could do that. I thanked Dr. Crockett, and he walked me out.

We were almost back to the "magic admittance" doors, and I had to ask.

"Tell me something, Doc."

"What?"

"What's the deal with the skirt you were wearing when you first came in?" I suddenly realized how much bigger Dr. Crockett was than me. His arms were long and thick. I suspected that if he wanted to, he could hurt me very badly.

"It's not a skirt. It's called a lavalava. It's traditional in Hawaii and the Polynesian South Pacific."

Whatever you say.

I thanked him for his help and quietly left the hospital with a lightness in my step and grim determination tightening my heart. I was the happiest I'd been since—well, in a long time. I was happy that Anderson would be okay, happy that I would see her again. At the same time, I knew that she was supposed to have been the fourth kill. That upset me. I didn't want to admit it, but I found myself caring for her. Even more scary, I liked caring for her.

Someone wanted something protected, something kept secret. They wanted it bad enough to kill anyone that got in their way. Even a small-town detective.

I didn't know why, but I would find out.

* * *

It was late now, and I didn't go home. I went back to Rockwell to sleep there. I was too wound up to sleep, so I studied up on Korea. Anderson's attacker was still out there, so I didn't want to sleep at home. I got some books and read a lot. Probably should have done that when the FBI sent me to Korea.

I discovered that Korea was split into occupation zones by the victors of World War II, much like Germany had been. This was the case because for thirty or so years before WWII ended, Japan considered Korea a colony. More than considered. To Japan, Korea was their little redheaded cousin that no one liked. They treated Korea accordingly. Apparently the two countries still do not like each other. The author related an incident from the early 1990s. The assistant to the undersecretary of agriculture for Japan was visiting Seoul. At the time, it was the highest level of talks between the two countries since the occupation. A lot of South Koreans didn't like that, and massive protests were held. In Seoul, at the Occupation Memorial, a man, screaming that his grandparents were killed by the Japanese during the occupation, stabbed himself with a ceremonial dagger. Such was his discontent with the assistant undersecretary's visit to Seoul. The author cited this as an example of the hostility between the two countries. That jived with what my gang friend had said back at Anderson's house.

Korea was split along the thirty-eighth parallel. Two separate capitals were set up: Seoul in the south, and Pyong Yang in the north. The United States and its allies assumed responsibility for the southern half, the USSR the north. All was quiet until June 25, 1950. In the early morning hours, the North invaded the South.

On June 27, 1950, the United Nations voted to condemn the invasion and promised to assist the sovereign nation of the Republic of Korea. The United States took the lead and appointed General Douglas MacArthur of the army as the supreme commander of all friendly troops on the peninsula. But for a while things didn't go as hoped. The United States was not prepared in either men or equipment. As a result, the troops—more precisely, the United States Marines—were pushed south until they were pinned inside an area surrounding the port city of Pusan. It became known as the Pusan Perimeter. Pusan is the largest port city in the country, and the United States Navy controlled the seas. For a while, it was feared that Pusan would end up as the "Dunkirk for the United States." But the marines would not be pushed into the sea. The USMC saved South Korea. *Semper Fi*, baby.

On September 15, 1950, the elements of the marine corps and army, along with several South Korean units, staged an amphibious landing at a small (at the time) port city just west of Seoul. It was Inchon. The North Koreans were caught totally by surprise by what the author called one of the most successful and daring amphibious assaults in the annals of war. Seoul itself was recaptured shortly thereafter. Inchon was so successful that by the end of the year, the North Korean army, or what remained of it, was pushed back to a small reservoir called Chosin. On the far side of Chosin stood the vast frontiers of Manchuria. The Chinese counterattacked with their North Korean ally and drove the marines south.

Despite the success of the Inchon landings and the valor of the soldiers, Korea turned into a nightmare of bitter cold in the winter, scorching heat in the summer, stalemate at the front, and casualties everywhere. An armistice was signed on June 8, 1953, that ended the fighting, but not the hostilities. A demilitarized zone was established, and it is still the border between the two Koreas. Technically, the two countries are still at war, and men are still killed along the DMZ. Every few years, the South discovers new tunnels dug by the North that extend beneath the DMZ and open up several miles into South Korea. The tunnels have rails laid down and are wide enough for tanks to drive through.

It took decades, but eventually the South emerged from the shadow of the war and became an Asian economic power. It is still a staunch ally of the United States and has fought alongside the United States in many conflicts. The author of one of the books I read related an anecdote from his days in Vietnam. He said that the toughest troops in Vietnam were not the Viet Cong, but the South Korean marines.

Go marines. How do you say *Semper Fi* in Korean?

* * *

I went home early in the morning and packed my bag. I showered and all that too. My weapon was always within reach. I thought about Anderson and wanted to hear her voice.

I'd arranged for a single red rose to be sent to her. I found the phone number for UVRMC, and hoping she was awake, I called. After a few transfers and some waiting, I finally got her on the phone. She was awake and sounded great. Tired and weak, but great nonetheless. She thanked me for the rose.

"The rose is beautiful. You didn't have to, Grant."

"Yeah, I know, but I wanted to. And you know I had to." We talked for a long time—well, in relation to our previous phone conversations. Which were nonexistent. She asked if I was handy.

"Grant, are you handy?"

I don't even know what that means. I'm afraid of housework, I got a C minus in a high school wood shop class, and I almost destroyed the family pool when it was going in. So I told her yes.

"There was something funny, Grant."

Funny? "Funny how, Anderson?"

"When they were in my house, one of them spoke to me. Knew my name. I heard his voice. It was funny. Weird."

I didn't interrupt. She went on. "His voice had an accent, and he wanted to know how I liked living in *the* Spanish Fork."

That is weird.

"It was like he didn't speak English. I mean . . ." She drifted off. Probably from the pain medication and trying to concentrate through it. "Like English was a second language to him. Am I making sense?"

"You are," I said and left it at that. How would she know if he had a Korean accent? What is a Korean accent, anyway?

"Grant, did you come by the hospital?"

"Yes."

"Did you give me a blessing?"

"No."

"I thought I heard your voice . . ."

"I wanted to."

"That's nice of you, Grant. You could have."

We didn't say anything for a few moments.

"Anderson, I have to tell you something. I mean, last night, at your house, I thought I may never see you again, and—well, I'm glad you'll be okay. And I was hoping that maybe you would agree to—" I couldn't spit it out, so I started over. "I mean when you're completely healed, would you . . ."

She cut me off. "Grant, are you trying to ask me out?"

Trying?

No. I was failing.

"Yes."

"Maybe it's the morphine talking, or the pain. Probably the pain, but sure, I'll go out with you. On one condition."

"What's that, Anderson?" I asked.

"Catch them. Stop them."

"Promise. I will. I got one of the punks that shot you."

"I know. I heard from a patrolman that you were the first one on the scene."

"I was."

"Why, Grant? How did you know?"

That needed a week or more to answer. I didn't have that long. "I just did," I said quietly, my voice cracking under the weight of my emotions. I knew she would persist, so I added, "I gotta go. I'll keep in touch. Don't worry. You're safe now." I hung up.

I was almost sure that our Asian janitor and the person behind Anderson's attack were one and the same person—Cook's North Korean terrorist.

I've learned that all terrorists want the same thing. They want to bring attention to their cause by disrupting the normal routine of the world and will do it with indiscriminate violence. Like that bomb in Italy that brought the Olympics back to Salt Lake. To be honest, I didn't care where my terrorist was from or what his geopolitical views were. I couldn't care less. In the end, we have to stop all of them.

I was only concerned with one.

The killer had his chance to kill Anderson. He failed. Even with his hired gang members. Now she would have around-the-clock protection. She was safer in the hospital than she would be at home.

Before I left, I made a few other calls. I called the Utah County medical examiner's office. Then I called in a few favors with some old friends from the Bureau. I even remembered to contact my pal Agent Cook.

"Cook, this is Grant."

He sounded happy to hear from me. "What's taken you so long to call me? I thought you knew the number." Maybe happy isn't the right word.

"Relax, Cook. I'm calling now." We really are buds.

"All right. Do you know anything, Grant?"

I know lots of things: Big Foot is real, and he lives with my ex-mother-in-law; the Loch Ness monster is really a child's blow-up sea monster; and that "Champy" monster in Lake Champlain is just that—a monster.

"Grant!"

Oh, yeah. "Nothing firm yet. I suspect the man responsible for a series of killings in Utah County is our North Korean friend. He is mean, ruthless, and desperate to keep something hidden. You should find him and say hi."

"Series of killings?" he asked.

"At least three."

"Three . . . You're sure it's him?"

"Yes. I've seen him, Cook. I spoke to him. I know his face. I'm heading to Korea myself; maybe I can find some answers there. I've arranged to meet someone."

"Who?"

"An old friend. FBI. You know an Agent Williams, Cook?"

"Dozens. Keep me informed."

"Will do."

I made sure I had Anderson's hospital phone number written down and on me. I drove back to Rockwell. I quickly reviewed the plans for Conductor's trip with Scott and the rest of my team. We were flying to Seoul, and from there he would attend six meetings throughout South Korea. Two in Seoul, two in Pusan, and two in Taejon. I made sure my team was ready to go.

Then, with the rest of the team, I escorted Conductor to the airport, and we took off.

I couldn't wait to see Conductor try *kimchi* soup.

* * *

The flight over was long, flying against the rotation of the earth. I slept through most of it. I had that dream again. In front of that bank in Denver. We stumbled on it. Only two Denver PD cruisers were at the scene. We didn't have Kevlar vests on. I wanted to help. We got out. I heard shots. Two or three hit our car. It was government issue, which meant I didn't care and it would require paperwork to get the repair work authorized. I started to tell Dan he would have to deal with the paperwork when I noticed something was wrong. Dan was wrong. He was bleeding from the chest, his face twisted in pain and confusion.

I went to him. I didn't need to shout for someone to call an ambulance; I could hear a cop near me doing just that.

"Dan, you're bleeding," I said. It was bad. Experts say that in times of stress we find it comforting to state the obvious because we control the obvious.

He smiled weakly. "Grant, man, next week, we're going back to the res. You with me?"

"I am. It's gonna be a blast, Danny."

I could actually see his life slipping away. It was eerie and terrifying, watching his life dissipate. Knowing I couldn't help or stop it from happening. His skin went chalky, his breathing erratic. His eyes glossed over. There was more blood. Lots more. Soaking his shirt, covering my hands. "Hang on, buddy. It's going to be okay. You'll make it." Experts also say it's important to give the victim a reason to live. "Hey, this time let's camp out under the stars. We'll take some dates. I bet the night sky is awesome on the res. You're going to be fine."

His eyes closed.

"Stay with me, Dan! Stay alive!" I yelled. I screamed. I pleaded. I cried. My tears mixing with the red.

I held him, and everyone else was gone. We were alone.

I watched him die. It was my fault.

Dan was gone.

It was my fault.

His eyes snapped open. He stared at me, his eyes not seeing me. I nearly dropped his head on the pavement. He was dead, but he was staring at me. His lips moved. I could hear his voice. He was telling me something, but I couldn't hear him.

I begged him to speak louder. But he didn't. Couldn't. I bent down to hear. He spoke again, and still I couldn't hear him.

The sky on the horizon turned an angry red. A blast of wind hit us, a wall of heat behind it. I could see it destroying, consuming everything in its path. Total devastation. The heat was closer, coming for me.

"Peter."

"What? Dan? I can't hear you!"

"Wake up, Peter." I felt a hand shaking my shoulder.

I jolted awake. Sweat drenching my face. I was on the plane. Conductor was there.

"Peter, I want to talk," he said.

How do you say no to that?

You don't.

chapter 8

The smell hit me when I got off the plane. It still smells, well, different. Not stinky-feet bad or anything like that. Just different. It would take some getting used to. Again. I wondered how I must smell to forty-five million South Koreans. I missed my Polo cologne.

Everything at the airport went smoothly. The customs official that searched my bag was a tad bit nosey, I thought, but I didn't say anything. The president of the Korea Seoul Mission met us at the earliest possible point. Because of security restrictions, that meant he almost had to meet us outside. I didn't catch his name; it's not my business. I need to be clear on this. I am a security agent—not a missionary, a PR man, or a tour guide. I see someone, anyone, and place them in one of two categories: no problem, or potential problem. The majority of people who meet Conductor when I am with him only have one of those two designations. If someone falls into the wrong category, *then* I take special notice of that person. The president of the Korea Seoul Mission was "no problem." That's all I needed to know.

We escorted Conductor to his hotel. The mission president drove one of the mission vans. Conductor does not like to spend money on taxis or rentals. He prefers to rely on the hospitality of the Church members. Usually, this isn't a problem. It wasn't now. I was with Conductor, and the rest of the team rode in the second mission van that was behind us. On the plane, I'd briefed Conductor on what was happening with the case in Spanish Fork. I told him I'd arranged to meet an old friend at the U.S. embassy who might be able to help. We agreed that I would concentrate on the case while he took care of some Church business with the local leaders. I was confident my team could handle it without me. After he was checked in and settled, I went in search of a taxi. I found one at the front of the hotel.

It was a ride that brought back memories of my first stay in Korea. The sheer number of cars, buses, mopeds, bicycles, and people on the road was awesome. And the way they drove was frightening. At least it was to me. My taxi driver seemed fine with all of it. We passed a few things I recognized: McDonald's and a Taco Bell.

Seoul is a massive modern city. Subways, skyscrapers, and other evidences of the modern world are everywhere. You can find almost any American fast-food restaurant. That doesn't make Seoul a modern city. But they're here, and I'm sure they're a welcome sight to weary tourists. Seoul has all the problems of a large city, and not everyone is able to afford, or has access to, modern amenities. Because Seoul is the capital of the Republic of Korea, it is home to the foreign embassies and is the heart of Korea's national government infrastructure. Within a mile of the American embassy are the ancient royal palace, national police headquarters, the Korean Joint Chiefs of Staff, and the Korean CIA. Now the Korean CIA is known as the Department for Internal Security, or DIS. The English, Canadian, and other embassies are close by as well. The U.S. embassy is a focal point for many things in Seoul. Most of it not good, from a certain point of view. Not mine. I think a little anti-American riot is a good thing now and then. It helps to keep the cops on their toes.

Student dissident leaders try every year to riot in front of the embassy itself. Most of the time, they get a few city blocks away, and that's it. Because of where the American embassy is located, the Korean government keeps riot police on duty at all times.

There are two kinds of riot police. One is dressed like a storm trooper from *Star Wars*, except the riot cop's armor isn't white. The other riot cop doesn't wear armor. He wears a blue denim jacket. Of the two types, the "denim jackets" are the ones the rioters fear most because they're all black belts in tae kwon do and they clean up behind the storm troopers. If you are a rioter, you don't want to get left behind—literally behind the storm troopers—because the denim jackets will find you. The plain-clothes riot cops are on duty at all times, and the storm trooper version is just minutes away. They take the threat of danger or damage to the American embassy very seriously.

Driving to the embassy, I was hoping to see a riot or two. But I learned from my taxi driver that it wasn't the right season for riots. The season was still a few weeks away. I think he said that it was still too cold. I may have misunderstood him. In any event, I didn't see a riot or smell any lingering tear gas along the route that the taxi took. The taxi dropped me off as close to the embassy as it could get. For security reasons, that meant I had to walk about a tenth of a mile to reach the main gate.

The main gate is made of steel, by the looks of it, and covered in black. About ten feet tall, with spikes along the top, and wide enough for two small cars or one large car to squeeze through. It is actually two gates that slide apart at the middle. They were both shut. No padlock was visible, but that meant zero.

To the right of the gate is an entrance, big enough only for two people to fit through at the same time. It looked like the beginning of a tunnel, but I could see the other side. The embassy walls go right to this smaller opening. A thick slab of reinforced concrete as high and deep as the embassy wall separates the car gate from the pedestrian entrance. This makes it look like some giant ice cream scoop has taken a chunk out of the wall and left an entrance. It too is gated, and here I stopped. I didn't have to knock. I'd probably been watched from the second the taxi dropped me off.

"Can I help you, sir?" a voice from nowhere asked.

"Yes," I replied to no one. "I have business inside."

A tall marine appeared behind the gate and looked at me. "American citizen?"

"Yes, corporal," I said in my best American accent.

Whatever that is.

"What business?"

"My own business."

I heard a buzzing sound, and the gate slid back into the wall. I walked through and nodded to the marine who had determined I was American enough to get in.

He stepped into a clear, probably bullet-resistant booth. A second marine was there.

The other one spoke to me via a speaker. "Passport."

I was tempted to flash my FBI credentials and tell the spiffy guards in their clean dress uniforms to mind their own business. Agent Cook would have just loved that.

A metal drawer slid open, and I put my passport in it. It reminded me of using the drive-through at a bank. My new friend inspected it and returned it the same way.

"Enjoy your time at the embassy, Mr. Grant," he said.

"You too." I walked on through a metal detector. It beeped. I was armed, so it should have beeped.

The first marine that spoke to me stepped out and approached. "Excuse me, sir."

Now I flashed my FBI credentials. "Special Agent Grant, FBI."

The marine stopped in front of me and inspected my ID. Then he turned smartly on his heel and walked back to where he came from.

I went into the compound.

The embassy itself is pretty drab-looking. Seven stories thick and too wide. It looked like it was overweight. Too short for all of that bulk. Lots of cement gives it a gray look. To the west is a smaller five-story building. It too is gray. It is the residence for the embassy employees.

My appointment was in the embassy itself. A large American flag hung from an upper story and lent some color, but not enough. There was no breeze for it to wave in.

I walked in the front door. A rather pretty woman sitting behind an attractive desk greeted me. The desk was probably oak, and her hair was probably auburn, but I wasn't sure on either count.

I don't know squat about wood.

"Welcome to the United States embassy, Mr. Grant," she said.

The marines must pass on all visitor identification.

I would.

"Thank you, Ms. . . . ?"

"Thompson. Miss Thompson. What brings you to our little piece of America in the heart of Seoul?"

"I have an appointment to see Special Agent Williams, FBI senior attaché."

"Agent Williams is expecting you. She asked that you be escorted to the meeting room. Before we go, are you armed?"

"Yes. Why?"

"All personal weapons must be checked here before you are allowed into the embassy. You can pick it up here when you leave. I will take it from you now." She held out her right hand, and without thinking I handed over my Glock.

"Thank you, Mr. Grant." She put it in a large drawer in her desk and locked it. "Follow me, please."

I did.

We went to an elevator on the first floor and took it down a few floors. We got out, and I followed her down a hallway. After a few turns, she opened a door. Miss Thompson and her auburn hair walked back the way she came.

I went in.

The basement safe room was not very big. It was mainly used by intelligence types. His Excellency, the Ambassador, used a much larger and more opulent safe room on the third floor for his briefings. The basement room was swept twice a day for listening devices and was furnished sparsely. A single long table, metal, with six large captain's chairs around it stood in the center of the room. At the far end of the table sat a man I didn't know.

Whoever he was spoke to me. "Take a seat, Agent Grant. Agent Williams should be here soon. In fact, she's late." I sat, and forty-five seconds later Williams walked in through the same door I had.

I'd known her for a long time. She was the FBI attaché for the embassy; she replaced me as the junior attaché and is now FBI senior attaché. She was about seven years older than me and, if I may say, much prettier. Five foot eight, blond hair, blue eyes, around 130 pounds, and one of the best agents I'd ever worked with. She had not left Korea after being posted here and from all accounts did not miss the States one bit. Some people like the foreign duty stations, and some, like me, do not. My tour in Korea overlapped with hers for a few months, and we had both lectured at the academy at the same general time. Stephanie "Will" Williams was a good friend for much of my time in the Bureau. I was about to find out if she still was.

The other person, a middle-aged man with graying black hair, was still unknown to me. He wasn't in uniform. He was dressed casually. Too casually for the Bureau. My gut said he was CIA, or some other spook agency.

Will spoke first. "Hi, Grant." She nodded her head at the stranger. "This is Tom."

"Just Tom?" I asked.

"Yes," Just Tom said.

Yep. Spook.

"Why don't you tell Tom what you have?" Will suggested.

He was bored while I talked, until I got to the Korean connection. So was I.

"Do you believe this punk?" Tom asked me.

"Good question. Yes, I do. He was in a lot of pain and had no reason to lie. It's not like he was betraying his gang or something. And his comment about the guy wigging out when he was called Japanese rings true. Plus there is that janitor I ran into and that stuff Anderson recalled."

Will interrupted, "But why would a Korean want to kill Americans in America? Assuming this janitor you saw is not the man that no one's seen in over twenty years. We're allies."

"Tom, why don't you field that one?" I suggested.

"Did you get a look at this guy? Assuming that he's real, did you see him?" Apparently Tom didn't want to field that one just yet.

"Yes. I did." I related in more detail the incident with the fake janitor at the Utah County ME's office.

"So. How do you know he just wasn't a very uptight janitor?" Tom said.

"I checked with them, the Utah County medical examiner's office. They don't employ any Asian janitors, let alone Korean. It was him. Whoever he is."

Will cut in. "How can you be sure, Grant? It could have been anyone."

"I'm not sure. But I don't believe it was just anyone. It was him. I know it."

Just Tom pulled a small cell phone from his shirt pocket, flipped it open, and spoke quietly and quickly.

He stood and said, "Come with me."

Will did.

So did I.

We didn't go up or down any stairs, so I assumed we were still in the basement. We went through what seemed like a maze of hallways. We ended up at a door with three red lights above it, which was marked:

AUTHORIZED ACCESS ONLY

I looked at Tom. He wasn't wearing a lavalava. "Are you authorized? Because I know I'm not."

Tom gave me an annoyed look and slid a card through a slot near the door. The three red lights turned green, and the door hissed open.

We walked in, and I said in my best James Earl Jones/Darth Vader voice, "Tom. I am your father."

Will told me to shut up.

"Shut up, Grant."

Okay.

This was a much more impressive room than the safe room. Lots of computers, techies in white lab coats, screens, digital imaging equipment, and the like. It was what I term a "high-tech room."

"Is this the embassy's extra-special safe room?" I asked.

Tom pointed to a seat in front of a large computer monitor and told me to sit.

"Sit."

I sat.

He sat at a desk next to me, also with a computer monitor. He touched it, and it instantly came to life. He navigated his way through by touching the screen.

My monitor came to life. "What did I touch?"

"Nothing, Grant. Just sit there," Will said.

My monitor screen was divided equally into six spaces. Each space was filled by a face.

"You see him?" Tom asked.

"Who?"

"Your janitor."

I studied each one closely, slowly, for a few minutes.

I didn't see him.

I shook my head, and the six faces disappeared and were replaced by six more.

Again, I checked each one carefully.

I shook my head. Six more faces appeared.

After a few minutes I said, "The face on the top right is familiar but is too young to be the janitor I saw."

"Are you sure?" Tom asked.

"Yes. Too young," I said again.

The other five faces disappeared, leaving the top right. It filled the screen, then started to change, to age.

"Stop," I said. "That's him. That's the man I saw."

"Will was right about you, Grant. You do have a great memory. The first twelve photos were just your average Korean street crimi- nals. The next six were known North Korean sympathizers and

North Korean operatives. Are you sure that he is the man you saw and spoke with?"

For a spook, Tom didn't pay much attention. "Yes, that's him," I said.

"That man, Mr. Grant, is Kim Song Su. He is one of Pyong Yang's most dangerous employees. The only confirmed picture we have of him is the one you noticed—a university ID picture. The South Korean DIS gave us that photo only last week. I don't know why they withheld it for so long. Maybe they wanted to nail this guy on their own. Kim Song Su did assassinate the South Korean president back in the eighties. Believe me, the DIS wants this guy bad. They claim they almost had him once. In France, the early 1990s. But he escaped. Anyway, he defected to North Korea sometime in the late seventies."

"Why did he defect?"

"Ever been here in the spring, Grant?"

"Spring? Sure, it's great. Flowers blooming, lots of tourists. What's your point?"

"Every spring, like clockwork, the college students riot. They hold massive demonstrations, protesting government decisions. Usually, the riots turn violent. They throw bricks, Molotov cocktails—mostly at the riot police, who respond with tear gas, clubs, and, in extreme situations, rubber bullets." He saw I was getting impatient and held up a hand.

"Spring 1976 was one such situation. It happened in a city in the southern part of South Korea, in Kwang Ju. A massive riot was under way when the authorities finally showed up. But these were not riot cops. They were commandos from the Korean army. Instead of firing tear gas and rubber bullets to disperse the rioters, the commandos fired real bullets. Seventeen students and bystanders were killed. It became known as the Kwang Ju Massacre and grew into the rallying cause of South Korean students everywhere for decades to come.

"Ironically, the Americans were blamed for allowing this to happen. The UN commander in South Korea has control over all ground forces on the peninsula. He has final say on when and how many troops on the Korean peninsula move. The commander then was an American. At the very least, the reasoning went, he could have prevented the commandos from moving. But he did nothing, and America was blamed.

"So for this reason, and various other fabricated ones, Americans are not very popular in Kwang Ju. The North Koreans have found this, and democracy with its many freedoms, very useful. They recruit some of their best agents from that part of 'their country.'

"In the spring of 1976, Kim Song Su saw his father and older brother killed in the massacre. He was just fourteen. By spring 1977, his mother was dead too. I'm guessing she died of a broken heart. After that, Song Su lived with an uncle. But apparently the uncle didn't show any real interest in the boy.

"He became a loner at school. But he tried to turn his lack of friends into a positive. He studied hard, and did well enough in high school to earn a scholarship to Kwang Ju University. He hated America, but he was not stupid. The South Korean—no, the American puppet government in Seoul still felt guilt over the massacre, and as a result had given the local colleges and university additional scholarships. They paid his way through school so he could throw rocks at the police.

"From what we can tell, college allowed him to meet people that felt and thought as he did. That's about the time he came to the attention of the South Korean government. The South Koreans were actually going to pick him up, I mean heading to his apartment the next morning, but he escaped to the north. He was too anti–South Korea for his own good. We're fairly confident he had the help of a sleeper/recruiter agent at the university. Most likely a professor. The DIS did capture such a man, but that's all we know. No one has seen the man since he was picked up by the DIS in the early eighties."

I almost added, "Just a few hours earlier and maybe we wouldn't be here." But I don't like what-ifs; they're too convenient. So I didn't say anything.

"What happened?" Will asked.

"We don't know. The South Korean DIS will only tell us that he disappeared. He is by far one of the North's top field agents. He was trained by the old KGB in Moscow, at the American and Western Europe School. Our good friends the Soviets also trained him in what used to be the city of Leningrad but is now St. Petersburg once again. And the Chinese trained him at their Internal State Security facilities in Beijing. He speaks Korean, Chinese, Japanese, Russian, German, and English. We have pinned some ten assassinations on him." Tom glanced down at some papers in front of him. "And we have confirmed only one failed assassination in his career."

"Who didn't he kill?" I asked.

"That's not your concern."

"It is now. Who?"

Tom obviously didn't want to tell me. Why, I don't know. So I guessed.

"Was it Reagan in '81?"

"No, it wasn't Reagan. John Hinckley shot Reagan. You know that. Just sit there and listen to me, Grant."

Okay.

Tom went on. "We have never caught him. No one has. But we would dearly like to. Counting yourself, we have three witnesses able to identify him."

"Maybe a fourth." I told him about Anderson.

"The gang member is one too, but I doubt Spanish Fork or Utah is interested in letting him go free because he saw an international terrorist."

Will spoke up. "I called our office in Salt Lake to have them feel out the locals for that possibility. Not interested. But they did offer some information. The punk Grant captured has a name: Roberto Mojica. He's a known gang member from Layton, north of Salt Lake. He and his gang buddies call themselves VLR."

Tom interrupted. "What does that stand for?"

"I think something like *Vario Layton Rules*. But don't quote me on that. Anyway, Roberto has a rap sheet with the Layton and

Bountiful PDs. When he was reminded that he was seventeen and would be prosecuted as an adult, he started volunteering information to the Utah County DA's office. VLR was contacted by our North Korean friend late last November or early December. They agreed to help him do some jobs, and he promised them guns. Lots of guns. Grenades too. They planned to use the guns to wipe out a rival gang, at least Layton PD suspects as much. They did some jobs all right, but they won't get the guns for it. He claims that's all he knows."

"Not a bad move on his part," I said.

"What do you mean, Grant?"

"Well, this Kim needed some muscle in order to kill, but he had to limit his own exposure. By using a punk street gang, he accomplished both. But this time, he'd bitten off more than he could chew, and too many people got to see Kim Song Su up close and personal. We know what he looks like now. What we don't know for sure is why he's killing."

No one said anything for a few minutes. I think all of us were wondering the same thing. And afraid of the answer, or lack of an answer.

I spoke. "What, Will and Tom, is a North Korean terrorist doing in Spanish Fork, Utah? Why did he torture and kill two seemingly innocent men? Why did he kill the medical examiner just hours after I was there? Why try and kill a local police detective that has never been outside the intermountain United States?"

CHAPTER 9

No one responded.

My gut hurt.

Finally Tom spoke. "You aren't FBI anymore, Grant. I know this a temporary assignment for you. I shouldn't tell you this, but you're already in this too deep. We need all the help we can get. I can't think of a better reason to not tell you."

I could give you some, Tommy.

"Have you ever heard of the *Enola Gay*, Grant?"

"Sure," I said. "It was the B-29 that dropped *Little Boy* on Hiroshima. Just days later, a second atomic bomb was dropped on Nagasaki. WWII ended soon after."

"That's right. Have you ever heard of the *Morning Glory*?" he asked.

I looked at Will, then at Tom. "No, I haven't. Should I have? Did it drop the bomb on Nagasaki?"

"No, it didn't. It never dropped a hydrogen bomb. It did, however, carry one," he said.

"I don't understand. Will, what is he talking about?"

Will looked at me, shrugged, but didn't say anything.

Tom touched his monitor again, and mine changed. Kim Song Su's face disappeared and was replaced by an atlas map of the two Koreas.

"Shut up and listen to me, Grant."

I did.

He talked.

"In 1951, General MacArthur was the supreme UN commander on the Korean peninsula. By the end of March, he was fired by President Truman. Do you know why he was fired, Grant?"

I thought I was supposed to be quiet.

"Grant, did you hear me?"

"Yes. Sorry, Tom. I don't know exactly why he was fired. I assume it was political."

"Political? Yes, you could say that. MacArthur did not agree with Truman's views of the war. He knew that the Chinese were involved and wanted to take them out. Truman stuck to his directive to keep the war limited to Korea only. MacArthur publicly disagreed with the president. Do you know what the real chasm between them was, Grant?"

"MacArthur wanted to use nuclear weapons against the Chinese," I said.

"That's right. MacArthur knew that the only way to *win* in Korea was to nuke the Chinese."

"But," I pointed out, "he never did. Truman canned him."

"He did. MacArthur was replaced by General Ridgeway. But—"

I don't like those kinds of "buts."

"But what?" Will asked.

"Before I tell you two, I must impress on you that what you are about to hear is a national security secret and that I could lose my job for telling you. If it wasn't for Will, I wouldn't tell you, Grant. In any event, you should guard this closely. I mean *very* closely."

Thanks, Will.

"What if I told you that MacArthur, before he was fired, ordered a nuclear attack against the Chinese?"

"It never happened," I said.

"The attack did not come to fruition. But I assure you both that General MacArthur did order just such an attack. A B-29 out of Yakuza Air Base, Japan, was sent to do it."

"The *Morning Glory*?" I asked.

"Yes, Grant. The *Morning Glory*."

Will jumped in. "What happened to it? If it was sent, where did it go?"

"We don't know," Tom responded.

"What do you mean, 'We don't know'?" I hate that phrase even more than "but."

"The plane disappeared off the radar scopes just before entering Chinese airspace. Somewhere over the Sea of Japan. We think it crashed in the ocean. We were intercepting North Korean and Chinese radio traffic throughout the entire war, and they never mentioned the plane. They mentioned shooting down a lone B-29 on the date the *Morning Glory* flew. They never mentioned finding an American hydrogen weapon. My personal belief is that some kind of mechanical glitch happened and the pilot was forced to ditch in the Sea of Japan," Tom said quietly.

"Got any evidence to back that opinion up, Tom?" I asked.

"No."

"So it is possible that it was shot down. Shot down with a nuclear—"

"Hydrogen," Tom corrected me.

"Shot down with a hydrogen bomb in its belly?"

"That's right, Grant." I don't think Just Tom liked me.

I don't know why. I liked him just fine.

"To this day, the United States doesn't know where the plane is?" I persisted.

"No, we do not," he said.

I don't know where the "we" came from.

"Who *does* know where it is?" Will asked.

"We have a general idea, and so do the Japanese. The South Koreans don't know about it. And the North does."

"North, as in North Korea?" Will said.

"Yes," Tom responded.

"How did they—"

Tom cut Will off. "I'll get to that shortly."

"Tom, what happened to the bomb? And don't say we don't know," I said.

He just looked at me.

I looked back. "Wait. You mean that a B-29, carrying a nuclear, I mean, hydrogen payload, disappeared off the coast of North Korea in 1951? And North Korea, a known terrorist state, probably knows where it is? This just gets better and better, Tom."

"We think it was North Korea."

"Do they have the bomb, Tom?"

"You mean the one from the *Morning Glory*?"

"No, Tom. I mean the one that my grandma made in her kitchen last week. Yes, *that* one!"

Tom looked pretty upset, but I was too, so I didn't care.

"We don't know. Maybe. Probably."

"Tom, how does this missing plane and its weapon tie into a small town in Utah?" Will asked.

Now that was an intelligent question.

"Six months ago, we managed to intercept a partial message to Kim Song Su, from his superiors in Pyong Yang. We were able to make out bits and pieces."

"Can I see it?" I asked.

"No. You can't, Grant."

"Can I hear it?"

"No."

"Can Will see it?"

"No, she can't either." Tom was not playing nice.

"What did it say?" I tried one more time.

"We were able to identify two words that were, for us, a bit ominous: *poktan* and *yong.*"

"My Korean is kinda nonexistent, Tom. What do they mean?"

"Bomb and dragon. We think it means they have the bomb, and that it has something to do with a dragon. Dragon could be a metaphor or a code word. It could be an actual dragon of some sort. Like something in a parade, or a statue somewhere. Dragon may be an NK phrase for America. It could just as easily be a mistranslation. We didn't have much to work with."

"Tom, why are you so sure that this word means *the* bomb?" I asked.

"Have either of you ever heard of the *USS Pueblo*?"

"No," we said together.

He paused for a second. Maybe debating whether to continue or not. He did. "It was a U.S. Navy ship attached to the Seventh Fleet. It was basically a trawler that was used as an intelligence-gathering ship. Lots of sensitive equipment and information on board. In January of 1968, it was searching off the coast of North Korea in the Sea of Japan."

"What was it searching for?" I asked.

He looked at me, silently imploring me to be quiet. "We had reason to believe that the *Morning Glory* may have been in the area. Or possibly parts of it. We were just looking, hoping to get lucky."

"Why didn't the navy just go in with a task force or something and find and remove it?" Will asked another good question.

"That would have been great. The North Koreans, Chinese, and Russians would have demanded what we were looking for so close to North Korean territorial waters. How would they have taken the news that, seventeen years earlier, the United States had decided to nuke the Chinese? It was the height of the Cold War; we couldn't admit that.

"Think about it, Grant. How did the U.S. react to those Russian missiles in Cuba? If the Cuban missile crisis *almost* started a war, then this would have definitely done it. Talk about an international incident! The decision was made to search for it as quietly and covertly as possible. We didn't need to actually see the plane or the bomb. We just needed to locate it, determine where it was. And then later, covertly, remove the payload."

"You mean remove the nuclear weapon?" Will asked.

"Yes. I mean the nuclear weapon. But it backfired."

"Hydrogen," I said.

"What?" Tom looked seriously miffed.

"It was a hydrogen bomb, not nuclear," I said.

Tom took a deep breath. "We'll just agree, for convenience, to call it nuclear. Okay?"

Will and I nodded.

"It was never found?" I asked.

"No. It was not found, Grant. And yes, Grant, it was kept top secret."

So, instead of openly admitting to it and possibly finding the plane and its weapon, the U.S. kept quiet, and a rogue country now had a nuclear weapon. "What happened?" I asked quietly.

"The North Koreans didn't like the *Pueblo* being so close. They claimed it was in their waters. We denied it. This was before the days of global positioning systems. Was the *Pueblo* in their waters? Probably at one point. All I know is the *Pueblo* was well within international waters when the North Koreans attacked it. The crew knew the information they had was, to say the least, very valuable to the NKs. They had some time, but not a lot. It was a fishing trawler. It had no weapons and no defensive capabilities. Their only hope was to escape. But the *Pueblo* wasn't built for speed, and they didn't escape. No help came either.

"The North Koreans attacked the *Pueblo*. They fired upon it, forced it to stop. A lot of the sensitive stuff was burned by the crew before *Pueblo* was boarded, but not all of it. Somehow, the information about the *Morning Glory* was not entirely destroyed. The NKs towed the *Pueblo* to Wansan, their nearest port.

"It took a while, maybe too long, but we arranged the release of the crew. I think two men died; I'll have to check my facts on that though. The ones that didn't die were beaten and mistreated. What we couldn't arrange for was the return of the information that the *Pueblo* carried. Nor could we verify what actual information the NKs had about the *Morning Glory*. We hoped we'd gotten lucky. Maybe the NKs had found nothing about the *Morning Glory*." Tom breathed deeply and didn't speak. No one did for a few moments.

I prodded, "But they did, didn't they?"

Tom picked up the story again. "The North Koreans hit the jackpot. All they had to do was locate and recover a ready-made American nuclear weapon. We think that it was sometime two years ago; they found the plane and the weapon."

"Where at?"

"About seventy miles north of where the *Pueblo* was. They have the bomb, and their top spook is seen killing people in Utah. Now, you answer a question for me, Grant. What begins in Salt Lake in three days?"

"That would be the eleventh." I thought for a second. Three days? Then it hit me. I couldn't speak. I swear my heart almost stopped. I'd been afraid before, even terrified once or twice. But what I felt now was beyond terror, if that's possible. The entire picture came into focus. I didn't know exactly where the bomb would be, but I knew the city it was probably in. The city it would destroy, the millions of people it would obliterate.

The winter Olympics opened February 11 in Salt Lake City, Utah. The North Koreans were going to detonate a nuclear weapon, and the whole world would see it live on TV. They would kill the president of the United States, in his own country, along with tens of thousands of his fellow citizens.

I looked at Will and Tom. "This is not good."

Tom responded, "No, Grant, it isn't."

"How big of a weapon is this, Tom?" I asked.

"By design, in terms of power and yield, much larger than the ones dropped on Hiroshima and Nagasaki. Compared to current standards, and the probable condition of the weapon, not as bad as you might think. Physically, it is smaller and lighter than the ones dropped on Japan. Much easier to transport and conceal."

Super. Less than a decade after the end of the Second World War, we'd figured out how to make bombs smaller *and* much more destructive. I was thrilled.

"So, it could be anywhere?" Will said.

"I don't think so, Will. Our guess is that they plan to detonate it at the winter Olympics."

She cut Tom off. "But they would kill their own athletes."

"No, they wouldn't, Will. The AP reported a few days ago that North Korea was not sending a team to the games. They boycotted the LA summer games in '84, Seoul in '88, and Salt Lake the first time. So this was not totally unexpected. The team they did send to Atlanta in '96 was small and didn't even stay in the athletes' village. For these Salt Lake games, they're claiming that they don't want to corrupt their athletes by exposing them to capitalism."

"Or radiation," I added. "That would be deadlier this time, right, Tom?"

"Yes, Grant. The North Koreans probably are boycotting the Salt Lake games because they don't want to eliminate their athletes and dignitaries in a wave of heat and destruction."

He made it sound much worse than I did.

"I thought North Korea could make its own nukes. Why do they need this one?" I asked Tom.

"Plausible deniability. Everything about this weapon screams it was made in the USA. The amount of plutonium, the purity of it, the radiation signature. Once it detonates, there will be no hard evidence to link it to the North Koreans. They use an American weapon on American soil. No witnesses, no trace evidence to point to the NKs."

"Why not just use an ICBM to deliver it?" I persisted.

"Our best estimates and intelligence show that their ICBM program isn't capable of sending it that far into the U.S. interior. Ten or fifteen more years, and maybe they could use an ICBM. But not today. Their goal would be to hit both the U.S. and South Korea."

Will jumped in. "There are plenty of Americans and South Koreans just across their border. Just one narrow DMZ away. Why not drop it on Seoul?"

Made sense to me.

"They wouldn't. You need to understand and appreciate the Korean psyche. First, they wouldn't nuke their own country. Would the U.S. nuke New Hampshire?"

Maybe.

Massachusetts might.

"The NKs see the peninsula as one country, their homeland. Secondly, Seoul is more than just the capital of South Korea. For both Koreas, it is the ethnic, spiritual, and cultural center. It is literally the heartbeat of the peninsula. The NKs don't want to wipe it out. They want to possess it.

"No, the only place they can strike at both the United States and South Korea is in the United States. The Olympics make it that much easier for them. Not only will the South Korean Olympic team be there, but so will a number of the Republic's government officials. The rumor is that their president may even make an appearance, a show of unity with ours.

"The DIS, for its part, has stepped up its active interrogation of suspected and known NK sympathizers. If anything was going to cross the DMZ, they would know about it. But nothing is."

"But how do they deliver the bomb?" I was afraid, but determined to stop this from happening. "How do they do it? You see, I live in Salt Lake, and so do another million or so people. Can they launch it from a sub?"

"No. We don't think so. They might have purchased an older Russian Delta-class missile boat, but those are expensive. Odds are the Russians would only accept U.S. dollars or English pounds as payment. Maybe the Euro dollar, but they don't have that kind of money. We know they have some very old Russian Whiskey-class missile subs that they bought in the early 1970s. But they are obsolete and almost always in port. Too expensive to send out on regular patrols. Too noisy too."

"But, Tom, this wouldn't be a normal patrol." I don't know much about subs, but I know that.

"Right, Grant. But I can assure you both that we know exactly where *all* of their missile boats are. They are constantly followed, and they are nowhere near the U.S. coast. The U.S. coast is a dream for them. A dream they will never realize. Even if they have managed to acquire a Delta, we know they don't have the missile system for submarine-launched ICBMs. And assuming that a North Korean sub somehow got within striking distance of the United States, it would be blown out of the water before it could strike."

"Then how do they plan to get it there and detonate it?" I persisted.

"That is the question. Kim Song Su is still in Utah, as far as we know. You, Grant, can ID him on sight. You need to be in Utah too. Three days is not a lot of time."

"No, it's not. I'll see what I can do."

"Good. If you need my help getting back to the U.S., come back to the embassy and ask for me," Tom said.

"What should I do? Ask the marine guards at the front gate if I can see Just Tom?" I was fishing for a last name.

"That would be fine," he responded.

chapter 10

Our meeting was over. Tom and Will escorted me back to the safe room where it all began. Then Tom disappeared. He didn't say good-bye, or good luck.

I was already missing him.

Conductor wouldn't be expecting me until eight the next morning at the hotel, so I had some free time. I needed to get away and think. About what, I wasn't sure. I had so much to choose from: Jason Russell, President Taylor, Kim Song Somebody, nuclear death, Dan Begay, and Anderson. I'd left my Billy Joel CDs back in Utah, so I decided to do what all tourists do, even though I'm not a tourist: shop. Will suggested I go to an area of Seoul called Itaewon. I wasn't really looking to buy anything special, but I took her advice. Plus it's a part of Seoul I actually visited a lot the first time I was here.

We actually shared a cab most of the way there.

Will had some business at a place called Yong San. She explained that it's the largest American army post in all of South Korea and the headquarters for the U.S. Eighth Army. All of which I knew. On the post there's a theatre, a supermarket, Burger King, McDonald's, a department store, and a bowling alley—not to mention two convenience stores. Little America in the middle of a foreign country. I was tempted to stop and get a Big Mac or a

Whopper, but I was already in a taxi and wasn't sure I could get another. Did the Big Mac from McDonald's on Yong San taste different from one off post?

I didn't find out.

I'm watching my weight anyway.

"What does it mean, Will?"

"What, Grant?"

"Young San? Does it mean American army or something like that?"

"It's not *young*, it's *yong*." The vowel was long, like in *oak*.

"Okay. *Yong* San. What does it mean?" I asked again.

"Dragon Mountain. Pretty cool, huh?"

Yeah, that's it. Cool. "But what if it was Young San? What then, Will?"

"I don't know, Grant. Didn't you learn anything about the language when you were here?"

I looked at her sheepishly. "No."

We didn't say much the rest of the way. Something was bothering me. Tom had said something. It suddenly dawned on me that it was important. I just couldn't remember it. I hate it when that happens. I have a great memory. All good cops do. We have to. Once, I was investigating some murders in Sacramento, and I remembered—

"I said good-bye, Grant. This is my stop. I paid my fare and enough for your solo ride too. Good luck." Will was already out of the cab, and then she was gone.

* * *

Itaewon was just a short ride from Yong San's main gate. The taxi dropped me at the bottom of a small hill and drove away. I followed a road up the hill. At the top of the small hill, people and shops were all that I could see. It was brightly lit. Plenty of lights. And despite the dark of night, shoppers were everywhere. American GIs and civilians were everywhere. I think there were more Americans than Koreans.

Korean shops and street vendors were all desperately trying to get the attention of the shoppers, mostly in vain. "Hey, GI, got good stuff. Very cheap." "USA, number one! Feel this. You like? Cheap for you, GI. Hey, USA!" Some vendors were jumping right out in front of shoppers and accosting them. "Hey, Miss America, come my store. You like, I promise." This situation went on for what looked like about a mile down the road.

I could see several clubs that were closed now, but advertised beer, *soju*, rice wine, and girls. Girls dancing. Girls drinking. Girls doing all sorts of things. It was 6:30 p.m. The bars and clubs probably opened in just a few hours. I didn't want to be around here when they did.

Wendy's and Taco Bell looked very busy. I didn't see a talking Chihuahua, and I didn't stop for a Burrito Supreme.

I saw so many illegal shops that my mind was nearly spinning. There was Han's Music Store. It was an outlet for poorly copied CDs and tapes. Name it, and Han had a fake, illegal, bootleg copy of it. I almost bought Billy Joel's newest. But I figured that since he wouldn't get paid for me purchasing a poorly made illegal copy of his work, it wasn't worth it. I checked out Chang's Clothing and was amazed at the quality of the fake Nike jogging suits I saw hanging from the racks. Not that I like jogging much. But they were good fakes.

Betty's Leather Goods looked promising, and I went in. Betty wasn't around, but there was plenty of leather. For a minute I thought I'd magically been transported to Kansas City, or at least Tijuana, Mexico. Unfortunately, I left my ruby slippers in Utah, and I was still in Betty's store. I always thought I'd look good in a black leather jacket, riding a Harley or some other bike. I saw lots of brown leather jackets and even a few purple and blue ones. But no black. Anderson looks good in black, so I kept looking. I finally found one I liked and decided to buy it. I tried to haggle about the price like everyone else was doing.

"Hey, how much is this jacket?" I asked a woman who could've been Betty, or her Korean cousin.

"Hey, GI. You like jacket? Very nice jacket. Try it on, GI," she said.
"How much is it?"

"How much is jacket, GI? You want buy?"

"Yes, Betty." Whatever her name is. "How much is the jacket?"

"That jacket cost much. One hundred sixty-five dollar."

"How about eighty-five?"

"Eighty-five dollar? No way, GI. Hundred fifty."

"A hundred?"

"No. How much you got, GI?"

"Hundred twenty-five."

"That jacket, hundred twenty-five. You like?"

"Yeah, I like it." I gave her the money and walked out. I only hoped Anderson would like it too. This was a new phase for me, buying a woman gifts. Hadn't done it in a long time. I hoped I hadn't screwed up.

I didn't find a Harley store.

The street was crowded; it looked like it always was. One big perpetual crowd of shoppers and sellers. With the new jacket over my right shoulder, I joined the crowd and tried to look cool.

Or was it hip?

People were still everywhere, and walking was slow and dangerous down the busy sidewalk. I felt like an ant in a colony, trying to get someplace when all the other ants were in the way. Someone pushed me from behind, and I stumbled to the ground. I scraped my right knee pretty bad, and I admit that it hurt. The pain blinded me initially to the fact that whoever shoved me also took my new jacket.

I turned around in time to see a teenage boy run down a side alley. I gave chase as fast as I could. I don't run super fast and my knee wasn't cooperating. To successfully complete the FBI Academy, you have to pass a physical fitness test: crunches, push-ups, pull-ups, shuttle run, and the dreaded timed distance run. When I went through the academy, I had to run two miles in under eighteen minutes. I almost failed it twice, but never did. I think I did leave a lung somewhere on that track though.

And that was over ten years ago.

The alley had thinned out, but my target stayed just far enough ahead that I couldn't grab him. As I ran, I realized I was lost. The alley was long and winding, and when my thief took another side street I followed. Soon we were the only people on the small, cramped street. Houses with orange tile roofs dominated the view in all directions. A very narrow street, somewhere in a city of over twelve million people, was deserted except for the two of us. I soon found out why.

He rounded a blind corner, and I lost sight of him. I came around the same corner, and it was a dead end. My jacket was on the ground; the would-be thief was gone. I bent down and picked up my jacket.

I wasn't alone.

Three men, dressed in black from head to toe, barred the way. They fanned out, slowly closing the gap between us. From their look, I knew they didn't want to sell me something or engage me in witty conversation. I had nowhere to run and resolved to take out a few of them before they got me. I bent down on one knee, the non-throbbing one, pulled out my Glock, and shot the lead one, then another.

I thought I did anyway. They came at me still, like ghostly apparitions. I fired at the ground in front of the lead one, but nothing happened. I would have panicked then, but didn't. By then it was too late. One of them kicked me in the head. It was so fast I didn't have time to react.

Well, I did black out.

The beeping of my watch alarm woke me. It was set for 9:00 p.m. I'd been unconscious for almost two hours. I didn't know where I was. But I was alive. Someone wanted information from me. That was the only reason I was here and not lying in that alley. My head hurt, and I needed some aspirin. Lots of aspirin. Maybe ibuprofen. I slowly realized that my hands and feet were tied. I was standing up, tied to a board or table. A bright light was blinding me.

"Good, awake now. Can you hear me?"

"Yes. Who are you? Where are you?" I asked.

The light was turned off. I still couldn't see, but knew that in a few minutes I would be able to.

"Better?" the voice asked me.

"Yes. Who are you?"

"I ask the questions, Mr. Grant."

It can't be a good sign if I was tied down and the only talking bad guy was being polite to me. "Fine. I'll just call you Skippy. Now, Skip, what am I doing here?"

A hand lashed out and slapped me. "I ask the questions." I was slapped again. "You respond."

"Okay. Let's play," I said. I was getting mad. I was hit in the stomach, but the ropes kept me from doubling over. That made it harder to breathe, the punch, I mean.

"Yes, now quiet. Good. What do you know about Jason Russell?"

I could make out three men, still dressed in black, and their faces still covered. I was slapped again. "What do you know, Mr. Grant?" Skippy was near me. His voice had a funny accent. English wasn't his native language, and he was uncomfortable speaking it. Exactly what Anderson described to me over the phone. A third time I was slapped.

"I ask, what do you know about Jason Russell?"

I didn't respond. I was thinking, assessing. I offered a quick, silent prayer. I didn't expect angelic intervention like Daniel and his lions. But I was hoping for some ideas. One came to mind. "Jason who?" Playing dumb is usually a strong option for me. Maybe it's the way I look or something. I was punched in the right cheek. I guess it wasn't such a strong option this time.

"I'm getting tired of that." My cheek was cut and bleeding. "Hey, Skip. I shot you. Why didn't you go down?" I had to stall.

"I will tell you why. Here in Korea, we have resources you only dream about."

"I dream a lot, Skip."

He started to slap me again. "Wait, Skip. I'm sorry. Tell me how."

He lowered his hand, clenched it, and hit me in the face. I tasted blood inside my mouth, from the right cheek. I convulsed in pain and cried out. I wasn't hurt that bad, but when he hit me, I jerked against the ropes that held me down.

"I will tell you that the desk of your precious Miss Thompson is not secure. Your gun has blanks in it. You will not need it again."

Skippy must like redheads, 'cause Miss Thompson, U.S. embassy employee, is not my precious.

The pain made it difficult to think, but I put it together. While Thompson was escorting me downstairs, someone tampered with my gun. Someone in cahoots with Skippy and Kim Song Su. But who? How many traitors were there? She couldn't have been gone that long from her desk. I didn't bother to check my gun afterwards; I just assumed that it was okay.

Never assume anything.

Skippy and his black-clad cronies assumed that I only carried one weapon. My .25 was still strapped to my right ankle. I didn't turn that one over to Thompson. I knew it was loaded with real bullets. That was one mistake. Unless Skippy and his boys had found it, removed it from my ankle, emptied it, and then replaced it. That was possible, but I needed a break. Skippy wasn't that smart.

"Peter. May I call you Peter?"

"Not unless you want me to kill you."

He smiled at that. Maybe he thought it was ironic. Or an empty threat from a soon-to-be-dead man.

I was serious.

Skippy was holding a long, thin knife. More like a thin dagger. The blade looked about eight inches long, and very sharp. The tip sparkled in the dim light of the room. "This is the DanDo. It is actually Chinese, but for centuries the Brotherhood has used the DanDo for our purposes. We use it for the GoMun."

"Brotherhood? I thought you pinheads are called comrades." I earned another vicious punch for that.

"I will enjoy this, more than I should. So smug. I hate Americans. I hate you. *Miguk shiloy!*"

"Yeah, well, I'm having a great time in Korea. Nothing but good thoughts. People are really friendly," I mumbled.

He touched the tip of the knife, delicately. "It is ancient form of torture. A very effective form." His *f*'s sounded almost like *p*'s. "We use it to learn many things. Things the victim does not want to tell. You do not want to tell your secrets. I want to know what you know. I do this by using the GoMun. It is painful. Do you like that?"

Just my luck. Skippy was a sadist. "Porm? You mean form?" Skippy looked really mad now, but he regained his composure. If you can call what he was doing composed.

"A day is coming when fire will rain down from heaven and destroy the Mother Land's enemies. Then, the Mother Land will be one Land, united and strong. It is almost here. You will not live to see it. It will be bloody!" Skippy smiled a stupid toothy grin. His teeth were yellow and black.

"Ever seen a dentist, Skippy?"

He hit me in the right side of my mouth, and I knew that I would need to see a dentist when this was over. I spat out a tooth and felt blood trickle down my chin.

Skippy must have been upset with me. He looked like he wanted to kill me, without the torture.

"You will not die quickly, Peter, that I promise."

"Just get on with it, you twit, and quit telling me about it."

Skippy smiled at me again and, instead of killing me, kept talking. Mistake number two. "The GoMun. It will not kill you. It is most painful. You will beg for death. The blade goes here." He pointed at my right underarm and ran his fingers down the blade edge. "If you tell no lies, then it is quickly pushed in. I decide if your answers are lies."

The only thing I would beg for would be for him to just be quiet.

"Make no mistake; it will be most painful. Finally, many hours after I grow tired of your . . . scream for mercy, I will push it all the way in." He sneered at me. "I will slit your throat, with DanDo still in you. I will kill you."

You gotta hate that. "What if I just tell you everything I know right now?" I suggested. My right hand wasn't tied securely, and I could almost pull it free. Mistake number three. They'd done a poor job of tying me up. They thought I'd already lost. But I had to wait for the right moment to act. For all my glibness, I knew I was close to death. I knew I only had one chance.

One chance to live.

I was in charge now, despite my predicament. Skippy was listening to me and responding to what I said. He'd talked too much, was too arrogant. I wasn't even—

Skippy's right hand smashed into my right eye. "I grow tired of waiting, Mr. Grant. Tell me what you know. And tell me now!"

I shook my head and tried to clear it. I opened my mouth, stretched it. A few more shots like that, and I was as good as dead.

I had trouble speaking and mumbled a few words.

"I cannot hear you, Peter Grant. Where is your silly language now? Where is your, how do you say, macho? You have lost, and soon all will be over." He leaned in, close to my right ear. "Answer my questions, no lies, and I promise kill you quickly." He said it like it was a special favor he would only do for me.

I mumbled, "Thank you, Skippy. You know your breath stinks?"

"To put you in the mood, I tell you something you do not know. Perhaps it might loosen your tongue. I was in Utah. It was beautiful. I met Jason Russell. Did you know, before he died, he told me everything? The GoMun is most efficient. He broke his promise and told someone. Told someone." Skippy broke off his narrative and looked away for a minute. "What did the artist call him? Ah yes. President Taylor. President Taylor." He spat the words at me. "Jason Russell broke his promise. I tortured him. I killed him. Just as I will you."

I looked closely at Skippy. "You're not Kim Song Su."

Skippy stood there, almost looked dumbfounded. He quickly recovered. "You know the name, Kim Song Su? You are right, I am not Song Su. He is my superior officer. He allowed me to kill Jason Russell. It was a painful death. Song Su watched and approved.

Then Song Su watched and tracked the Taylor man. Song Su is master of the GoMun. He used it to destroy Taylor. It is sad that Song Su is not here to see you die."

"Too bad for him. I was hoping to meet him. Maybe shoot him. Where is he? Salt Lake? Where's the bomb at, Skippy? What's it got to do with the dragon?"

"Dragon? There is no dragon. The rest is not your concern. The GoMun is."

Skippy thought he was in control, thought he'd won.

I started to sob, my body to shake. My words came softly, quietly. Skippy couldn't hear me. He yanked my head off my chest by what was left of my thinning hair. "I cannot hear you, American pig." The words stopped, and he threw my head against the table.

Again my words came softly, quietly. Skippy leaned down, his ear near my mouth, about six inches away. "Speak up or I will use the DanDo now. The GoMun will begin!"

My right hand came crashing down on his neck; his body crumpled to the floor. His two "Brothers" ran at me. I quickly freed my left hand and reached my right ankle. My gun was out, and the closest Brother fell dead with a bullet in the head.

The other turned and ran.

My head was spinning, dizzy, and I was in a lot of pain. I steadied myself against the table, untied my ankles.

I was free.

I thought about killing Skippy but didn't.

Using the ropes that had been around my ankles, I tied his hands behind his back, then picked him up by his shirt. I pulled his mask over his head and slapped his face a few times. His eyes opened, without recognition, wondering what was happening.

My beaten face filled his vision.

"I'm not gonna kill you, Skippy. But it will be painful." I fired two shots. One into the stomach, the other into his right knee. "Don't call me Peter."

I left him there, with more of a chance to survive than he'd given Jason Russell.

I didn't know where I was. I stumbled out of the building that was supposed to have been my tomb, and was thankful for the blackness of night. More thankful that I was alive. There was at least one more assassin out there; for all I knew he was waiting for me around the next corner. I did know that I was alone, and injured. My head was throbbing, my jaw hurt, and my right eye wasn't focusing all that well. It was probably starting to swell. It was cold too. It felt like it was below freezing, but only barely.

I also knew that at the very least I needed to get away from this building. From what I could see, it was an old warehouse that had been abandoned for some time. A small street ran in front of it. To the left the road disappeared into the darkness, and to the right it disappeared into a fog of lights and people. I went right.

My head was really hurting. The road I was on kept going and going, but I never seemed to reach the lights or people. I half wondered if maybe I hadn't imagined the brightness, but told myself that what I could see was real. I had to believe, because I had nowhere else to go. I kept moving.

The road sloped up, gently at first. I finally started seeing other people. Lots of other people. It was as if Seoul suddenly burst into being around me. I saw buses, cars, and taxis. I tried hailing a taxi, but none would stop for me. I can't say I blame them. I wouldn't stop for a foreigner that looked like his head had been through a meat grinder. But from now on, I will. The road was steep now, and my progress was slow.

I didn't look behind me. I saw a few police cars and even a few foot patrolmen. I considered stopping them, but ruled against it. How could I communicate with them? I could try to get across the name of Conductor's hotel. I guess that *Hyatt* sounds the same in Korean as it does in English. Or maybe it's some vulgar swear word. I wasn't desperate enough to risk offending a policeman with my own ignorance.

By now I was at the top of the hill, and I could see even more of the massive city that is Seoul. It sprawled out in all directions, crawling over and around the hills that once surrounded the ancient city. I couldn't see all of it, probably only a very small portion of it. From the looks of the buildings, I had to be in a residential area. Homes, stores, public baths, and churches were all I could see. The churches were all topped by neon red crosses. Thousands of them dotted the night sky, casting an eerie luminousness over the city.

But on a smaller hill to my left I noticed something different. I thought at first it was a figment of my imagination, and I closed my eyes, daring it to disappear. Then I opened them again, and it was still there. Rising above the red hum was a gold statue, one I'd seen many times before, its brilliance keeping the red neon lights at bay. It beckoned to me like a lighthouse, a light of welcome, a safe harbor. It represented my salvation.

My only chance?

The road I was walking on went right by it, but at the base of the hill. It was only a half mile away, and I was confident I could make it. Strength returned to my arms and legs, and my vision was crisper. I picked up my pace, keeping my eyes on it. It gave me hope, and from my hope I drew strength.

"Mr. Grant!"

A voice from far behind called out. The accent was funny, wrong. I knew who it was. It wasn't Skippy, but one like him. I turned back to look, still walking, and could make out two figures coming at me. They were Korean, and they were in a hurry. In a hurry to catch me.

My legs protested, but I ran anyway.

"Mr. Grant . . . Stop, please . . . It is useless . . . You have nowhere to run."

I didn't know how many were behind me, and I didn't care. Yet I knew at least two were after me. Two too many. I ran past pedestrians, food vendors, and outdoor markets, the sidewalk overflowing with people and their nightly business.

My breath came in short spurts, and in the cold, my lungs ached with a dull pain. The road sloped down at a steep angle, and I was running faster.

So were the goons behind me. Still I ran, my lungs begging for a break. In the cold I must have looked like an old steam train spewing out a lot of smoke. I covered the distance and made it into the shadows faster than I thought I would.

I couldn't see the statue, or the edifice that it topped, anymore. A large brown church was built right up against the road, almost as if to prevent motorists and pedestrians from seeing what lay behind it. A small road shot up to the left, in the direction I wanted to go.

I checked over my shoulder and thought I saw my two would-be escorts trip over a cucumber vendor. I went left and ran for my life. The small road was steep, my knee was tightening up, and my lungs burned. After about seventy-five yards up the road, I stopped and hid in the blackness offered by a building and its shadow. I was pretty sure I hadn't been seen.

I tried to control my breathing. I took in large gulps of breath. It was colder now, and the cold burned my lungs. For the next few minutes all I could hear was the rhythmic beating of my heart. It filled my ears like a jackhammer.

I checked my watch: 10:06 p.m. Then I checked the road: it looked clear, but I couldn't be sure. I didn't need to be. I checked my gun, the one with bullets in it: seven shots left. I didn't have my Glock. I never saw that gun again.

I was wounded, but not dead. My gun was small and limited, but deadly. I was still in the game, but I had to find some help.

I stayed in the shadows and made my way farther up the road. It was deserted. The houses along it were shut and dark, except a few with interior lights.

The nearest streetlight was about a tenth of a mile ahead. After another five minutes of trying to move only in the shadows, I was at the light. It marked a four-way intersection. No stop signs that I could see. The road wasn't marked very well, and it was wide enough for one car in either direction. I looked back and couldn't see the main street that I'd started from. The side road I'd taken must have curved up at an angle. That made me feel a little better.

"Well, no time like the present to press my luck," I said softly.

I had to be close to my goal now. I could feel it. I knew it was probably closed, but my plan was to climb over any gate that barred the way and sleep on its grounds until morning. It was the best I could come up with. I probably couldn't climb, but would make the effort if I got the chance. Not a great plan, to be sure, but better than what Skippy wanted to do to me.

I sprinted across the lighted area and ended up against a brick wall. The wall stood about six feet and wrapped around a four-story brick building. The lowest floor, probably a basement, was lit up, and the light was visible through some ground-level windows. With the little amount of light the windows offered, I could make out a sign on the corner of the brick wall. It looked vaguely familiar, but in the dark—and in Korean—I wasn't sure. Still, I had the distinct feeling that it was familiar to me, or should be. There was a gate, and it was unlocked. I went through, closing it silently behind me.

Four figures appeared at the first-floor door, and I froze. I wasn't afraid. The light from the basement was shut off, and one exterior light came on. The doorway was glass, and I could make out dark suits and trench coats. I melted into what shadows were available, but it was futile. As soon as they came outside, they would see me. I grabbed my gun and waited for whatever was to come.

The door opened. "Very funny, Elder Johnson."

Someone laughed. "I thought so."

They were speaking English.

They sounded American.

They were missionaries.

I stepped into the light. "Elders, can you help me?"

Their questions came quickly.

"Who are you?"

"What are you doing here?"

"What happened to your face? Man, you don't look so good."

If I could trust anyone to help me, it would be missionaries. I just didn't want to tell them too much. I really didn't want to tell them anything. I wasn't going to endanger their lives just to save mine. Although technically, by just talking to me, they were now in danger.

I spoke slowly, not because they looked dumb, but because my mouth and lungs hurt. "My name is Peter Grant. I'm employed by the Church, and I need your help." I didn't sound very convincing, and I'm afraid that my appearance counted against me.

"What can we do?" they asked together.

"How far away is your mission president?"

"Far? He's not far at all. He lives around the corner. We were just headed there."

"Good. I'll walk with you, if you don't mind."

One of them, a tall, blond young man, spoke up. "Wait a minute. What do you do for the Church?"

"I protect the area president."

They stared at me in the dark. One of them said, "I hope he's in better shape than you."

"Me too, Elder. Now answer a question for me." I pointed to the tall blond guy. "What's your name?"

"Elder Johnson."

Elder Johnson wasn't only tall, he was huge. He looked like an offensive lineman for BYU. Godzilla in Korea. He must have been a sight door-knocking.

"Well, Elder Johnson, what is this building?" I gestured to the building behind him.

"This? This is the Shinchon chapel."

Yes, it was a chapel. It had seemed familiar. The sign must have been the name of the Church in Korean.

"I'm kinda cold, fellas, so if you'll lead, I'll follow."

With that, they filed out into the road and went left.

I followed.

The mission president's home was only a slow four-minute walk from the Shinchon chapel.

"Elder Johnson, tell me, what's his name?" I asked.

"Whose name?"

"The mission president's name."

"President Nicholson. He's from Portland, Oregon. He's a good egg; you'll like him. Here we are."

We were outside a three-story house surrounded by a high fence. A small gate was the only visible entrance. One of the missionaries—not Johnson—pushed a few buttons on the gate, and it buzzed. Then it opened. We filed through.

The yard was small, about five by four feet. Right in front of me was a steep staircase that ended at the main door. To my right was a small path that led to a basement level. Elder Johnson spoke to me.

"Wait here."

I waited at the base of the stairs while the missionaries went up.

Not more than two minutes later, Johnson reappeared and motioned to me to come up.

I went up.

Inside the door was a small entryway and shoes everywhere.

"Take your shoes off," Johnson told me.

I did.

I was finally inside.

The main floor was laid out like this, as far as I could see. In front of me was the main room. It doubled as a dining room. The carpet was silvery blue. The room was filled with china cabinets and other nice things. It was dominated by a large oak (I guess) table, circled by eight chairs. Beyond, through a doorway, was the kitchen. To my left was an office, and to my right was a smaller office. It was really a nook with a desk in it. At the end of the table was a big man. He walked to me.

"Brother Grant, is it?" He extended a large hand.

We shook hands. His grip was strong, his eyes filled with questions and doubt.

"Yes, President Nicholson, it is," I responded.

"I have to admit that I have some serious doubts about you and why—"

I cut him off. "Ephraim has black eyes, President." Because the missions of the Church are spread throughout the world, mission presidents called to certain foreign missions are taught some security phrases. For example, if the missionaries in South Korea needed to be evacuated, Church headquarters would telephone the mission president (or reach him another way) and tell him to "pack the books." This would tell the mission president that he had only forty-eight hours to have all of the missionaries under his responsibility ready to evacuate the country. About 185 missionaries. If the mission president was told to "send the books," then he had forty-eight hours to get every missionary out of the mission and every foreign missionary out of the country.

All mission presidents are taught the one I had just used. Ephraim is a code word used only in extreme emergencies. The color of his eyes indicates the degree of seriousness. Red is the least serious, black the most.

He looked at me, then spoke to the missionaries. "Elders, thank you for checking out the chapel. Please travel home safely, and do so quickly."

"But president, we wanted—" Johnson started.

"I didn't ask what you wanted, Elder Johnson." President Nicholson's voice was stern, and there was no further discussion. The missionaries left.

We were alone.

"So, Ephraim has black eyes, Brother Grant? I prayed I'd never hear that. By the looks of it, you do as well."

"Thanks."

"How can I help?"

"First, do you have a bag of ice and some ibuprofen? My head hurts."

We went in the kitchen, and he fixed up a bag of ice for me and gave me some ibuprofen. I popped it without water and pressed the ice bag as delicately as possible to my right eye. We walked through the dining room into his office. We sat in chairs facing each other, then I filled him in on what I thought I could tell him.

"Why are they trying to kill you?" he asked when I finished.

"Who said they were trying to kill me?"

"Have you seen your face, Brother Grant?"

"I can't tell you." Just Tom had sworn Will and me to secrecy. I couldn't tell President Nicholson everything. "But it has nothing to do with the Church or missionary work."

"I'm glad to hear your opinion on that, Brother Grant." He idly stroked his chin. "This is odd. Their attacking you. I've never heard of street criminals assaulting an American unless it was near an American military post or connected to the American military in some other way. They must really not like you to attack an American like this."

Yeah, that's what it is, odd.

"Do you think they saw you with the missionaries, Brother Grant?"

"No. I don't think so. I'm pretty sure they didn't. But to play it safe, you may want to transfer them to different parts of the mission, or maybe even home."

"Good idea. I'll think about it."

"I need to get hold of the area president. Where is your phone?"

"You don't need a phone. He's sleeping downstairs."

"He's what? He was supposed to sleep in the hotel." Conductor liked to be with missionaries as often as possible. It made nice memories for them, and Conductor loved it. But it created potential nightmares for security junkies like me and my associates.

"He's been here about three hours, and he went to bed only thirty minutes ago. Two of your security men are with him. Do you want to wake him?"

I probably should have. "No. Let him sleep." A rested Conductor is a happy Conductor.

"If you don't mind me asking, how did you end up outside the Shinchon chapel? I mean, I know you were being chased, but how did you know which road to take?"

"I didn't." I told him what I'd seen from the top of the hill and how I'd hoped to find *it* instead of the missionaries.

President Nicholson smiled. "Come with me."

I followed him up the stairs to the third floor. The stairs were narrow but not too steep. At the top he went into a small room. The hallway continued on, but we stayed in the tiny room. The room was dark, and I couldn't see much.

"Is there a light in here?" I asked.

"Yes, but you don't need one." President Nicholson pulled back a curtain.

Outside the window, it was close. I'd never seen one this close before. I knew it wasn't close enough to touch, but I was tempted to reach out and try anyway. The lights shining off it made it seem even larger, almost to the point of filling the window.

It was the angel Moroni. The statue that topped the Seoul Korea Temple.

I'd reached my goal.

For the first time in what felt like weeks, but was really only hours, I relaxed. We stood there in silence for a few minutes. I didn't know this man, President Nicholson, but I took comfort in not being alone and in our common beliefs.

I followed him back downstairs.

I slipped on the next to last step and crashed to the floor.

CHAPTER 11

"Peter, can you hear me? It's time to leave."

The voice was familiar.

"We have a plane to catch."

I opened my left eye, the pain-free one, and saw Conductor. I was lying down and tried to sit up, but Conductor's hands were on my shoulders and he kept me down.

"Don't get up. I understand you had a busy night," he said simply.

"Yes, sir. You'll have to excuse the condition of my face."

He smiled at my morbid humor. "I already have. You should have woken me last night, Peter."

"Yes, sir. I didn't want to disturb your rest."

"Better my rest than my breakfast. President Nicholson has related what he knows. What you told him. I want to hear it from you."

"Are we alone?"

"Yes. You are on the couch in President Nicholson's office. The door is closed. We are alone, but talk softly."

I did.

I told him everything, even the stuff about the *Morning Glory*. I chose to ignore how Just Tom would feel about that.

I figured if I couldn't trust Conductor with that particular national security secret, who could I trust? After all, he lives in Salt Lake City too.

He didn't say anything at all, at least, not what I expected. Maybe I was hoping for him to provide an answer to the problem that loomed before me, before all of us. Something along the lines of where the bomb is. Or maybe where I could find Kim Song Su. Preferably both. It's an easy trap to fall into. Shouldn't he be able to tell me where, when, and how? But it's a trap of laziness. My job existed because of necessity, and I had to do my part. The revelation part could have been done when I was hired. In any event, he didn't magically pull a rabbit out of his hat and tell me how to solve this.

Besides, that rabbit-out-of-the-hat thing is just a sleight-of-hand trick.

"Can you identify this North Korean? If you saw him in a crowd of people, would you recognize him?"

"Yes. I would."

Conductor looked into my eyes, and I felt my heart swell in my chest. He didn't speak for what seemed an eternity.

"Can you stop him?"

I held his gaze. "Yes. I can."

He didn't ask me if I was sure. Maybe he should have.

"Then we need to get you back to Salt Lake as quickly as possible."

"When do we leave, sir?"

He looked at his watch. "In about two and a half hours. Eleven thirty. After my meetings yesterday, I decided to cut my visit short."

"Just like that?"

"Yes, just like that. I can do that, you know." He smiled at me. "I'll be coming back soon. I spoke with President Nicholson and three stake presidents this morning, and it was agreed I would come back after the Olympics. I enjoy it very much in Korea, and I love the Korean Saints. I visited here the first time in the 1950s. Just after the war ended. Korea was a different country then. The ravages of the war left this land broken and destitute. A wasteland. So much devastation and deprivation . . . Didn't your father fight in the Korean War?"

"No, sir. He was here, but not as a soldier. He was a cook on a ship. He never made it to Seoul."

He continued. "By the end of the war, not a single building in the city stood higher than one story. And there weren't very many of those. The homeless were everywhere because everyone was homeless. I helped to coordinate the Church's relief efforts here: food, water, medicine, blankets. This land has recovered miraculously. The Korean people are strong, especially the Saints. I even knew the first Korean member of the Church; his name was Kim Ho Jeek. The members here affectionally referred to him as the Korean Joseph Smith because he was the first Korean member."

Conductor looked away for a brief moment, maybe remembering what this beautiful city looked like in the 1950s. "I attended the temple dedication here, back in the mid-eighties. It is a crowning jewel on a city that rose from the ashes of war and despair. The temple sits on a well of fresh water. It supplies the water for the baptismal font and the water for the temple workers' apartments that were built on the property too. Did you know that?" He wasn't really asking me a question, so I didn't answer. But I knew he'd attended the Seoul Temple dedication. The water thing was news to me. He kept talking. "This land, the people, have been special to me since that first visit. I love the food. They have this *kimchi* soup you should try before we leave." Did Conductor just say he loved the food? *Kimchi* soup? Maybe I had a concussion.

"One more thing, sir."

"What, Peter?"

"I need to see a doctor."

"You may not have seen, but a doctor was here for several hours tending to you. You have a slight concussion but nothing of immediate danger. Your right eye will heal; the swelling is already down. You will need to see a dentist, I'm afraid. There looks to be some extensive damage to the right side of your jawline, but it's not broken. A tooth is missing. He left some medication for the pain."

"You remembered all that?"

"No. I had the doctor write it down." Conductor held up a yellow notepad with the doc's notes on it. "Next time, let them hit you on the left side of your face."

I'll remember that.

"Just one more thing," I said.

He gave me a mock look of exasperation that said he would allow only one more "one more thing." "What, Peter?"

"Can I take a shower before we go?"

"If you hurry." He was enjoying himself.

I'm glad someone was.

I had extra clothes in my suitcase. My things, along with the other team members' stuff, were now at the mission home. Or so I'd been told. But my things weren't at the mission home. My suitcase was missing. I couldn't find it. It wasn't where President Nicholson thought it was supposed to be. No one knew where it was. I found out that it never actually came over from the hotel. I picked it up at the airport, and I carried it into my hotel room. Now it was gone.

"This is just great. My bag has been stolen." I had a pretty good idea who was responsible. Skippy and his goons had somehow gotten it. Losers. But that didn't make sense. Nothing was making sense. Someone had messed with my weapon while it was at the embassy, and now my luggage was missing. I'd think about that later. My head hurt too much to concentrate.

I still needed a shower though. President Nicholson loaned me a pair of sweats. They were too big, but I put them on anyway. The shower felt great. I felt invigorated.

* * *

The biggest airport in all of Korea is Kimpo International Airport; it's just outside Seoul. It is massive and imposing. There is security everywhere. I don't mean men and women in gray slacks and dark blue blazers carrying two-way radios and magic wand metal detectors. Security at airports outside the United States means armed troops at all times. Kimpo is no exception. Plenty of troops everywhere, for all to see, armed with submachine guns.

As a security man, my job is to protect Conductor's life. I normally hate airports, despite the presence of armed troops. Criminals are not usually too bright when it comes to seeing the obvious: cops with big guns. Armed good guys are not a deterrent; they are only a challenge. And anyway, in my line of work, the same job the Secret Service has provided for American presidents since 1901, we don't deal with normal criminals. We deal with zealots. People that honestly believe in what they are doing. They believe so passionately that self-sacrifice becomes just another element of the job. It is true that sometimes this belief can be caused by a form of dementia. What they believe is irrelevant. What caused the belief is irrelevant.

What is relevant is that they kill anyone they deem to be a threat to their ultimate goal. Or the kill itself is the ultimate goal. History is replete with people murdered by zealots. American Presidents Lincoln, Garfield, McKinley, and Kennedy are just a few of the long list of victims of zealots with a gun and a plan. Others, like Ford and Reagan, are attacked and wounded. Most of these attacks, the successful and nonsuccessful, occur in public places. Places like train stations, theaters, public plazas—and airports.

Conductor is a public man. The faster and larger the Church grows, the more difficult my job is. The more of a target our subjects become. I don't mean to leave the impression that they are as much a target as the president of the United States. They're not. But it only takes one nutcase.

I anxiously waited for the plane to lift off. The most dangerous place for a subject to be is sitting in a plane on the tarmac. Waiting. After that, he is no longer the target. The plane is. A plane is bigger and easier to blow up. Whether it is a shoulder-mounted rocket fired at the plane or a small handgun fired at point-blank range, the end result is almost certain death.

We don't have the resources of the Secret Service. We can't scout out all possible locations for a gunman to hide, or order areas of a city blocked off, or seal off entire buildings. We use what we have, which usually amounts to our own experience, concerns, and the protocol that is established. Every general conference of the Church we enlist the aid of members in and around Salt Lake. We have a big meeting in the Tabernacle and hand them a few photographs with names of individuals we think might show up. This is very helpful when more than a hundred thousand people cram into downtown Salt Lake for the various sessions of conference.

Despite our lack of resources, we do our job well. Very well. I trust my team. Truth is, they're all as good as or better than I am. The hard part isn't taking the proverbial bullet for the protectee. The hard part comes before that: preparation. And in that respect, each member of my team is a professional. We're prepared to take that bullet. But we know the more preparation we do, the less likely it becomes that one of us will have to take a bullet.

Soon, but not soon enough, we were leaving Kimpo International Airport. With the plane in the air, I had one less thing to worry about. Now I was free to think.

I had a dead artist and a dead art teacher who taught the dead artist in high school. But their student-teacher friendship was more than a decade old. Did it really matter? No, it didn't. I knew now that Jason Russell had told Taylor something.

There was a dead medical examiner that had discovered a physical connection between the previous two and a wounded detective that had been investigating the second death. We'd been planning to investigate the first victim, Jason Russell, when she was attacked. It all went back to Jason Russell.

I was missing something, something I knew was important. Was it something Skippy had told me? The pain medication, something called Ultram, was making it hard for me to remember clearly. It was something about Russell and Taylor. What had I learned?

"What was it?"

"What, Grant?"

"Nothing, Scott. Just thinking out loud." Scott had a good career in the FBI. He has what I call "Steve Martin hair." It's almost luminous white. Not gray or blond—white. He is a fanatical jogger and is in probably the best shape of anyone I know. That includes current FBI rosters. He has a large family, four girls and one boy. His wife's name is Debra. I met her once and called her Debbie. I never did it again.

I fell asleep. The Ultram had done its job. I had crazy dreams. Anderson and I were married and living in her big house in Spanish Fork. We had two daughters and a golden retriever named Gandalf. The crazy part is this: I fixed up the house. I painted it (I painted the trim some color called Navajo red). I patched up the roof, and the old house looked great. Anderson told me it looked like it was almost brand new, and she really liked it. It wasn't a dream; it was a fantasy.

I had one nightmare too. Dan Begay again. It was the same dream. Dan still died in my arms. It was a one-in-a-million shot, and it hit Dan. I watched him crumple to the ground, dying, and I ran to him. Then I was holding him, telling him everything would be all right. I told him he was fine, that he would live, and we both knew it was a lie.

Then suddenly he was gone, and I was in Salt Lake, looking for my new North Korean friend. I failed and never found Kim Song Su. I never found him because I was desperately searching for Brigham Young. Of course, he died a long time ago, and I didn't understand why I wasn't looking for Kim Song Su. I should have been. My searching was in vain. I never found the bomb. There was a large explosion, and I saw a mushroom cloud over Salt Lake. A cloud of destruction and death over Temple Square. I failed Conductor, Anderson, Agent Cook, and millions of people from around the world I didn't even know. A feeling of guilt covered me, assaulted me, and I wanted to disappear. Just before the destructive heat wave struck me, I woke up.

I put the Ultram away. I would deal with the pain without medication. I had plenty of my own nightmares without an artificial source triggering new ones.

By my watch, it was 6:00 p.m., Thursday evening in Korea.

"Scott, what time is it?"

"Where at?"

"Anywhere but Korea," I said.

"We already passed the international date line. Every few hours that we travel west, the time is earlier. So I don't really know exactly what time it is right now. I do know that we will reach the continental United States before we left Seoul."

"Say again?" I was confused. How could we be in the U.S. before we left Korea?

"The time change. You get to live today twice. So instead of it being Friday when we land, it will still be Thursday, the ninth."

Cool.

Then it hit me. I remembered what Skippy told me. Taylor was killed because Russell told Taylor what he was *doing*. Russell was an artist. A sculptor. He must have told Taylor what it was he was creating. Taylor was the second kill. Whatever Jason Russell had told Taylor, it stopped with Taylor.

I had to know what Russell knew. I had to know what he told Taylor. But more than that, I had to know what Russell was creating in that shop of his in Springville.

Attacking Anderson was a natural progression in the chain of destruction and misery caused by Kim Song Su. I should have seen it coming. I'm not a rookie, and I blamed myself for the attack on Anderson. If we'd been more prepared, then she wouldn't be in the hospital recovering from gunshot wounds. No, not "we." I have the experience and smarts to know that she was a target well before it happened. I could've been there. From now on, I would be.

I knew everything Anderson did. In fact, I knew more. I'd actually seen Kim Song Su. I could identify him. If anything, that made me more of a target. I wondered if he was the one who got away at Anderson's house. I'd been stupid to wander around Seoul and go shopping. I was also lucky. Luckier than Skippy. Sometimes it's better to be lucky than smart.

Usually I go for smarter.

A few things still eluded me. How did a Korean War–era nuclear weapon fit into all of this? What did a dragon have to do with Salt Lake City? I thought Just Tom was right about the bomb, but I still needed some answers.

"Hey, Ken." Ken Jones is retired Secret Service, and his hair is gray, not white. He was one of Reagan's and the first Bush's favorite Secret Service agents.

"What, Grant?"

"Trade me seats."

"What? Why?"

"I need to use the phone."

Jones was sitting next to the phone, and I wanted to use it.

"Okay."

We switched seats. After getting comfortable, I picked up the phone and called Rockwell. Anyone can call Church security. Only the agents on the security teams know how to reach Rockwell. I dialed the number for the front lobby of the Church Office Building.

Sister Wilkins answered. "Church Office Building. This is Sister Wilkins. How may I be of assistance?"

"Rose, it's Grant. Get me Rockwell."

"Authorization?"

To reach Rockwell, you have to go through the Church Office Building. The only way to actually reach Rockwell is with the proper security phrase. It changes monthly, and I had to think for a moment before I could remember February's.

"Teancum is hunting for the king."

"Just a moment, Agent Grant."

The code phrase always incorporates a heroic figure from the Book of Mormon. Three of my favorites are all found in the book of Alma: Captain Moroni and his chief lieutenants, Lehi and Teancum. They were an inspiration for their people. I get the feeling when I read about them that the Nephites knew that with Captain Moroni at the head of their armies they could not be defeated. But this is only true because of faith. Their faith and Moroni's faith. Lehi and Teancum were no less heroic in my estimation, and Teancum is one of my favorites. I think all young men in the Church, at some point, wish they could be like Captain Moroni or his second-in-command, Lehi. Me, I always liked Teancum. This month's security authorization phrase was a reference to the Lamanite-Nephite war in the book of Alma and the role Teancum played in it.

She patched me through. After two rings, it was picked up.

"Yes?"

"This is Grant."

"Hey, Grant. This is Simms. How are you? Heard you had a rough night. You all right?"

News travels fast.

"Good. Yes, and yes. You busy?"

"You know the answer to that, Grant. But I can give you a few hours."

"Good. I need you to do something for me."

"What's that? Where are you?"

"I'm with Conductor. Check out an art shop in Springville. I don't know the name, but the artist's name was Jason Russell."

"Was? Is he dead?"

"Yes, he is, and his shop burned to the ground last year. Officially the fire and his death are still open cases. Try to find out what he did. I mean, what he created. Find out all you can about him, okay?"

"Sure. When do you get in?"

"I'm not sure. Just leave whatever you dig up on my desk, and I'll get it when I get there."

"Can do."

"One more thing. I know this sounds crazy, but try and locate any dragons in the Salt Lake area."

"Dragons?" He sounded incredulous.

"Yes, dragons. Don't worry about paintings or drawings. Look for a big dragon. Big enough for you to hide inside, okay?"

"Yeah." Simms hung up.

I was tempted to call Anderson. I wanted to know if she liked Navajo red. I put the phone back, closed my eyes, and thought about Anderson.

I liked thinking about her.

I picked up the phone again and called her. Her voice was music to my ears. Of course it could have been the radio that was on in her room when she first picked up. I told her what I learned about Russell and Taylor. Then about the two Korean words Just Tom had given me. I didn't mention the bomb, just that I needed to find a certain dragon.

"Thanks for keeping me in the loop, Grant."

"No big deal, Anderson. It's good to hear your voice. Do you like Navajo red paint?"

"What, Grant?"

"Nothin'. How's the shoulder?"

"Stiff and sore. The Percocet helps with the pain. So, when do you go dragon hunting, St. George?"

"Soon as I find my lance."

"Maybe it's a young dragon. You know, a minor." She laughed at her own joke.

"It's not *young*. It's *yong*." I said it with the long vowel.

"What does it mean, Grant?"

"I told you. Dragon. The other is probably a code word for . . . something else. Look, I gotta go. I'll call again. Be safe, Anderson."

"You too, Grant."

I hung up.

The total flight lasted some thirteen hours. Much quicker than the flight to Korea. Everyone, including myself, was asleep when we stopped in Anchorage, Alaska, to refuel. I admit I didn't sleep very well. We were there for about two hours. After refueling, we lifted off again and headed for home. A few hours later, we were nearing the United States.

I'd never seen the Columbia River from the air. I saw it now, spilling into the Pacific Ocean. Even the small oval windows of the plane did little to hinder its beauty. Washington, on the left, and Oregon, to the right, seemed only to serve the mighty Columbia. I couldn't say anything, other than, "Beautiful." It looked just like it does in an atlas. I was amazed that the atlas people had gotten it right, and my amazement was overshadowed by the beauty of it all.

The captain spoke over the PA system. "We will soon be flying over Portland, Oregon. Local time, Pacific standard time, is 10:30 a.m., and the temperature is a chilly 41 degrees. Welcome to the United States, and thank you for flying Mormon Airways." The pilot thought he was being funny. I think I saw Conductor smile. We flew over Portland, the City of Roses, and past Mount Hood.

Mount Hood juts out like a massive spike sticking out of the earth. It is the crown jewel in this part of the Cascade Mountains, the highest point in Oregon. Our plane flew right past it, and I had to cover my eyes because of the brightness of the sunlight reflecting off its snow-packed sides. All too soon, it was gone.

Two hours later, we were landing at Salt Lake International Airport. I was hoping the pilot would buzz the golf course that sits near the airport. That would have been cool. But he didn't. Because of the time difference, it was only 11:40 a.m. By the time we cleared customs, it was just after 12:30 p.m.

I didn't have a lot of time.

chapter 12

Conductor went home. He lives in an apartment on an upper floor of the Gateway Apartment Building, where a lot of other General Authorities live, including the prophet.

I went with what was left of my team back to Rockwell. Conductor is only escorted by security when he is making public appearances. It doesn't matter if it is South Korea or Temple Square. He didn't have public appearances planned until the eleventh, in the early evening. He was not attending the Olympic opening ceremonies. Before the Olympic ceremony, as part of the celebration, Conductor was scheduled to preside at a gathering on Temple Square. It was going to be a busy night for Church security and every other law enforcement person in or around the city.

Given the situation, Conductor had relieved me of my job-related responsibilities. I thought of protesting, but didn't. If Kim Song Su wasn't found in time, it wouldn't matter what anyone was doing.

I was free to hunt down Kim Song Su.

First thing I did at Rockwell was check my desk. After that I took a shower and changed into a fresh set of clothes that I kept at Rockwell. I sent the sweats back to Korea a few days later. Then, I went back to my desk. Simms did the research for me, and he didn't find much. It was grim reading, and my stomach turned, but

I trudged through it. Jason Russell's death was still officially unsolved, and the burning of his shop was still attributed to arson. Rags from his shop were soaked in lacquer thinner, placed behind the dumpster at the rear of his shop, and set on fire. The whole structure went up pretty quick. Because of the chemicals used by Russell, the fire was unusually hot and the fumes very toxic. The Springville Fire Department could only watch it burn to the ground. The next day, Jason Russell's body was found in the charred rubble.

Simms had managed to dig up a few photos. The first was of Jason Russell himself. I'd been so busy that I hadn't actually seen a picture of him. Normally, that's one of the first things I like to find. It helps me to identify with the victim. The photo I was looking at showed a smiling, blond-haired man.

A note written by Simms and attached to the top photo read, "He was talented and had a bright future. He was regarded as one of the up-and-coming artists in the Intermountain West. Because of his talent, and the circumstances surrounding his death, the value of his work has gone up considerably." The photos were all of his work: children playing, George Washington and Abraham Lincoln standing together, a bust of Joseph Smith, and other pieces of art he'd sculpted. I don't know art, but I would have to agree with Simms's note. Russell was good.

The last page said he could not discover what it was Russell had been working on when he was killed. Russell apparently kept all of his records at his work, and all were lost in the fire. Simms found some dragons, but nothing large enough to hide himself, or a bomb, in. But I would check all of them myself.

Before I did that, I called Anderson. She was still in Provo at the hospital.

She sounded great.

"Hey, partner, how the heck are you?" My gut hurt. I was actually nervous! My throat was tightening up.

Maybe I'd caught the flu.

"Good, I think. How are you?"

"Better than I was in Korea." The swelling in my right eye was almost gone.

"Why?"

I could've said something romantic like, "Because I'm nearer to you," but I didn't. I'm not sappy. At least I try not to be. "I'll tell you some other time."

"Tell me now. What happened?"

"I made a stupid mistake and left myself exposed. I went shopping, bought you a leather jacket. A nice black one. But I lost it."

"What happened, Grant?" she persisted.

I told her. "Some associates of the guys that attacked you did a number on my face. Messed it up pretty good. I can't tell you what they wanted over the phone."

"Is it still messed up?"

"My face? Nothing more than normal, except for the missing tooth. My jaw still hurts."

She almost laughed. "Is it an improvement?"

She was laughing at me. At my pain. "Probably. Want to see?"

"I do. How did you escape, Grant?"

"I got lucky and outsmarted them."

"You were lucky. That's easier for me to believe than you outsmarting them." She laughed again. It was more of a giggle. I liked the sound of it.

"Seriously, Grant, it's good to hear from you. How's the dragon hunt going?"

"I'll fill you in later."

She hesitated. "Is everything all right?"

Sure, other than my face and a missing tooth. Oh, and as long as you know nothing about a possible nuclear winter. "I've just got a lot on my mind. I don't mean to be short with you. You'll be there through the weekend?" The mountains would probably shield most of Utah County from the initial blast of a nuclear detonation in Salt Lake. Somehow I felt better knowing that even if I failed, Anderson would live.

"Yeah. Doc says that I'll be okay. My shoulder is major sore and stiff. Just like the last time you called. I can't move it at all, and it still hurts."

"Bullets will do that to you. That's why I never got shot in the FBI. Don't move it if it hurts."

"Thanks, Grant. Will you come visit?"

I wanted to go see her right then and there. But I couldn't.

"I will. Soon as I can. Promise. Listen, I gotta go now. I'll call you later. It's good to hear your voice. Talking to you, it helps."

"You too, Grant. Bye."

I hung up after she did.

Then I called the Salt Lake office of the FBI. I figured I should talk to Cook and enlist the FBI's help. He still didn't sound happy to hear from me. We agreed to meet at 3:30 p.m., at Temple Square. He wanted me to come to his office, but I told him I wouldn't do that. I know how the FBI works. All feds have the same ego problem. They think they are always in control. If I'd gone to his office, I would have lost the independence I needed to look for Kim Song Su in my own way. By insisting on meeting him on my terms, I made it clear that he could not control me. At least, I thought I was doing that. I could have just been irritating Cook more than normal. Well, that was okay too. His agreeing to meet me also demonstrated that the FBI still had no idea where to find the bomb or Kim Song Su. If they did, he would have been totally unwilling to work with me. I know. I was in Cook's position for a very long time.

I had time for one more phone call. Technically, it was a call I had no business making. Over the years, I'd done many of them. Too many. But sometimes the call can be very beneficial. I checked my notes and found the number. I hoped she would be home, but maybe she'd decided to leave and live with one of her kids. With her husband gone, she didn't seem to have many ties to the area. I called Ann Taylor, wife of President Taylor.

It rang four times, and I was tempted to hang up. On the sixth ring, it was answered. It was a man's voice that answered.

"Hello."

"Hello. My name is Peter Grant, and I am trying to reach Ann Taylor."

"I'm her son. Does my mother know you?" His voice was guarded. Protecting his mom.

"She doesn't, but I really need to speak with her."

"I'm sorry, but my mom, she's pretty upset right now. She's not in any condition to talk to you. Good-bye."

"Wait. Please, don't hang up. I don't know your mother, but I think she'll want to talk to me."

"Really? Why?"

"I'm investigating your father's murder."

Her son was quiet. Then he asked, "Who are you?"

I told him. "My name is Peter Grant, and I'm working with the Spanish Fork Police Department. Please, can I speak with your mother?"

Her son could say no and hang up. I knew that, and so did he. He didn't say anything else to me. It was quiet.

So was I.

I could hear voices in the background and could make out only part of it. I did understand "Here, Mom."

Ann Taylor was on the phone.

"Who are you, and what do you know about John?"

"My name is Peter Grant and—"

"You are not the police detective that came out here."

"No, I am not."

"Who do you work for?"

I didn't have the time to explain. "The FBI."

"Oh." She seemed confused for a moment, but quickly recovered. "What do you want to know?"

I offered my condolences, which were sincere. No one deserved to die the way John Taylor had. Then I jumped right into it. "Did your husband keep in touch with a young man from Springville named Jason Russell?"

"Jason? Of course he did. John took Jason's death very hard. He was like another son." Her voice cracked and broke, having to speak about her husband in the past tense. When she spoke again her voice was firm. This was a strong woman. "They were very close, and now they're both . . . I'm sorry."

"Don't be. I am terribly sorry to be bothering you. I need you to try and remember something for me."

"What? I'll try."

"I know you will. And I know this must be difficult. Thank you. Before Jason died, did he meet with your husband? I mean, close to Jason's death?"

"Two weeks before he died, Jason came over for dinner. He didn't have any family left in the area, and he came over about once a month for dinner."

"Did he seem upset that night? Distracted?"

"I don't understand. I thought you wanted to know about John."

"I do. This could help me. Help me catch the person responsible for your husband's death."

Her question was quick but accurate. "Is Jason's death linked to my John's?"

I was prepared for that. "Possibly, but only in a peripheral, incidental way. Please take a minute and try to remember what Jason was like that night at dinner."

She was silent for a good minute. "He was normal. Normal for Jason."

"Okay. Good. Did anything unusual happen that night?"

"Unusual? How?"

"I don't know, Mrs. Taylor. Does anything stick out? Anything at all." I didn't want to coach or prod her, but I was out of time. Almost.

She was quiet again. "Nothing strange. No, nothing. Unless you count talking as strange."

"What did they talk about?" My heart was thumping against my chest.

"Nothing much. Church history."

"Church history? Are you sure?" I was confused now. I was hoping that maybe it was that last night at dinner that Jason

Russell mentioned his work to John Taylor. But Church history made no sense at all. "Are you absolutely sure?"

"Yes, absolutely. I remember it clearly. It was Jason's last night in our home. They stayed up late talking about Brigham Young, Church history, and art. John was Jason's art teacher in high school. Jason was always asking John his opinion and advice." She paused, took a deep breath. "I'm sure that's what they were talking about. I went to bed at 10:00 p.m., like usual, and they stayed up late talking."

"Did Jason ever give your husband any photos of his work, or did they ever share design plans or anything like that? You know, consult together on some of Jason's work?"

"Yes. They consulted a great deal together. We have many photos of Jason's work. We, I mean, I even have some original pieces of his work. We felt like Jason was another son, and those feelings were reciprocated by Jason. John was like a second father to Jason."

"May I come see some of the work of Jason's that you have?"

"Sure you can. I don't know why, but you may if it will help you. You wouldn't be the first one."

The Spanish Fork police officer who told Ann Taylor about her husband's death must have looked at the stuff too. "When may I come down?"

"The house is kind of full right now, because of John's funeral . . ."

I cut her off. I had to see it today. I would apologize for interrupting her family's privacy another time. "How about this afternoon?"

"Now? It's already almost one thirty."

"I know, and I don't mean to be pushy. But this could be very important. I'm in Salt Lake. I can be there in about an hour, if that's all right."

"My sons may not like it, but it's my house. Come on down. Do you need directions?"

"I do."

She gave them to me.

"Thank you, Mrs. Taylor." I hung up. I would have to stand up Agent Cook and the FBI. I was sure Cook would understand.

The drive took an hour and ten minutes.

I was back in Utah County, and when I passed Provo I wanted to stop and see Anderson. I'd make time for that later. Maybe on the way back. I was off the freeway now, heading for my destination. The Taylor home is on the outskirts of Springville. I passed a sign that said someplace called Mapleton was a few miles ahead. That sounded inviting. I took a right turn, heading away from the mountains, and about a mile from the main road was the Taylor home. It was a white split-level house. I think split-level homes outnumber chapels in Utah.

There were five cars in the driveway. Most of the license plates were out-of-state. Probably her children's cars. I parked on the opposite side of the street and walked over to the house. The lawn was covered in gray and white snow. The walkway was small and narrow, and I slipped on some ice and almost fell. But I didn't. I stepped up on a small porch and knocked on the front door.

A disheveled man wearing khaki slacks and a dark blue button-down shirt answered it.

"You Grant?" he asked. His blond hair needed to be combed. He didn't look happy that I was there.

"I am." I offered my hand and we shook. "I'm here to see your mother. You are?"

"She's waiting for you downstairs. I'm Donnie. Follow me." He left the door open, and I walked inside the Taylor home, closing the door behind me. A flight of stairs was just inside the front door. The left side went up, and the right down. Donnie went to the right, and I followed him. He wasn't very talkative, which I could understand. But I sensed that he was angry I was there. I can't say I blame him. The walls, on either side, were nearly completely covered with pictures of the Taylor family. I even noticed Jason Russell in a few. The stairs led to a finished basement.

Part of it must have also been the entertainment room. To my right there was a big-screen TV, two leather recliners, and a home theater system. Donnie went to the left.

He stopped outside a door. "My mother agreed to see you. I don't know why. She's under a lot of stress, and she's trying to bury her feelings about dad's death. She shouldn't see anyone. Even the bishop left. Don't upset her, Mr. Grant."

"I won't."

Donnie turned and left. I went in the door.

It was a big room with carpet on only half the floor. There was no furniture, other than two wooden bar stools. On the uncarpeted area was what looked like a work area. Tools, saws, and lots of other do-it-yourself stuff adorned a peg-board above a workbench. The workbench was packed full of things, but was clean and orderly. The exact opposite of my garage. An older woman sat on one of the bar stools.

"Mrs. Taylor?"

"Yes, Agent Grant. Call me Ann."

"Will do. Please just call me Grant." Ann Taylor was a pretty woman. Her hair was gray, silvery, but full. Her blue eyes were red from days of crying. Her skin was free of blemish, and she wore little makeup. I could see why a young man at BYU had found her attractive all those years ago. A lifetime ago for Ann Taylor.

"After we spoke, I rounded up all of the things that Jason had given us over the years. Everything I could find is there." She waved at the workbench.

I went to the workbench and studied Jason Russell's life work. Most of the items looked like miniatures of larger pieces. He must have given his "parents" at least some of the study models he'd made and used over the years. I looked at all of them closely, and Ann did not disturb me. It took about twenty minutes. Finally, I asked, "You're certain that this is everything? Nothing is missing?"

"Everything he gave us is there. Yes."

Good. "Can you tell me which one, or ones, he gave you near the end?"

Ann got off her stool and joined me at the workbench. She didn't hesitate. "That one there." It was a miniature statue of what looked like Brigham Young. I thought for a minute that I'd seen it before, but dismissed the thought just as quickly. It was missing a base and had an unfinished look to it. I think artists would have called this a study model. I called it unfinished.

"Where's the base?"

"Jason told us that he didn't want to work with one. I assumed that eventually he would have made one. I mean for the actual statue when it was finished."

That made sense.

"Do you know who he was making it for?"

"I don't. He said he couldn't tell us. It was a secret. We didn't push him on it."

That must have been what he told President Taylor. Jason Russell told John Taylor who he was working for. And it got them both killed.

"Do you know if he finished it?"

"I don't. Didn't the shop fire destroy it?"

"I don't know. Maybe." Simms didn't mention anything of Russell's that survived the fire.

"Did Jason enjoy fantasy books or sci-fi stuff?" I asked.

"I don't know. He could've."

"Would he have sculpted fantasy figures or objects?"

"Like what?" Ann looked interested. Anything to take her mind off her pain.

"I'm not sure. Elves, dwarves, dragons, pixies, that kind of thing?"

She smiled. "He didn't. Jason may have enjoyed fantasy books as a young man, but that stuff was never in his art. He did do some comic book stuff, but those were pencil drawings. He loved Batman. He did those a long time ago. I don't even have that stuff."

"That's all right. I don't need to see them. Thank you for your time." I started to leave, but stopped. Something was bugging me. I could almost see it, understand what it was. "Has anyone else been here to look at this stuff?"

"Yes. Why?"

"Was it the officer from Spanish Fork?"

"No. He said his name was Yakamura, and he said he worked for Church security." My heart went cold. "A short little man. He was here just a few days ago, but he didn't stay very long. My sons were rude to him. I tried to help, but he didn't really ask me anything. Everything on the workbench now was spread throughout the house, and he just walked around looking at stuff. Do you know him?"

I did. But there is no Agent Yakamura that works for Church security. It had to be Kim Song Su. The Taylor family was lucky to be alive. "What did he look like?"

"Funny you should ask that. His hair was jet black, and he had a bushy mustache. He had a cane too. I know I shouldn't feel this way about someone that works for the Church, but he made me uncomfortable. I was relieved when he left. He looked nice, but felt bad. It's difficult to explain. I felt better when he was gone."

We walked upstairs.

It had to be him. The cane and mustache were just part of his disguise. Kim Song Su had already been here, but he hadn't found what he was looking for. I was sure that if he had, it would be gone now, and the Taylor family most likely would be dead.

Ann opened the front door. "I'm sorry I wasn't able to help more."

"You have," I said. I thought about warning her, but how? I didn't want to scare her. I took a chance. "Have you had the funeral?"

"Yes. Yesterday morning."

"Do you have somewhere you can go?"

"You mean, like a vacation?"

"Yes."

"My son Donnie wants me to come and stay with him for a few weeks. I was considering it."

"Do it. Leave tonight."

"Tonight? I couldn't possibly do that."

I interrupted her. "Sister Taylor, Ann, there is no Yakamura that works for LDS Church security. I know there isn't. Whoever he was, he was not what he appeared to be. Your instincts about him were correct."

"Then who was he?"

"I don't know. Leave tonight." I didn't know what else to say. Maybe after all this was over, I would come back and explain it all to her. In the end, all I really did was scare her. The one thing I didn't want to do.

I walked away, across to my car.

I drove away, still searching for a dragon with a bomb.

I found my way to the Springville Police Department headquarters. I walked in the front door. It was small, like the one in Spanish Fork. There was one officer behind a high counter.

"May I help you?" he asked me.

"You may. I need to report something."

"What?"

"The last few nights, I've seen something strange at my neighbor's house."

The officer, Baker was his name, gave me a blank, disinterested look.

"My neighbors, the Taylors, well, her husband was killed up by that mine." I was doing my best to sound like a local yokel, but what the heck is that? I told him the address. "There is this strange man—I think it's a man anyway. He's been sneaking around."

Baker grabbed a notepad, but didn't seem to really care. I was too tired to put up with this. "Can you describe him for me? Any distinguishing marks?" Yeah, he kills people. Oh, and he has access to a nuclear weapon.

"He was short and had black hair and a mustache. He had a cane."

Baker wrote it all down, like it was a math equation he didn't care about.

Maybe it was the jetlag finally catching me, but whatever it was, I was losing patience fast.

"Anything else?"

"Well, it's just that, I really like the family, and I would hate for anything to happen to them. After what has happened to Mr.

Taylor, I just don't want them hurt anymore. I guess the whole neighborhood is watching out for them."

"Well, you filed a report, and we'll keep it on record. Thank you. I'm sure they're fine. Have a good day."

That's it? They would keep it on file? I lost it. Sorta. I leaned across the counter and whispered something.

Baker couldn't hear me. "What did you say?" He leaned closer.

I spoke loud enough for him to hear me.

"This isn't a game, Officer Baker." I threw my ID on the counter, and the FBI flexed its muscles. "Keeping it on file isn't enough. Do some drive-bys. Watch their house. If anything happens to Ann Taylor, Officer Baker, I will be upset. And you don't want me upset. I tried to be nice, but you're so thickheaded and slow you didn't catch on." All I wanted was for him to act like a cop. To care. "Look, Officer Baker," I said, "we're on the same side. And I could use your help. I'm hunting a maniacal killer that is short with black hair and a cane. Watch the Taylors. Enlist the sheriff's office if you have to. Get Deputy Millhouse out here. Do whatever it takes. The short man with the cane already killed her husband. I don't want her to die by his hand too. Do you understand?" My voice was calm and at the same volume level. I didn't sound upset or act upset. I didn't yell or threaten. I just told him what I wanted. Nice and simple.

"I understand. Who are you?"

"The tooth fairy." I grabbed my ID and walked out. I'd done all I could to protect Ann Taylor.

No, I hadn't. I was going to stop Kim Song Su.

Maybe break his cane too.

* * *

It was dark outside. Had been for a while. Rush-hour traffic had come and gone. My watch told me it was almost 6:00 p.m. I was tired. Agent Cook was probably pretty mad at me. I'd call him in the morning. After I had left the FBI, and moved to Utah, the

Salt Lake FBI field office hosted a little dinner in my honor. Cook had been there. He was tall, six two. Blond hair and blue eyes. I remember thinking he looked like a living breathing version of Apollo or some other Greek deity. Come to life right off the pedestal he was sculpted on. He acted like a Greek deity too. He was making a noise. He wouldn't stop. Man, Cook, shut up!

BEEP!

BEEP!

"What the heck?" I swerved back into my lane and avoided the F-150 that was blaring its horn at me. I'd fallen asleep. While I was driving. That's not good. I made it to the freeway. I rolled my window down all the way and put in a Billy Joel tape. I turned it up loud, and I sang for all I was worth. I didn't sound good, but it kept me awake. I could make it to Provo, but there was no way I could make it back to Salt Lake. I decided to stop in Provo.

I took the Center Street exit again and headed east. I kept singing along to Billy Joel, nice and loud. People walking along the street stared at me like I was strangling a cat. Who cares. I already know I can't sing. I crossed Fifth West and then University Avenue. I came to Ninth East and turned left. I passed lots of businesses that catered to the student population at BYU: fast-food joints, gyms, supermarkets, clothing stores, and apartment complexes everywhere. Soon I was passing BYU itself. The campus sits high on the bench of the mountains. It is a picturesque scene. Ninth East curved to the left, and I could see the Provo Temple perched on the mountainside. The mountain, in fact, the entire mountain range from Spanish Fork in the south to Ogden in the north, was covered in snow. On the west side of Ninth East, directly across from the temple, was the Missionary Training Center. The MTC is full of thousands of young men and women preparing for their missions around the world. In between the temple and the MTC is a huge open field. Missionaries use it for football, softball, soccer, walking, running, and just sitting. It offers a great view of Utah Lake, and the whole valley. In the cold months, it's pretty deserted.

I was lost. I was at the MTC, but I wanted to be at the hospital. The MTC is a nice place to be, and I have good memories of it from my own experiences as a young missionary. But I didn't want to be here now. I continued past the MTC and the temple, and the street took me back to University Avenue. On the corner I saw a twenty-four-hour convenience store, and I pulled into the parking lot.

Mine was the only car in the lot. I walked in, and the bright lights actually hurt my eyes. I could see a young woman cleaning a frozen drink machine. There's no Slurpee like a clean Slurpee. The only way I would clean one of those was if I was getting paid to do it.

"Could you help me, please?"

She turned away from her work, looked at me, and smiled. "Sure. What can I do for you?"

"I'm trying to find something. I need directions."

She left the frozen drink machine and walked behind the counter. She was blond, maybe it's called platinum blond, with brown eyes. Her T-shirt proclaimed she was "Property of BYU Football." Maybe she played defensive line, although she was kinda small for that. If she was three inches taller and fifty pounds heavier, she could probably play cornerback. But that may be a stretch. Cornerbacks have to be quick.

"Did you hear me?"

"What?"

She gave me a look that said I needed to work on paying attention. "Where do you need directions to?"

"The hospital," I said.

"Which one? There's one in Provo and two in Orem."

"Provo. UVRMC. How do I get there?"

She gave me directions, and they didn't sound too difficult. I walked back out to my car, started it up, and headed for what I hoped would be the hospital. I made it to Fifth West and turned left. Traffic was surprisingly heavy. Provo has too many cars and not enough roads, I decided. I soon came across the hospital on my left, and I turned into the parking garage. I parked and entered the hospital.

The lobby was big and spacious. The western wall was glass and offered a nice view of a small garden. There was a nice statue of children playing with their mother. I walked over to it. It was titled "Mother and Her Children." The sculptor was listed as Jason Russell. I stared at it, studying the work of a young man I was trying to help posthumously. It was good. Real good. And his life had been snuffed out by a man from North Korea who killed him because Jason Russell was no longer any help to him. That made me mad. I don't like being mad. It upsets me.

I kept walking. Then I saw the Patient Information Center. I walked over to it and stood in front of a high counter. I could do this one of two ways. I could use my FBI identification or try another route. A large woman with straight black hair, dressed in light blue scrubs, was working at a desk behind the high countertop.

I cleared my throat.

"Can I help you, sir?"

"Yes, you can. I'm looking for a patient. I need her room number."

"Visiting hours are almost over," she said disapprovingly.

"I know. I've been away on business, and I just flew in. Please."

"What is her name?"

"Anderson. She's a police officer."

"You a cop too?"

"Yeah." I showed her my ID.

She typed some information into a computer and said, "Room 355."

"Thank you." I had already seen the elevators. I walked over to them and pushed the number 3 on the panel. At the third floor, the doors opened again, and I stepped out and followed small signs on the wall that indicated where rooms 350 through 375 were. Sooner than I expected, I was at room 355. There was a sheriff's deputy sitting outside the door. He stood up when he saw me.

I pulled my ID from my breast pocket. "Easy, deputy. I'm Grant, FBI. I have official business."

He stared at my ID, then he stepped aside.

"I didn't know the FBI was concerned with this."

"I take the shooting of Detective Anderson very seriously, deputy."

Which is true. I do. Just not for the same reasons the FBI might. I walked into her room and closed the door behind me. It was dark and Anderson was asleep. I sat in the big chair next to her bed.

I fell asleep.

chapter 13

"Grant, wake up."

I made a sound, but didn't open my eyes.

"Grant, you need to wake up."

"I am awake." I didn't open my eyes.

"No, you're not. Open your eyes and look at me."

I opened my left eye. I was in Anderson's hospital room. She woke me up and was staring at me. "What are you doing here, Grant?"

"I promised to come see you. Here I am. It's good to see you, Anderson." I smiled at her. I was a mess. "What time is it?"

"It's good to see you too. Ten thirty."

"Ten thirty? I needed to be up hours ago." I sat up and rubbed my eyes.

"You slept for a long time. I saw you last night. One of the nurses was going to wake you and make you leave, but I told her it was okay. You slept through two nurse checkups and one from the doctor."

"I have a gift for sleep."

"You do. The bathroom is over there." She pointed with her left hand.

"Is my hair messed up?" I probably looked horrible.

"Yes."

"You have a brush, Anderson?"

"I haven't brushed my hair since I checked in, Grant. Check the bathroom. There's probably something you can use in there. And if you meant toothbrush, tell me which one you use. The color."

"Why?"

"So I don't use the same one."

Oh. I hadn't lived with someone in a long time. It's amazing how quickly you forget the little things. Isn't it?

I went in the bathroom and looked in the mirror. I looked horrible and felt that way too. I had the nightmare again last night. The one with Dan. But it was different this time. It started the same. We were in Denver, outside that bank. Dan still was shot, and I held him as he died. The pain was still there. Suddenly we weren't in Denver anymore. I felt the blast of wind again; I could see a wall of heat, like a tidal wave, heading for us. Then Dan vanished. I was alone. The tidal wave of heat and destruction was heading for me. I covered my head with my hands and knelt down. Just before it consumed me, it was gone.

I opened my eyes and looked around. Then I recognized Salt Lake. The familiar skyline backed by the Wasatch Mountains. I recognized places in the city. I was above the city. I could see all of it. I could make out Temple Square. The Conference Center and Church headquarters. Then it came out of nowhere. No one was prepared for it. The wall of heat hit the city like a massive tidal wave crashing into a shoreline. Temple Square was consumed first. The state capitol, the Delta Center and the Salt Palace, the mall, all of downtown Salt Lake was a boiling mass of destruction and pain. The University of Utah, up on the hill, was hit too. But it was destroyed after the other places. I remembered that quite clearly. I was sweaty and the memory of it was slow to leave me.

I turned the water on. I stuck my head under it. It was cold, and I jerked my head back. "Man, that's cold."

Anderson called from her bed, "Quit complaining, Grant."

I found a towel and a comb in a drawer. After combing my hair, I washed my face. It was still sore. I had to make sure I didn't touch it too hard, which is harder to do than it sounds. I would have a nice shiner around my right eye for another few days. At least the swelling had gone down. Shaving the right side of my face would not be easy either. I found a purple toothbrush and used it.

Anderson was asking me something. ". . . concerned, Grant. What happened to your face?"

At least someone is. I know my ex-wife isn't.

"Korea, and I used the purple toothbrush."

"I'm serious, Grant."

So am I. "I told you already. I was stupid. I was alone and exposed in the open in a city totally unfamiliar to me. I was jumped by some bad guys. I think they're connected with what happened to you and the others. Do you know about Dr. Sherman?"

"Yes. I'm sorry. She didn't deserve that."

No, she didn't. No one deserved that.

"How is the attack on you in Korea connected with what happened to me?"

"I'm not sure." I didn't want her to know about Kim Song Su or the bomb. That might upset her.

It did me.

"But how did they, whoever they are, know you would be in Korea? Did someone tell them, or was it just a coincidence?"

I stopped what I was doing and walked out of the bathroom. That had me stumped. "Good question. I don't know. I intend to find out." Odds were the person who had tampered with my gun had also tipped those goons off that I was on the way. Only a few people knew I was going to Korea. I didn't want to believe any of them would betray me and the United States. But that's why it's called "betray." By definition it had to be someone I trusted, someone that I knew. It had to be someone who took the pledge of loyalty to uphold the laws of the United States and to abide by and protect the Constitution, just as I had. Cook was right. It had to be someone inside the FBI.

"How do I look, Anderson?"

"Like you slept in a hospital chair all night. And you were wrong. That attack on your face was not an improvement. How do you think you look?"

I don't know. How about great? "Not good, and thanks for the pep talk. I need to go, Anderson. I'll call when I know something."

"Promise?"

"Yes, I promise."

I walked to her door and was about to leave when she stopped me. "Grant, it was great to see you. Really. Thank you for coming. I appreciate it. Look, you're welcome anytime to sleep in my chair."

We stared at each other for an awkward moment. I wanted to go to her and hold her in my arms. But that would probably hurt her, considering the condition she was in. So instead I said, "When this is over . . . give me a chance, okay?"

"Sure," she said.

"Bye," I said.

"Go to work, Agent Grant."

I walked out of her room and made my way out of the hospital. I found my car where I left it. The drive to Salt Lake would take forty-five or fifty minutes.

I exited the hospital parking lot and turned left onto Fifth West. I knew for sure that if I went this way I would run into Provo's Center Street. From there I could get back to I-15. I made it and headed north for Salt Lake.

The rest of the way back I thought about dragons around Salt Lake City. There aren't many. Because of traffic, it took me an hour and a half to get to Rockwell. I should have realized that traffic would be heavier. After all, the Olympics would open tomorrow. The entire world would be focused on Salt Lake for the next few weeks.

I hoped.

At Rockwell, I called Agent Cook.

"This is Cook."

"Cook, it's Grant."

"Well, how are you? The prodigal son finally calls."

"I'm fine, and you are not my father."

"Grant, you weren't in Spanish Fork last night, were you?"

"Why?"

"An Officer Baker called and reported that an FBI agent threatened him. It wasn't you, was it?"

"No way, Cook. I'm not FBI anymore. You know that."

"I know you're not FBI anymore. I've been trying to reach you."

"You have? Should I feel special or get a restraining order?"

He ignored that remark. "You stood me up yesterday afternoon. Do you carry your cell phone with you?"

"Yes, but I don't answer it. Do you want to meet today?"

"You know I do, Grant. We have much to discuss. What time?"

I looked at my watch. "Two o'clock. Temple Square. Crossroads Plaza entrance. Can you make it?"

"Yes. Question is, will you show up? Oh, and I heard from a friend of yours."

"Maybe. See you at two. Who called you and claims to be my friend?"

"Some guy named Tom. Said he saw you in Korea. He filled me in. We have a serious problem. He said you got roughed up too."

That's certainly one way to look at it.

"Two," I said, and hung up. Then I went to a small bathroom, one with a shower in it, and I showered. I changed clothes again. I was running out of stuff at Rockwell. Maybe I should go home.

I decided to walk to Temple Square. Salt Lake is a beautiful city. The streets are wide and clean. Just like all large cities, Salt Lake does have crime. It is not paradise. Well, I've been to Los Angeles, and I would say that Salt Lake is closer to paradise than the City of Angels. Despite the crime, there is still a wholesomeness to the city. The streets are, for the most part, pretty safe. Nightfall does not mean the criminals and thugs own the city. But you couldn't pay me enough money to stay the night at Pioneer Park.

The walk from Rockwell to Temple Square is pretty short. Technically, Rockwell is a part of Temple Square. I went in through the Crossroads Plaza entrance. Sister missionaries were manning the gate. Maybe that means they were womanning it. I'll have to ask Anderson.

"Welcome to Temple Square," one said to me.

I smiled.

I found a bench that gave me an excellent view of the gate, and I sat down. I had a few minutes to think, and took advantage of the time. I was missing something. Something that Tom said at the embassy in Seoul? I thought about dragons.

"What did they mean?" Dragon could easily just be a North Korean code for the United States. The message the CIA intercepted simply said that the bomb was in the United States. Or that it would be used in the United States. It could mean anything or nothing. I was giving myself a headache. A sure sign that my limited number of brain cells were about to burn up. Luckily, Agent Cook had just walked into Temple Square.

I waved him over and stood up.

We didn't shake hands. We just sort of nodded at each other. Even with a North Korean terrorist running amok in the city with a nuclear weapon, "guy protocol" still had to be honored. He still looked like Apollo. I still looked like the Minotaur. Some things never change.

"Cooker. How are you?"

"It's Agent Cook, Grant. Nice shiner."

Whatever.

"You should see the other guy. Anyway. I discovered some interesting things last night."

"What about?" Cook looked interested. He should.

"A man named John Taylor and a friend of his named Jason Russell."

"And?" Cook sure was impatient.

"I think it's important. They probably knew Kim Song Su."

"Knew?"

"He killed them both."

"How do you know that?"

"I do, okay? Taylor was the man found at the mine. Russell was a student of his at Springville High School. Kim Song Su and his

Brotherhood misfits tortured both of them. The Utah County medical examiner, Dr. Sherman, is Kim Song Su's handiwork too."

"He killed three people?"

"Yes. The question that I think we should answer is *why* he killed them. He had to have a reason. If we find out why, then we might find Kim Song Su and his nuclear bomb." I thought it was flawless reasoning, and I thought I already had a lead.

Cook didn't think so.

"I don't think so. I have another idea."

Really? Why doesn't that surprise me?

"Let's chat. I need your help to track down a terrorist. You can identify him on sight, so I need you to come with me."

"Where are we going, Cook?"

"For a drive. Let's go."

"I don't think so, Cook. You tell me what your plan is, and if I want to help you, I might."

He looked pretty miffed at me. "Okay, Grant. My plan, such as it is, is to go to certain spots around Salt Lake City and look for Kim Song Su. If we get lucky and you see him, then we can grab him."

I smiled. I almost belly-laughed. "*That* is your plan, Agent Cook? To go looking for one man in a sea of millions?"

He still looked miffed. I don't think he'll send me a Christmas card. "Not all of it. We have every available agent working every angle possible. And we have thousands of these being passed out to every police department and sheriff's office in Utah." He showed a flyer the FBI had produced with an age-enhanced version of the picture I recognized in the basement of the embassy. Probably got the photo from Just Tom. "All we need is time."

"Time is the one thing we don't have."

"At least we agree on that, Grant. Will you help?"

I stood up and looked at Temple Square. The angel Moroni stood atop the Salt Lake Temple. It was from here, in my nightmare, that the cloud of destruction began.

"Yes. Let's go." I had nothing to lose. I mean, other than my life. Besides, I intended to check the places Simms provided for me anyway.

We walked back through the gate and past the peddlers on the other side. His car was a short distance away. It was parked in a tow zone.

"They should've towed it," I said.

Cook just smiled. "Get in, Grant."

He pulled away.

"Where to first, Cook?"

"There is a Buddhist temple in Sandy that has some stone dragons in front of it. It makes sense to look for possible locations of the bomb. Our prey will probably be near."

I nodded. It also made sense that our terrorist expected us to do just what we were doing. My gut told me it would be a waste of time. Maybe that was personal revelation too. Our prey wouldn't be anywhere near a Buddhist temple.

The drive was long and slow. Cook didn't take the freeway. He said he liked surface streets better. Dork. We didn't talk much. I was thinking about my nightmare. The University of Utah kept sticking out.

"Hey, Cook, where are opening ceremonies going to be held?"

"At Rice-Eccles Stadium. The University of Utah."

That must be it. It stood out in my nightmare because it was the focal point of the whole thing. The center of it all. "Has anyone checked it out?" I asked.

"Yes. The president will be there. It's the safest place in the country right now. There is a team of FBI agents up there right now along with the best the Secret Service has to offer. State and local police are working with them. They're using bomb dogs and radiation detection equipment and anything else that will point out if a nuclear bomb is at the stadium. Not to mention the CIA also has some agents up there doing their thing. Rice-Eccles will be swept clean, and then swept again."

Something was still gnawing at the back of my mind.

It was starting to hurt.

We eventually made it to Sandy and found our destination. It was a small, one-story, off-white building. A waist-high stone wall enclosed the whole place. The monks at the Buddhist temple were not happy to see us. I don't blame them. We buzzed the only gate we could find, and waited. We identified ourselves, and the gate opened. A little man with a shorn head and glasses met us just inside the gate. His glasses were perfectly round. Some of his friends, I assumed they were friends, joined us.

The first thing I noticed was the clothes they were all wearing. These monks didn't dress anything like the Buddhist monks I'd seen in Korea. In my taxi rides through Seoul to the embassy, I passed many Buddhist temples and monks. They always wore gray. The monks I saw now were not covered in gray. I think some of them were wearing jeans too. I figured it was because they were in the U.S. I honestly didn't know why they dressed differently, and I didn't ask.

Another thing was the lack of their symbol. I'd seen it on every Buddhist site in Korea. It looked like a swastika, but was not quite the same. (I'd seen plenty of swastikas in the FBI. We busted a great number of Nazi punks.) The Nazis were never in Korea. I knew that from history and my study of the country. I had asked Will about it when we were at the embassy together in Seoul. She told me the story that she had been told.

It went something like this. When Hitler was ascending to power in Germany, he wanted a symbol for his party and followers. By chance, he stumbled across the symbol of Buddhism and liked it. He inverted it, called it the swastika, and made it an international symbol of hatred and fear. Sounded like a good story to me. But I don't know if it's true. Anyway, this Buddhist temple didn't have any symbols that had been stolen by the Nazis or that could be misinterpreted by ignorant people.

They protested, but they let us search anyway. Cook was pretty arrogant, and he bullied his way in. He has the people skills of a dead frog. The stone dragons in the front courtyard were harmless. There were plenty of carved and painted dragons around the exterior of the building. But they too were harmless.

I was right; it was a waste of time. So were the stone dragons in front of the Salt Lake City Library. The ceremonial dragons at the

Asian Gardens restaurant were too small to hide anything. (They are carved out of wood. I don't know which kind of wood, only that they are wood.) But we checked them anyway. The rest of the day with Cook was exactly the same. A waste of time. We didn't find a bomb, or even a firecracker, anywhere. And I never saw Kim Song Su. I wasn't surprised.

We stopped wasting our time at 7:30 p.m. It was dark, and we were both tired. My body was fighting sleep again. We ended up at Rice-Eccles Stadium.

"Come on, Grant. Let's check with the team here."

Okay.

We went in through the main entrance on Fifth South. A Salt Lake City police officer was manning the gate. I was sure he wasn't alone. I looked around me. Chances are that at least some of the high points in the area would be converted into sniper's nests. If they hadn't been already. The Secret Service would make sure of that. Armed Utah National Guardsmen openly patrolled in and around the stadium. Security was tight. We had to pass through a series of metal detectors. We set off every single one. My personal opinion, it was because Cook is actually some weird Frankenstein monster. But that's just a theory. The troopers seemed to think it was our weapons. Probably. A Salt Lake City police officer insisted on patting us down, even after we flashed our FBI IDs.

Cook seemed slightly indignant at the pat-down but didn't say anything. He put his ID away and nodded his head in my direction. "He's with me. Do you know where Agent Williams is, officer?"

The officer seemed real impressed by that. Oooh, another FBI man. "Up there somewhere, I suppose." He meant the stadium. He obviously wasn't intimidated by FBI credentials. Good for him.

His answer only angered Cook.

Apollo was upset.

You gotta hate that.

"Up there somewhere? Why don't you use your little radio and find out? I'm in a hurry, and I'm getting cold, Patrolman . . ." Cook read his name with barely disguised disdain. ". . . Harris."

Harris turned away and spoke into the radio attached to his right shoulder. He had a short conversation with someone on the other end. He turned back to us. "Williams is over there." Harris pointed to a lower-level concession area.

Cook walked away.

"Thanks, Harris," I said.

It was a longer walk than it looked.

The size of the stadium caught me off guard. My sense of perception was screwed up, but after a few minutes, I was used to it. I was just a few feet behind him when he rounded the corner of the concession area. The concession area stood beneath some of the stadium's massive red steel girders. I followed Cook around the corner and almost bumped into a group of men and women wearing cheap suits and overcoats.

It was the FBI.

Cook introduced me. "Everyone, this is our witness, Mr. Grant." That was it. He didn't mention my twelve-plus years of service in the FBI or how good of an agent I'd been. I mean, still am. Unofficially, of course.

Someone I couldn't see said, "Cook, you jerk. Everybody here knows Grant."

Everyone in the group, five other agents, all acknowledged me and said, "Hi," "Hello," "How are you?" "Good to see you," and, "Sure is cold out here." I doubt they all knew me, but I wasn't going to make the correction. I couldn't see who properly introduced me. Then I did. It was Will! She looked tired.

"Will, what are you doing here?! I left you in Seoul. I mean you left me in that taxi in Seoul." I grabbed her arm and steered her away from the small group. Cook had to gather reports from his underlings anyway.

"I just got in this morning. The director thought it would be best if I were here. I guess 'cause we're dealing with a North Korean terrorist, he thought the FBI's liaison in Seoul would be helpful. So, here I am."

"It's good to see you. I'm glad you're here, Will."

"Good to see you too, and in one piece. I heard you had a little adventure after you went shopping. Did you get your leather jacket back?"

Cook jumped into our conversation. "How did it go, Williams? Find anything?"

"No. The state troopers helped us search this place top to bottom. We searched all day and into tonight, but found nothing. The dogs came up empty too. Usually that's a good sign, but not now. The radiation indicators are all normal too, or so they tell me. We'll do it all again tomorrow, for as long as we can. Did you get lucky, Cook?"

He shook his head. "Nothing for us either." He was right; we had no luck.

"What is the plan for tomorrow?" I asked.

"Same thing," Cook said.

"I have a suggestion. Why don't you and Will trade spots tomorrow?"

"Why?"

"Because, Agent Cook," I said, "we know how to work together. We've done it before. Will and I go back a long way."

Will jumped in. "That's a great idea, Grant. But it's your call, Cook. You're the agent in charge."

He thought about it. I think. "If it increases productivity and the chance of stopping this guy, let's do it. I have a meeting with the Secret Service at 6:00 a.m. to coordinate security for the president. Meet at seven thirty?"

That was the smartest thing Cook had done all afternoon.

I know, because I was with him all afternoon.

We agreed to meet at the stadium the next morning at 7:30. There was some small chitchat, but not much. My watch said it was almost eight thirty.

"I don't know about you young people, but us geriatric folk need our rest," I told them.

After some good-natured ribbing, Will and I left together.

"Where do you live, Grant?"

I told her my address then added, "Just take me to Temple Square. My car is there."

"Where's Temple Square?" Will had never been to Utah before.

I gave her directions.

"How's your Korean, Will?"

"Same as always. Terrible. Why?"

"Something is bothering me, that's all." Actually, it was gnawing at me again.

"What?"

"I want to know what a certain word means translated from Korean to English."

"Which word?"

I told her.

"Sorry, I can't help. I told you all I knew in the taxi a few days ago. Besides, Tom told you what that message meant in English. Tom was on the right track. CIA knows its business. Drop it, Grant."

"I know. It's probably nothing."

We were at Temple Square, and she dropped me off. People were everywhere. The city was filled to capacity, and the influx of Olympic tourists wasn't done yet. Young people, infants in strollers, mothers, fathers, grandparents, couples, small families, and large families were everywhere. From their look and the languages I overheard, not everyone was American. For the second time in four years, the world had come to Salt Lake: Canadians, Mexicans, Japanese, English, Germans, French, Nigerians, South Africans, Russians, Chinese, Poles, Italians, Koreans, Brazilians, Argentinians, and dozens of other nationalities filled downtown. It was an international smorgasbord of athletes and fans. North Korea was conspicuous by its absence. At least they were to me.

Opportunistic vendors were selling everything Olympic. Pins, hats, T-shirts, shorts, golf shirts, shoes, and hot dogs wrapped in Olympic napkins were being scooped up by the tourist crowd. A large banner with the Olympic rings on it was hanging from an upper floor of Crossroads Mall.

Temple Square looked like it was standing room only, despite the cold. It was a scene of organized chaos. The Olympics were in town, and the world had come to see it, again. Those that couldn't personally attend would tune in tomorrow night at 6:00 p.m., MST, to see it all begin. But what would they see?

"You're not going to be at the stadium tomorrow morning, are you, Grant?"

"Nope. I have to check some things out. Tell Cook I said hi."

"I hope you know what you're doing. Do you still hate cell phones, Grant?"

"Yes, but I have one."

"Carry it with you tomorrow in case anything breaks."

"I will. Thanks for the ride."

She drove away, and I strolled into the underground parking garage. Soon, I was back in Rockwell.

Rockwell isn't my home; it just isn't as lonely, so I spend as much time there as possible. I was looking for someone that spoke Korean, but I was failing. Most of us are returned missionaries, so this wasn't as bad an idea as it may sound. I found an agent who spoke Spanish, one who spoke Portuguese, one who spoke German, another who spoke Dutch, but not one who knew Korean. I'm sure that Portuguese is a fine language; it just didn't do me a bit of good. I needed someone who could speak Korean.

I was losing valuable time, and I knew I needed help. I had the bright idea to call Anderson. It was late, but I did it anyway.

"Hello?" Is it love when you hear a certain voice and as soon as you hear it calmness washes over you?

"It's Grant." Could it be love?

"I was expecting a call." She knows me. "This is becoming a habit, Grant."

"Is that bad?"

"No."

"I was just thinking, I need to talk some stuff out. Would you listen?"

"Sure. Go ahead."

"I've hit a wall. I need help with a language. Korean, specifi-
cally. You don't speak it, do you?"

"No. Didn't you live there for a while?"

"I did. Just over a year. But to be honest, Anderson, I spent
most of my time on base or at the embassy. It's not a language you
can just 'pick up' or something."

There was a pause.

"You already know where to go, Grant."

"I do?"

"Yes."

"No, I don't." My brain cramp was getting worse.

"You're kidding, right, Grant?"

"No." I never kid. Well, hardly ever.

"Think about it, Grant."

"I have."

There was another short pause. "The MTC. You know, the
Missionary Training Center. They teach, what, about a hundred
languages or so. I know you didn't serve a foreign mission, unless
you count Kentucky as foreign, but you did spend some time
there, right?" There are moments when you realize you missed
something you shouldn't have. And then there are moments when
you look like the world's biggest buffoon.

I said buffoonishly, "Yes, I did, Ms. Smarty Pants." I laughed as
I said it. The answer is always obvious after you have it. "Thanks
for your help." But in this case, it really should have been obvious.

"Don't be upset, Grant. Sometimes you get so involved that
you miss the obvious."

Did she mean us? I said hesitantly, "I don't want to miss the
obvious."

"Good. I don't want you to either."

"I need to go. I have another phone call to make." I offered
sincerely, "Thank you for your help." I hung up. I looked up the
number I needed, then called. Because it was so late at night, I
didn't have high hopes, but I called anyway. Someone picked up
after the first ring. I was impressed; it was after 11:00 p.m.

"MTC front desk." It was a woman's voice.

"I have a question, and maybe you can help me."

"I'll sure try. What can I do for you?"

"I need to talk to someone who can speak Korean reasonably well." I didn't really know what to ask for.

"I'm sorry. All of the missionaries are asleep, but you can call back in the morning."

"Thank you, but I would rather talk to someone that has actually lived there."

"All of the instructors are returned missionaries. Could they be helpful?" For it being so late at night, she sure was being nice.

"I think so. Can you tell me when the first class is held in the morning?"

"8:00 a.m.," she said.

"Thanks."

I hung up and walked down the hallway. I went back to the parking garage and found my car where I'd left it. It was still locked, and I could see no visible evidence that it'd been messed with. I got in and started it. It didn't blow up. I took that as a good sign. I drove home through the crush of pedestrians and cars that conspired with the snow to choke the downtown area. A fifteen-minute drive took me thirty. My house was dark and empty. Just the way I'd left it.

* * *

I turned my key in the door, went in through the front door, and locked it behind me. My .25 weapon was out, and I searched my home room by room. It's not that big, so it didn't take too long. I was the only one there, but I was still pretty edgy. I went to my bedroom and, in the closet, opened my gun safe. I picked up my spare Glock, made sure it was loaded, and took out two full clips. Then I reloaded my .25 and strapped it back to my ankle. I took something from my dresser drawer, went back to the front room, and sat in my most comfortable chair. It's a dark red leather recliner. I pulled off my shoes and socks and closed my eyes. My weapon was in my lap, and my watch was set for 3:15 a.m. This time, it would wake me up before I was tied up and threatened with torture.

I hoped so, anyway.

I had a feeling that I would see someone tonight.

Sleep came easily to me. Sudden exhaustion washed over me, and I was powerless to resist.

chapter 14

I could see someone. It was Dan. Dan Begay was there, but he wasn't killed by bank robbers. He didn't die in my arms this time either. He was at Temple Square, doing something, without moving. I know it sounds odd, but hey, it's my nightmare. I couldn't really see what it was he was doing. It was almost like he was standing a certain way. Standing still. His hands were held out, but beyond that, I couldn't distinguish anything. He wasn't calling or motioning to me. Then he was gone.

Colors of red and yellow and all shades in between filled my vision now. The cloud of death and destruction took Dan's place. It was noisy; the rushing wind, the sound of a freight train filling my head. It was almost unbearable, but through it all, I noticed something different this time. Temple Square wasn't destroyed. I mean, the cloud seemed to begin there, but the temple was unscathed. Before, it was always wiped out first, but not now. I tore my eyes away from Temple Square and surveyed the rest of the valley.

People, en masse, were dying everywhere. All of the valley was obliterated in a matter of minutes. Downtown, aside from the temple, disappeared in a burst of unbearable heat and destruction. Buildings for miles and miles around Temple Square were leveled flat or simply gone. The dead and dying were crying with a terrible voice, "Help us." Some were reaching for me, grabbing my clothes, pulling me into the cloud of death. Just before I was lost with them, I heard something. It was a noise. It was my alarm. I woke up and could feel beads of sweat rolling down my face. My body was sore and tense, as if I'd been lifting weights for over an hour.

I sat up and cleared my thoughts. I didn't turn a light on. I just sat in the dark and waited. I was expecting company. I was alive and I planned on keeping it that way. I waited for thirty minutes and nothing happened. I was confident that if Kim Song Su was going to try and take me out, it would have to be tonight. He wouldn't be satisfied with "maybe" doing it with a bomb. He would want to kill me, up close and personal. I was half hoping for him and half hoping for someone else. Preferably the someone else. I had a score to settle, and I would get a chance if who I expected actually showed up. The silence was broken, and I was instantly alert. A window in a back room had been discreetly cracked and broken.

I heard a noise from behind me. Someone was in my house, and I didn't invite them. Whoever it was, I couldn't see yet. I slid out of my chair and rolled onto my hands and knees. I checked my weapon, and it was loaded, with real bullets. Kim Song Su would not have been so sloppy as to make a noise. I knew who was here. It had to be the person who had betrayed me, the FBI, and the United States. The person who wanted to see a nuclear winter in Utah.

In my bare feet I made my way to the wall behind my chair. I went to my left, moving quietly toward my kitchen. There was no connecting door between the two rooms, just an opening slightly larger than a regular doorway. I made it to the edge and stood there with my back against the wall and my weapon in my right hand.

POP! POP! POP! POP! Four rounds whizzed from the kitchen and into the back of my chair. I stayed perfectly still and waited. My would-be assassin would not be satisfied I was dead until my body was checked and found lifeless. There was no sound in my kitchen, and still I waited. After ten minutes I heard a footfall in the kitchen, and then another. Soon I could see a gun and a hand. I waited until I could see an arm, then I struck with all my strength. I hammered down with my weapon-free hand on the arm and knocked the gun loose. Then I stepped into the doorway and, anticipating that when the gun arm went down the body would too, I brought my right knee up with a violent force and caught my attacker square in the face.

The attacker fell back, stunned. I reached around the wall with my left hand and turned the kitchen light on. Lying on my kitchen floor, dressed in black but not wearing a mask, was the person assigned to kill me. The person who betrayed me and knew that this betrayal could end up killing hundreds of thousands of people, maybe millions. That person just lay there. I looked at my attacker, my former friend.

"Hey, Will. I thought you'd never get here." I didn't smile warmly. "Looks like Cook was right. There was a traitor in the FBI, and her nose is bleeding. Did that hurt? Hope it did."

Her face was twisted into a hideous shape by hate and anger. She was breathing heavy. Score one for the good guys.

"I didn't want to believe it was you, Will. But it had to be. How could you do this?"

"I want a lawyer."

"I bet you do. Don't you find that comical? The country you betrayed, you want to invoke its constitutional protections. Well, I'm not the Supreme Court, and I could care less about your rights." I was mad. Mad at Will. What was wrong with her? Why? "Do you want to hear how I knew it was you?"

"No."

"Too bad," I told her. "You had access to my gun at the embassy. Somehow you were able to get into Thompson's desk. All you had to do was remove the real clip and replace it with blanks before she returned. You were late for our meeting, remember?"

"That's it?"

"No, Will, that's not all. You were sloppy. Your comments at the embassy, always trying to deflect me away from the truth. You asked me about what had happened to me in Seoul after I went shopping. You asked if I recovered my leather jacket."

She stared at me.

"You made a stupid mistake. No one at FBI knew about that. But you did. And I called you, Will, before I went to Korea. You knew I was coming, and you contacted your friends and arranged it all. You had my luggage stolen from the hotel."

She didn't answer that.

"I called you for help and you betrayed me to a psychopath. And not only me, but your country."

"My country?" Hate and disgust covered her face. It was kinda scary. "My father, he served his country in Korea and was killed in action. North Korean commandos crossed the DMZ, ambushed his outpost at night, and killed him. The United States Army covered it up, because the country couldn't afford another Korean War over the death of one American soldier. They said he died in a training accident. They forgot my father. They won't forget me."

"But that's not possible. The war ended years before you were born, Will."

"It has never ended. Don't you understand yet? The war never ended." She sounded really fragile now, and her voice was cracking. "My father was not in the official war. He was at the DMZ after the United States thought the war was over. And there his buddies, his friends killed him." Her voice reeked with sarcasm. She sneered. "They left their posts; they were drunk. They wanted to party, and they left him alone. He was the only one there and the only one killed. He died alone, betrayed by soldiers worried more about getting liquored up than their duty. The war was over, and the army killed my father. They told my mother nothing could be done. No one was brought to justice for my father's murder. And it was murder! It was covered up. My country murdered my father in cold blood. It destroyed my mother, and she never recovered. It killed her. She gave up on life. I was alone. I was ten years old, and my family was destroyed by the country that was supposed to protect them. I was orphaned by my country. My country ruined my life. Someone has to pay for that. They have to! Song Su offered me a chance to make amends. He told me. . ." She stopped talking.

"He told you what?" I asked.

"You wouldn't care."

"Oh, but I do care." I pointed my weapon at her. "What did he tell you?"

"He told me how his father and brother were killed. They were killed by his country, by soldiers that should have protected them. Don't you see, he and I are the same." She was recovering her senses now, and I saw her eyes darting around, looking for her gun.

I raised mine again. "Don't even think about it. You were right. I don't care what lies your boss told you. But I am sorry about your father and mother. So your daddy was killed in a war that was supposed to be over, and Stephanie Williams wants revenge. Wants to hurt people she doesn't even know, hurt them the way she was hurt. But do you really think your father would be happy with your plan to kill so many people?"

"Yes," she said feebly.

"You know better than that," I said. I didn't know what else to say. Will and I had worked together. She was a good agent. But she had a weakness, and Kim Song Su exposed it, exploited it, and now she was as corrupt as a rotted-out tree. I doubt Kim Song Su had asked her directly to betray her country and friends; if he had, she wouldn't have agreed.

Finally, she spoke. "You could let me go, Grant." She was on her hands and knees, pleading. "I could just disappear, and promise to never return. I could leave the United States and the Bureau. No one would ever know."

I admit I was tempted, but only for a split second. On second thought, I was revolted. "Wrong. I would know, and I can't allow you to escape. Your part is finished, Will. Just relax. Now be a nice traitor and tell me where your boss is. I have something I want to give him."

She stared at me. "He is not my boss, and he is not a psychopath. He is my partner. My equal. Kim Song Su is a dreamer and a patriot."

Now it was my turn to stare.

"Will, you're talking like you're in love with the guy."

Will just gazed blankly ahead.

"Will, tell me you're not in love with Kim Song Su." I thought I was going to be sick. Really, I wanted to vomit.

She could tell I was shocked. "He is magnificent, Grant. He sees things and understands people, tactical situations, strategic goals, political ideals, and the entire world. He is ruthless and takes what he wants when he wants. No one stops him. No one denies him. He treats me as an equal. We are partners. You could never understand how we feel about each other."

Maybe not, but I will stop him. I will deny him.

I promised Anderson.

"How did you pass the yearly psych evaluations at Quantico?"

"The FBI's vaunted tests?" She tossed her hair to one side. "It was easy."

"No, it's not. How did you do it, Will?"

She wouldn't answer.

"Tell me, Will."

"After I knew where and who to hate, I was trained by the homeland. Control my breathing, speaking flat, emotionless."

"Homeland? You mean North Korea? Are you a comrade now?"

"Shut up, Grant."

"Sorry about that. Wait, let me reconsider . . . no, I'm not. You were the FBI attaché in Seoul for how long? Six years?" It was easy for her there. No one would question her. And her movements, as long as they were discreet, would not be noticed. "Does the director even know you're not in Seoul? Probably not, huh? You never spoke to the director about coming to Salt Lake. Kim Song Su and his masters in the north sent you here to kill me."

"He does not have masters."

"Yes, he does. He's a puppet just like you. How long has he had you under his thumb?"

Again, no answer.

"When did you betray your country and your friends? The whole six years in Seoul? Or did it begin earlier? What was your price?"

"It began when my parents died. My price?"

"Yes, Will, your price. What did he promise you and your damaged psyche? Do you really think that monster loves you and all will be fine after he detonates a nuclear weapon in the United States? How screwed up are you, Will? You know we would hunt him down like a dog. And you too."

"Nothing. He promised me nothing. And the Americans would not know where to find us."

"I know when you lie, Will." I was amazed and sick to my stomach. She was as committed as Kim Song Su. Just as looney. "Let me guess. You know this is a one-way trip. You want to die together, don't you? Seal your perverted love with your lives?"

She glared at me.

"He first came to you when you were assigned as the FBI attaché in Seoul. At first you didn't really know who he was. He slowly reeled you in. Gave you gifts, asked small favors of the most important American law enforcement officer in South Korea. At first you may have even said no. But eventually you gave in. He confided in you. Told you his sad life story. Earned your trust and then told you he loved you. Tapped into your ego. He knew your background the whole time. Knew you were an orphan looking for payback. Do you love him, love that monster?"

She hissed, "He is not a monster. Look in the mirror if you want to see a monster. Who killed Dan Begay? You did. Song Su will kill you for this, Grant. Do you hear me? You will die. Unless you let me go."

"You expect me to cower and beg forgiveness because you think I killed Dan Begay? Because it was my fault Dan died, you expect me to help you? Think again, sister. I took you down, and your boyfriend is next."

I was done asking questions. With my weapon I motioned her to stand up, and I knelt down and picked up her gun. "I hope that perverted love and admiration will last you for twenty to twenty-five years, Will. Turn around."

She twisted around. I pulled some zip line from my back pocket and secured her hands behind her back. I pushed her in front of me, out of the kitchen.

"How did you get in, Will?"

"A back window. I was almost in when I slipped and fell. If I hadn't fallen, you would have been in that chair when I fired."

"You think so? You should have tried the front door. It's not locked. Don't feel bad, but I was hoping your boyfriend would show his face tonight."

"Where are you taking me?"

"It's a surprise. Let's go."

We walked outside and to my car. I put her in the backseat and tied her ankles together with some rope I keep in the car. Then I laid her on her stomach, and I got in and we drove off.

"Tell me, Will. You knew about the bomb. How could you agree to help the North Koreans?"

"Two reasons. All unofficial, of course." Now that she was caught, she was relaxed and seemed like she wanted to talk again. "First, money. Lots of money. Second, power. I'm no patriot, and I don't care about politics. But money and power, I care about that."

Whatever. Liar. "So you had a price. They bought you."

"No. I believed in their cause long before this was planned. They paid me for this, for the bomb."

Really? "How long have you worked for Kimmy?"

"Do not mock him!" she screamed.

"Testy, testy, Will." Believe me, I planned on doing a lot more than mocking. "Did you know Su is a girl's name?"

We didn't talk the rest of the way. When we reached where I wanted to go, I parked and helped Will out of the backseat. "I considered taking you to the FBI. But then you would disappear and live a long, healthy life in the witness protection program. I can't allow that."

I walked her up the front steps of the Salt Lake City Police Department. I used my FBI ID here and explained enough about her trying to kill me to the desk sergeant. He took her into custody. "Oh, and Sergeant, she's a traitor to her country." The sergeant gave me a bored look, so I used the other "T" word. "This woman is a terrorist, and she is part of a conspiracy to harm innocent people during the Olympics." That got his full attention. "But if I were you, I wouldn't call the FBI until after I called KSL. But that's just me. They might want to know the Salt Lake PD is holding a terrorist and a traitor. Her name is Stephanie Williams."

"Grant!" Will yelled at me.

I stopped at the doors. "Yes?"

"It's too late. You've already lost."

"No, I haven't."

When I walked out, I felt a great weight lift off my shoulders. I felt like singing, but not Billy Joel. Instead of Billy Joel, Church hymns were the object of attempt. I did more humming than singing, but who cares? "How Firm a Foundation" wouldn't leave my mind. I hummed it and sang it over and over on my drive. I went home. I was tired, and I had to get some more sleep. My watch beeped at me: 3:15 a.m. I changed the alarm from 6:00 a.m. to 6:30. I walked in my home and checked the rooms one more time, just to be careful. And then I crawled back in my chair and fell asleep.

* * *

Six thirty in the morning always comes too early. If I didn't have "save the world" on my daily task list, I wouldn't have gotten up. Not until eleven thirty anyway. Just to be sure, I checked my PDA. Yep, it was still there.

6:30 a.m. Prevent nuclear holocaust.

I'd have to sleep in another day. I rolled off the chair onto the floor.

I did a few sets of push-ups and tried to do three or four sets of crunches. It hurt more than usual because I was so sore, but I made it through the push-ups. When I was a kid, crunches were called sit-ups. Apparently sit-ups are bad for the lower back, so now everyone does crunches. That's fine with me, 'cause I think crunches are easier anyway. I did my sets and didn't even strain a muscle.

The morning light was gray, and it looked cold outside. A light snow had fallen during the night; it just dusted the old stuff. I went into the kitchen and made myself some breakfast. I'd been too busy to do any grocery shopping, so my refrigerator was pretty bare. I did have a few eggs, though, so I scrambled them up. The milk still smelled okay, so I poured myself a glass. I toasted some bread. That's actually a good breakfast for me. I should probably eat more healthy.

The thought occurred to me that I could just leave. If I left now, I could be almost to California when the bomb went off. It wouldn't kill *me*. I would live. But that's just too cowardly. I am many things, and a coward is not one of them. Besides, Anderson was here, and there was someone I wanted to meet. Instead of fleeing for my life, I took a shower.

The shower felt great; I just wished my body felt as good. More exercise would help me feel better. I needed to pump some iron. I'd rather pump it than take it as a supplement. I dressed and headed out. I stopped and went back in my bedroom. There on top of the dresser was my cell phone. I grabbed it, picked up my Glock in the kitchen by the stove, and went outside. February is cold in Utah. My jacket was still in my car. I put it on, got in, and drove away. The dashboard clock told me it was 7:40 a.m.

The snow from last night made the road slick, and I decided it was prudent to slow down. It took me about forty minutes to reach I-15, and it was clearer than the surface roads had been. The pre-Olympic opening day crowd was still in bed, and there wasn't much traffic on I-15. I made pretty good time on the freeway, and soon Murray and South Jordan were just snow-covered spots in my rearview mirror. South Salt Lake Valley slipped past my window at sixty-five miles per hour. But the Olympics seemed to follow me. It may have just been me, but it seemed like every overpass, business, and building had some Olympic art or decor on it. It was like that all the way past the state prison, over the Point of the Mountain, and into Utah County.

My car sped past Lehi and American Fork. Orem is Provo's sister city. Provo needs three more exits off I-15, but it doesn't have them, so I took the last Orem exit. I went east long enough to run into Provo, then I worked my way to Ninth East and the MTC.

The MTC is a busy place. The main entrance is reserved for dropping off missionaries and picking up their families after they say their good-byes. I didn't have to do either, but I parked there anyway. It was 8:45 a.m. A group of missionaries saw me, and one said, "Mister, you can't park there."

"Yes, I can."

I went in the front door. The main room is pretty large. The carpet is a deep forest green, and the walls are another color. It's a color that contrasts nicely with the floor. There are a few benches and some nicely done displays of various Church stuff. A few people were milling around. The information and administrative counter runs the length of the south wall. I went over there. There was only one person I could see behind the counter.

"Hi."

"Hello. Welcome to the Missionary Training Center. What can I do for you?" It was a guy, but he was even more polite than the woman who had helped me on the phone last night.

"I need to see someone."

"Who?"

"I don't have a name. I need someone that speaks Korean. Preferably someone that was a missionary in Korea."

"Can I ask what you need him or her for?"

"No."

"Why not? We have rules here. You can't just go anywhere you want."

"I'd like to tell you, but I can't. It's government business. FBI," I told him. I showed him my ID. The FBI was very involved with what I was investigating. My new friend didn't look convinced. "Look, it won't take long. I just need someone to tell me what a certain word means."

"What word?"

"Do you speak Korean?"

"No. I speak Spanish though."

Yeah, Spanish is just what I needed. "Then you don't need to know. Okay?" I smiled my best be-my-friend smile and waited.

"Just a minute." He pulled out a drawer and consulted a list. "Head over to Dan Jones, fourth floor, room 425."

"Dan who? What? Where?"

"The next building to the south. It's named for an early missionary of the Church. His name was Dan Jones. He was . . ."

It was rude, but I didn't stay to listen.

I went back outside and headed south. Dan Jones's building was only a hundred feet from the main entrance. It was six stories high, and I soon discovered that the only elevator in the building needed a key to operate it. I didn't have a key, so I walked. I reached the fourth floor and went in search of room 425. I found it. The door was closed, and I knocked.

No one answered. I tried the knob; it wasn't locked. I went in, and the room was empty. I counted seven chairs, and there were posters all over the wall. I don't know what they said, or what they were about, because they were all in Korean. I think it was Korean. But it may have been Egyptian.

"Where is everyone? How can missionaries learn Korean if they aren't in the room?"

I didn't know what else to do, so I sat in a chair and waited. Patience is not a virtue I was blessed with, so it was harder than it sounds. I sat still for about ten minutes. A small tiger on one of the posters was standing on his hind legs and had a grin on his face. It was eerie, so I changed seats. I swear his eyes followed me to my new seat, because after I sat down his beady eyes were staring right at me. He was wearing a small, round, red hat that had long ribbons of colorful cloth connected to it. It was just odd-looking. Almost as freaky as staring cows.

I walked over to it and pulled it off the wall. "Stupid tiger." I rolled the poster and put it behind one of the chairs. I sat down and waited some more. I found myself counting the seconds on my watch and comparing it to the second hand on the clock on the wall. I was getting annoyed.

I could hear voices, faintly. Someone was in another room. Of course! I hate it when I'm dumb. It only made sense that there was more than *one* roomful of missionaries bound for Korea. I left 425 and knocked on the door across the hall. It was 424.

A young woman with dishwater blond hair and a pink dress stuck her head out of the door. Her white name tag read *Sister Nagle*.

"Hi, Sister Nagle. My name is Brother Grant." I stuck my hand out, but she didn't take it. "I'm sorry to interrupt your class, but I need your help."

"My help?"

"Yes. You are the teacher?" Because if you're not, I'm just wasting my time.

"I am the teacher. What do you need?"

"Can we talk out here? It's pretty important. Please." I tried not to sound needy, but I probably failed.

"Just a sec." She closed the door, and I waited. She was short but not petite. I decided I would like her. I could hear talking on the other side. After just a few moments, the door opened again, and she came out. She closed the door behind her.

We walked down the hallway. "Okay, ask away, Brother Grant."

"I need to know what a word means in Korean."

"What word is it?"

"I was in Seoul earlier this week, sightseeing, and I went to some place called Young San."

"No, you didn't. It's Yong San; the *o* sound is long. That's the big army post in Seoul. We teach the new elders and sisters that it's the 'oak tree *o*.' Get it? Oak because the vowel sound is long."

I bet she is a good teacher.

"Yes, thanks. What does it mean?"

"Dragon Mountain. Is that all? If you were in Seoul, you could've asked someone there."

"I meant to, but I forgot. I didn't remember to ask until I got back." Getting beat up will do that to you. She turned back to go back to her class. "Wait. Just a second."

She stopped. "Is there more?"

"Just one more question. What if it wasn't *yong*, but was *young*? What if I mistranslated?"

"I've never heard of Young San."

"No, I mean, what does the word *young* itself mean?"

"That's easy. Spirit."

It's only easy if you speak the language. "Could it mean anything else?"

"Oh sure. It probably comes from Chinese and has lots of meanings. But the most common would be a name."

"Someone's name?" It was gnawing at my head again. Hard.

"Yeah. I had a companion named Young, Sister Young. She was from northern California. Her name in Korean, when it was written, was indistinguishable from the word *spirit*. That was her nickname even, Sister Spirit." Sister Nagle snickered. "She hated it."

I would have too.

Someone's name? I had the answer I wanted, and it was coming into focus. I had all of the puzzle now; I was sure of it. I just needed to think it out, make sure it all made sense. I checked my watch. It was almost ten o'clock.

"Thank you, Sister Nagle. That was all I needed."

I walked to the end of the hallway, and then ran down the stairs out to my car.

I would have stayed longer, but a piece of the puzzle I'd been working on fell into place. It was someone's name! It had to be. It was the only thing that made sense! Not a dragon. I remembered what Tom said in the embassy. He admitted that it could have been a mistranslation, a mistake, and he was right. A name! But who was Young? A man? A woman? I had an idea.

Just then my cell phone started chirping. I lost my train of thought. I answered it before I started my engine.

"This is Grant."

It was Cook. "Grant, get up here fast!" He was excited and agitated. I could hear it in his voice.

"Why? What's happened?"

"A University of Utah police officer was found dead this morning, only a few blocks from the stadium."

"Is it connected with our business?"

"Yes! It *is* our business. Two bodies were found inside a helicopter at an abandoned National Guard armory. One was the cop. The second one hasn't been identified yet. We were at the stadium when the call came in, and we made it there in under ten minutes. The cop—Officer Myers was his name—his body was found lying on top of a large wooden crate."

"So. How is this our business?"

"As soon as I saw the bodies and the crate, I had everyone back away and leave the bodies where they were. The crate is big, Grant."

Alarms were sounding in my head. "Big enough?" I asked.

"Yes. Big enough for a Korean War–era nuclear bomb to be inside."

I started my car and slammed it into gear.

"Keep talking, Cook. Is there more?"

"Yes. We had some of the records guys at the field office do some checking on the helicopter. It was air force to begin with. The air force designation is MH-53J. They call it the Pave Low."

"And?"

"The navy uses the same helicopter, with some minor differences. Their designation is MH-53E. Grant, the navy calls this thing the Sea Dragon." He was excited and was having trouble controlling his voice. "We found our dragon, and it has a bomb in its belly!"

My heart turned cold, ice cold.

"Are you sure it's the bomb?"

Cook didn't respond right away. "No. But a radiation team is here, and they picked up some levels of radiation emitting from the box. They were low, but consistent with what to expect from a weapon almost fifty years old."

Could I be wrong? Maybe it wasn't a mistranslation. Maybe I was wrong. I can't afford to be wrong. But if I was, then the problem was solved!

"But is it a bomb? I have to know! We can't screw this up."

Cook didn't like my attitude, and his voice was stern. "No, you don't need to know. You're not in charge, Mr. Grant. The FBI is, and we are not in the business of screwing things up. I only called you as a courtesy."

"No, you didn't. You came to me when you needed my help. You may still need it."

The line was quiet for a second. "We don't know for sure that it is a bomb, and we don't know that it isn't."

"When will you know?"

"We're waiting on a team from the Dugway Proving Grounds to show up. They're out in the West Desert somewhere. They should be here within the hour, and then we'll know for sure. But if you ask me, this is it. We found the dragon in time." His tone softened. "We do need you up here for something, Grant."

Typical FBI response. Come in like gangbusters and take control, and then try to appease the local cops by offering scraps from the mighty Federal Bureau of Investigation dinner table.

"What for?"

"We need you to take a look at the other body. You may be able to identify it."

"Why would I be able to do that?"

"The body is Asian, probably Korean. We think it may be Kim Song Su. But you're the only one around that can ID him."

I felt deflated when I should have felt elation. The bad guy was caught. The bomb was found. Disaster was averted. All of the questions were answered. We'd been looking for a dragon, and we found it. It even had a bomb inside its belly. Kim Song Su and the cop must have struggled, and in their fight both suffered lethal injuries.

"How did they die?"

"You mean the cop and the other guy? We can't tell yet. Given the possible exposure to radiation, I won't let anyone, including medical personnel, near the bodies."

"Did they kill each other?"

"We can't tell. We'll be able to go inside after the Dugway team gets here."

"Okay. I'm in Provo now. I'll get there as soon as I can. I have some news for you."

"What?"

"Did Will show up for work today?" I inquired.

"No. I assumed she was with you."

"She's not."

"Then where is she, Grant? I don't have time for this."

"You will make time, I think, Cook. She is in the Salt Lake City Jail."

"Where?"

"The jail."

"Why? What are you talking about, Grant?"

I filled him in on what happened.

"I can't believe it. No. Not possible. Agent Williams is a traitor? *The* traitor? She was working for Kim Song Su and the North Koreans? But she was the attaché; this doesn't make any sense."

"On that we agree. Maybe you should ask her about it."

"Yeah. I think I will. I can't think about that now. Get up here."

"Okay, but think for a minute, Cook. Kim Song Su knew what we were looking for. The FBI attaché in Seoul was his girlfriend, and the morning of the Olympic opening ceremonies we find just what we think we should find? It's too easy."

"I don't call the work we did 'easy,' Grant. Get up here. Now."

I didn't bother responding. I hung up and concentrated on driving. I made it back to I-15 all right, but I wasn't going to go anywhere fast. Traffic was at a standstill. It must be a wreck or something. I saw an ambulance and UHP cruiser driving on the shoulder of the freeway. I turned my radio on and found KSL. The morning news show was still on.

"It should be a beautiful night for the opening ceremonies tonight for the winter Olympiad. It will be clear and cold, but not too cold. The temperature will hover around freezing. The president and the rest of you had better dress warmly." I didn't care about the weather. I could see that. What I couldn't see was why I was stuck. I sat through a round of commercials and other advertisements. No one's car moved an inch. Finally the commercials ended.

"We're getting news of a major accident on I-15, somewhere around Orem. A listener phoned in on a cell and said that a tanker had lost control on the wet freeway and flipped over. If this is true, and we're waiting for confirmation from the UHP, it means that I-15, both directions around Orem, could be closed for hours. If they don't get it cleaned up soon, this could spell disaster." I turned it off.

I knew what I needed to. I wasn't going anywhere, for a few hours at least. This is not what I needed.

I slid a Billy Joel tape into the deck and thought about what I knew.

Question: Why was Jason Russell killed?

Answer: He was making something, for someone, and he told a third person about it. Odds are that Jason Russell was to be killed anyway once his job was finished. It didn't matter that he told someone else what he was doing. The moment he agreed to do the work, Kim Song Su decided Jason Russell had to die.

Question: Who was the third person?

Answer: John Taylor of Spanish Fork, Utah. He knew something he wasn't supposed to. He knew what Jason Russell was making. And that was enough. He didn't know for whom Jason was making it; he was killed simply because Jason told him what it was. I was wrong. It did matter that Jason told a third person. It mattered very much to John Taylor.

Question: Why was the Utah County medical examiner killed?

Answer: She discovered the only physical connection between Russell and Taylor. The wounds in the armpits were caused by Kim Song Su. No. Not all of them were. Skippy did it to Taylor. My pal Skippy. But I knew the type of weapon that had been used and that Russell and Taylor were both tortured.

Question: Why was Anderson attacked?

Answer: Because we knew about the connection between Russell and Taylor. And that connection put us on the right path to . . . the answer? We knew something that scared Kim Song Su, messed up his timing. And it scared him into a desperate act. But how did Kim Song Su know Anderson and I were involved? He saw us that day in the Utah County medical examiner's office and probably listened in on our conversation with Doc Sherman. Maybe Will somehow heard about Cook coming to me and passed the info on to Kim Song Su. Still, Kim Song Su was forced to act quickly, and he failed.

Question: Why am I constantly thinking about Anderson?

Answer: I don't know. But I like it. A lot. I have to make a conscious effort not to think about her right now. It's distracting me from my work. I'm glad I didn't have a girlfriend at home waiting for me while I was on my mission. Why do I only use her last name? Do I even know her first name? I'll have to think about that later.

Question: Why try and kill me in Korea?

Answer: Because I was there. I was just as much a target as Anderson, and I was stupid for not fully appreciating it. One dumb mistake nearly cost me my life. Must be more careful.

Question: Does Kim Song Su have a nuclear weapon hidden in Salt Lake City, ready to use?

Answer: Yes. I was going to say probably, but why try and fool myself. He had it, and I had to find it. He planned to use it, and I wasn't going to let him. My gut said the helicopter Cook and the rest of them had stumbled onto was just another diversion. Like Russell, Taylor, and Sherman had been.

Question: What time is it?

Answer: According to my watch, 11:30 a.m. I've been sitting here for over an hour.

Question: Why was I having dreams about Temple Square and Dan Begay, when everyone who should know agreed that the bomb was probably someplace close to Rice-Eccles Stadium?

Answer: I don't know. Mr. Spock would tell me that logic dictates that those who are supposed to know are in fact wrong. Very wrong. This being the case if Mr. Spock was a real person and not a member of a make-believe alien race on *Star Trek*. I'm not a doctor or a bricklayer, but he was right. Assuming that my dreams meant something real, then maybe the stadium shouldn't be where we, I mean the FBI, were focusing our attentions. Kim Song Su would know that, and he would use it to his advantage. How? By creating a diversion near the stadium.

We were dealing with a man that had killed repeatedly to keep his secret quiet. Something about the bodies and the crate was bothering me. It was just too neat, too easy. It was just the way the FBI liked it: all of the loose ends are tied up. The bomb is found before it explodes. North Korea can't publicly accuse the U.S. of attempting to nuke the Chinese without exposing how they learned about the bomb and what they did with it. Kim Song Su, international terrorist extraordinaire, is found dead at the scene of his most heinous would-be crime. Disaster is averted, the FBI gets a big slap on the back, the thanks of the International Olympic Committee, the state of Utah, the United States government, and the world community. It all made sense. Too much sense. I learned many things in the FBI. One thing I learned was it never made sense. Drugs, thefts, murders, serial killers, kidnappings, bank robberies, white-collar crime, it never made much sense. Very rarely did two plus two ever equal four. It usually added up to three or five.

I couldn't explain why my nightmare was explicit in portraying Temple Square as the center of it all. I thought about the whole Mormon connection. I am a member of the Church and have a sentimental connection with Temple Square. Temple Square is in the heart of the city, and in the hearts of Church members stands next to Nauvoo in affection. Is Temple Square the key? If it is, then the FBI is wrong, and Kim Song Su has a relatively unprotected piece of real estate where he can hide the bomb. Maybe already has.

BEEEEEEP!

A car behind me was honking. The cars that had been sitting in front of me were moving now, and the person behind me wanted to as well. I put my car back in gear and headed north again. It was slow moving, but it was moving.

My watch beeped at me: 12:30 p.m. I was hungry.

I flipped on my cell phone and tried to call Cook back, but I didn't. I didn't have his number. I tried *69, but that did nothing for me. My cell wasn't working at all. I looked and it was dead. I hadn't charged it last night. Man, I hate technology.

My speedometer said I was back up to thirty-five miles per hour. I actually had to use fourth gear now. Orem was behind me, and I was almost to American Fork. When I reached the first American Fork exit, I took it. I could see a store just off the exit. Where there are stores, there are phones.

I pulled up next to a bank of outside phones along the front of the store. None of the phones were being used, so I grabbed the nearest one. I slid some change down the machine's throat and called the FBI.

"Thank you for calling the Federal Bureau of Investigation."

"I don't care what your name is, or how long you've worked for the FBI, this is Peter Grant, and I need Agent Cook's cell number, and I need it now."

"Sir, I can't give you that information."

"Yes, you can. If you want to stop a lunatic from destroying the city, then you can. It's your choice, sister."

She hesitated, and then she was gone. I was swimming in a sea of expletives and anger when I heard Cook's voice. She'd connected me. Which is better than giving me his number. I love technology.

"This is Cook."

"Hey, Adonis, it's me."

"What do you want, Grant? I'm kinda busy up here."

"I know you are, but I think you're busy in the wrong place."

"What?" He didn't like the idea of a nonagent telling him he was wrong. "You must be off your rocker, Grant. I have two bodies, one of which is Kim Song Su, and a bomb inside a dragon."

"Are you sure?"

He didn't even think about it. "Yes. One hundred percent. Absolutely."

"You weren't two hours ago. How do you know it's Kim Song Su? You've never seen him! The bomb is just a crate with some low-level radioactive junk in it. You have nothing!"

He thought for a minute this time. "Nope. You're wrong, Grant."

I tried one last time. "Don't you see? He's giving you exactly what you want. He's showing you the picture you want to see. You're finding what you expect to find in the place you expect to find it."

"I agree. But only because what we want to see is the only way it can be. He's dead and you're wrong. Now get up here and help, or I'll have you arrested for impeding a federal investigation."

I didn't bother to respond. I just hung up again.

I got back in my car and headed for the freeway. It was still congested, and my dash clock said it was almost 1:00 p.m. I knew Cook was serious, and I resolved to go to Rice-Eccles Stadium. Maybe I was wrong; maybe it wasn't a mistranslation, and I was wrong. The only way to be sure was to look at the other body and positively identify it as Kim Song Su. If it was.

My gut told me it wasn't.

For once I prayed my gut was wrong.

chapter 15

Traffic was bad all the way back to Salt Lake. I mean, it normally is anyway. But today the extra thousands of people on the road because of the Olympics made it plain awful.

I didn't reach the stadium until nearly 3:00 p.m. I stopped in front of the main gate and walked up to the entrance. Officer Harris was on duty.

"Hey, Harris. Cold?"

He was wearing a heavy coat and had a badge pinned to the outside. "Nope. Warm as can be." He clapped his gloved hands. "What can I do for you?"

"Is Agent Cook around?"

"No, but there's tons of FBI types around."

"You gotta hate that."

Harris smiled. "Tell me about it. What do you want him for anyway?"

"I need to look at something for him, and I thought he may be around here."

"Not up here. He's down at Sunnyside."

I gave him a funny look.

"It's the old armory, down Guardsman Way. I've heard some strange stuff, man."

Really? The cop rumor mill is alive and well. "What strange stuff, Harris?"

He gave a quick look around and lowered his voice. "I heard there's a dead police officer and someone else. I hear it's a terrorist, and this officer died killing him before he could blow the city to kingdom come."

"That's quite a story, Harris. You believe it?"

"I'm not sure. Maybe. Do you?"

"I never believe anything I don't see with my own eyes, and I only trust my eyes half of the time. Always trust your instincts, Harris. See ya." I headed for my car, stopped, and went back. "You got a family, Harris?"

"Yeah."

"Kids?"

"Two. Why?"

"Go home when your shift is over. Hold your kids and your wife. Tell them how much you love them. Thank your lucky stars that some terrorist did not blow the city to kingdom come. Never forget how good it feels to hold your family and how close you came to losing them. Okay?"

He stared at me and nodded.

I got in my car and headed for Sunnyside Armory.

Cop cars were everywhere. The Salt Lake PD had blocked off the end of Guardsman Way. I rolled to a stop in front of it. A patrolman dressed in a warm bomber jacket and hat was motioning me to stop. He walked over to my window, and I rolled it down.

"I'm sorry, sir, but the road is closed. You will have to turn around and go the other way."

I was tempted to do just that. "But I have some business at the armory."

"What business is that?" Arrogance and condescension dripped from his voice. He reminded me of someone I don't like. No one special, or in particular, just someone I don't like very much. I'll just pick one . . . Millhouse. Yeah, he reminded me of Millhouse.

"I'm supposed to ID a body for Agent Cook of the Federal Bureau of Investigation. So, if you'd be so kind to get out of my way, patrolman, and move that roadblock, I'd appreciate it." My tone suggested that if he didn't comply, he'd be reassigned to guard an ice truck in Greenland.

He took a step back and spoke quickly into his radio. I heard him say, "Yes, sir," four or five times. He asked me, "Your name Grant?"

"Yes," I said sweetly.

He yelled to the cops manning the road block. "Move that thing back. Let this car through."

"Thank you, patrolman."

"Agent Cook is waiting for you."

Oh goody.

I drove slowly past the mass of assembled law enforcement: city, county, state, and federal. I made the right turn onto Sunnyside, and then I pulled into the armory's parking lot. I was forced to park and get out of my car. The lot was full of vehicles and cop-type people.

Cook materialized out of nowhere. Spooky. "You're late, Grant."

"It's good to see you too, Cook."

"Follow me."

Can do. "Is it real?"

"You mean the bomb, Grant?"

We passed police cars of every make imaginable: sheriff's Blazers and vans; SLCPD Luminas and Explorers; UHP Mustangs, Camaros, and Crown Victorias; and FBI Oldsmobiles. I always wanted a Mustang, but the Bureau wouldn't allow it. Everyone we passed gave Cook a wide berth. It was like they knew Cook had the plague or was FBI. Probably both. We were at a wide gate.

"Yes, I mean the bomb."

"Of course it's real." He pointed at the ground. "We found and bagged pieces of the lock that was on the gate. It was shot to pieces."

"How do you know it's real?" Cook was being evasive. I wanted to know why. "Do you think the university officer shot the lock?"

"No. Someone else did, and Officer Myers, that's his name, found it that way."

Makes sense. "You didn't answer my question."

We went on into the compound. The lot wasn't plowed, but now there were plenty of tire ruts to walk in. I was grateful, because I wasn't wearing boots.

"What question is that?"

"How do you know the bomb is real? Has the Dugway team confirmed it?"

"No. But it's real. I know it is."

"Why hasn't the Dugway team checked it out?"

"They got stuck in traffic. I-80 is a mess. They won't get here for at least a few more hours."

"Then how do you know it's real? Have you checked it out?"

"No. No one has been allowed inside the helicopter since early afternoon. But we've searched thoroughly around it. Myers's cruiser is still here too. The scene is secure, very little contamination. Relax, Grant. This is it."

We didn't speak the rest of the way. But I wasn't relaxed. I was getting cold. Wind was swirling around the lot, making it difficult to see and chilly. Eventually, I could see the massive Dragon inside a fenced compound. I also could make out the police cruiser, but nothing else. The police established a circular perimeter around everything, and the command post was within fifteen feet of the lonely and empty cruiser. We went to the command post.

Cook introduced me to the bigwigs. He started with a man of average build and average looks. His look screamed "Chief."

"This is Chief Miller, Salt Lake City PD. Chief, this is Grant."

"Hey, Chief." I stuck out my hand, but we didn't shake.

All he said was, "You're late."

Cook went on. "Captain Johnson, Utah Highway Patrol, meet Grant."

Johnson was tall, about six foot three, and his shirt was straining to contain and cover a large amount of bulging muscles. I think his arms are bigger than my legs. I expected to hear a thick Austrian accent.

"Good to meet you, Grant. Hope you positively ID our friend in there."

Nope, he's not Austrian.

He nodded at the helicopter. I think he did anyway. He didn't have much of a neck to nod with. We shook hands, and I tried to be tough and squeeze. I didn't squeeze much, but Johnson smiled.

There were other police officers standing around. I stood next to Johnson. I was full of questions. "Cook tells me the area has been searched."

Chief Miller responded, "It has. We didn't find anything, other than Myers's shotgun. It was found about twenty feet away from his cruiser, just lying in the snow. There was some evidence that he was probably attacked where he dropped the shotgun."

"What about another car or something?"

Miller stared at me like I was an imbecile. "Myers's car is right there."

"Oh, I see that, Chief. I was just wondering how the other guy, the other one who couldn't drive away because he's dead, I was wondering how he got here."

"Who cares?" Chief Miller sounded pretty mad.

"I think you should, Cook. Two bodies and one car. I think it's safe to assume that Myers didn't offer this guy a ride. Myers drove here. How did the other guy get here?"

"That's not your concern," Miller said. "Salt Lake PD is in charge of the investigation, not the LDS Church."

He was right. But I was working for the FBI.

"Did you find a gun?"

Miller looked like he wanted to explode. His face was red, and his eyes were starting to bulge. "What gun?"

I looked at Cook. "You want to tell him, Cook?"

"Sure. Grant means the gun that was used to shoot the lock on the main gate. Myers didn't do it."

Miller still didn't get it. "There is no second gun. The lock had to have been pried apart or destroyed some other way."

"No, Miller, it was a bullet from a gun. I saw the lock pieces that were recovered," Johnson said.

Miller didn't argue with Johnson.

I wouldn't either.

"It's probably inside the chopper. We've only been able to do a quick search inside that, and it's pretty big, lots of places to hide something."

Absolutely possible, but I didn't harbor much hope for finding it.

"Can we go in, Cook?" I wanted to see the scene.

"Yes. Been waiting for you. Wanted you to see it undisturbed. The radiation levels are low and not harmful unless you're exposed for a very long time. Let's go."

The four of us headed for the chopper, the Dragon. We went through a hole in the fence. There were plenty of footprints, and it was obvious that something, or someone, had been dragged across the snow.

"This wasn't here before." Johnson meant the hole in the fence. The hole in the side of the chopper was old. Most helicopters don't fly with gaping holes in their sides.

"How long has it been here?" I meant the chopper.

Miller responded, "I'm not really sure, a few years minimum. It can't fly, and everything important has been stripped: avionics, weapons, navigation systems. The hole was cut as an entrance by the National Guard after it was brought here. It made stripping it easier."

Cook and Johnson went in first. Chief Miller and I brought up the rear.

We fanned out once inside and examined the bodies. Cook turned Myers's body over.

"We need a light."

Johnson and Miller both produced large flashlights. The kind that can be used as clubs. Cook pulled out a small penlight from his jacket. Myers's shirt was covered in blood. Probably from a wound to the heart, but I was guessing. I went over to the other body, the one we all hoped was Kim Song Su. Johnson and Miller went with me. Johnson walked around to the other side. He ended up behind the body, and Miller was looking over my shoulder. Miller flashed his light on the face. I looked at it for a few seconds. It didn't look like Kim Song Su, but bodies always look different in death. I grabbed him by the shoulders and lifted to get a closer look.

"Be careful. This is still a crime scene."

"I am careful, Chief."

It wasn't Kim Song Su.

Johnson said something.

"What, Johnson?"

"There's something written on his back. I can't make it out. Turn it over."

Miller and I turned the body over, onto the stomach. Both flashlights illuminated the back. I could see a word, but couldn't read it. I knelt down and pulled the jacket tight. I couldn't believe it. It couldn't be. I let go of the jacket and fell backward.

"Who's Skippy?" Johnson asked.

"Cook, check beneath the arms!"

"What, Grant? The arms? What for?"

"Just do it. This isn't Kim Song Su, but I think he killed them both."

Cook was at my side, staring at the word *Skippy* written in black ink on the back of the body's jacket. "What does it mean, Grant?"

"When I was in Seoul, some of Kim Song Su's cronies captured me and tortured me. I escaped, but the man who interrogated me, I called him Skippy. This is him. It's a message." I rolled him onto his back and lifted his left arm.

"Message? From who?"

"Kim Song Su. We have to get out of here now! This is a setup. It's fake. The crate is not a bomb."

"Are you sure?"

"Did you find anything beneath the arms?"

Cook checked quickly without disturbing the body very much. "Myers has a deep wound in the left armpit."

I checked the right armpit, and I found it. "Skippy has one in the right one. Kim Song Su killed them both. This is not good, Cook."

I stood and walked outside. Everyone followed. "He knew we were onto him, and he knew we were looking for a dragon."

"But how? CIA gave us that information."

"I told you how." I didn't have time to play the blame game. Cook is a good agent, and whatever troubles he and I may have, I would not show him up in front of other officers. If it needed to be done, it could be done later behind closed doors. "It was Will. Will told him everything. The North Koreans could have fed CIA the bogus transmission. They know CIA monitors communications. How doesn't matter right now. We probably have very little time. He's almost won. Don't you see, he gave you exactly what you expected to find. Myers was just more bait." I stood up. "Everything serves a purpose."

Johnson jumped in. "He's kept us busy all day. We've been out of the way now for more than six hours."

"But where is he, if this isn't it?" Cook led us away from the chopper, back into the snow.

"I don't know, Cook. I need to think. First thing, clear this place out. All nonessential personnel. Get them back on the street."

Cook looked at me. "Right. I'm on it." Cook ran off, yelling orders as he went.

"There is a dead police officer in there!" Miller was all red again.

"Yes, Chief, you're right. The crime scene is yours, and the officer is one of yours. Well, more yours than the FBI's or the state's. Do a good job." I walked away. Johnson did too. Cook was barking instructions, and I went a ways off and tried to think. I didn't think much. Any second, I expected to see a giant mushroom cloud over Salt Lake, if I lived long enough to see it. My guess was that the heat wave would hit first so I wouldn't see the cloud rise over the city.

My watch beeped at me: 6:00 p.m. Conductor was dedicating a statue on Temple Square at 6:45.

I hoped.

Johnson walked over to me. "Had trouble seeing you in the dark. Think of anything?"

"No. My thoughts are all jumbled. I can't think of anything."

"Sometimes talking about stuff, unrelated stuff, helps me."

"Okay. Tell me about yourself, Johnson."

"What do you want to know?"

"Anything. Start at the beginning. But we may not have a lot of time, so skip the boring parts."

"I have a nephew on a mission."

"Where?"

"Funny you should ask. He's a big kid, played football for the Y before he left. Will when he gets back too. He must look like a moving mountain to the people."

"What people, where, Johnson?"

"South Korea, Seoul. He comes home in a month. I got a letter from him last week. His last area was near the temple in Seoul. He says it's not the biggest temple in the Church, but it's still beautiful."

It is. And he's right—his nephew is huge. The Elder Johnson I met that night in Seoul had to be his nephew. "How long have you lived in Utah, Johnson?"

"Well, my family came west with the pioneers. They left their homes in Europe after meeting the missionaries."

"In Austria?"

"No, Wales. They eventually ended up in Nauvoo. My great-great-great-grandfather was actually in the second company to reach the Salt Lake Valley. I always thought it would have been cool if he could have been with Brigham Young when he stood on Ensign Peak and said 'This is the place.' But he wasn't. Too bad for him he wasn't in Young's company."

That was it! I had another moment . . . a good one, not a buffoon one. I saw it all. It all made sense now. "Come on, Johnson!" I took off.

"Where, Grant?" He was running next to me.

"I know where Kim Song Su is, and I know where the bomb is. We can still stop him. Let's go. Where's your car?"

"In front."

We ran across the lot in the snow. We ran to save our lives and millions more.

It was a longer run than it looked. I slipped and fell once, but got up and kept running. I was out of breath and wheezing pretty bad. Maybe I should jog more. If it didn't kill me, it would probably do me some good.

"Where are we going, Grant?"

"Temple Square."

CHAPTER 16

Captain Johnson's car is a Mustang. Nice. The roads were packed, and if I'd been in my car, it would have been very slow going. But in the white UHP Mustang, with lights flashing and sirens blaring, we made pretty good time.

"Better call the cavalry, Johnson."

"Yep." He grabbed his radio. He switched the frequency from the UHP to a general law enforcement channel. "This is Captain Johnson, Utah Highway Patrol. All available law enforcement officers converge on Temple Square. This is a 417. Be advised that the suspect is a North Korean national. Consider him armed and extremely dangerous." Then he did the same thing through the UHP dispatch. He looked at me and put the radio down. "I don't know how much good it will do. I know for a fact we're spread pretty thin. I assume the other agencies are too."

They are.

"What's a 417?"

"Terrorist attack, Mr. Grant."

A few motorists, who apparently couldn't see flashing lights or hear a siren loud enough to wake the dead, were slow to get out of our way. This made Johnson mad. When a car didn't pull over to the right, Johnson would smile a funny smile.

"Taking a picture of the license plate?" I asked.

"Yes. There's a sensor in the front bumper that is activated when the lights are on. It senses when a car directly in my path does not move. There is a five-second buffer that the car has to move, and if it doesn't, the sensor tells a small camera to take a picture of the license plate. We mail the offender a ticket."

Good for you. That was always a pet peeve of mine. I hated it when people wouldn't get out of the way like they were legally obligated to do.

"How fast can you go in this thing, Johnson?"

"Sixty-five miles per hour."

"Sixty-five? Really?"

"Yes."

"How about during a pursuit?"

"More than sixty-five miles per hour."

Okay. I like this guy.

"What are we looking for at Temple Square? I don't know what the suspect looks like, and describing him won't do me any good. Unless he has orange hair. Does he?"

"No. Last I saw, it was black."

"So what do I look for?"

"I'm not sure."

"What do you mean, you're not sure?"

"We're looking for a new statue of Brigham Young. It's being dedicated in—" I checked my watch. "In about fifteen minutes."

"A statue?'"

"If I remember right, the statue is between the Tabernacle and the North Visitors' Center. The bomb is in the base of the statue."

"How do you know?"

"The 'anonymous' donor who commissioned the statue is our terrorist."

"Are you sure?"

"Yes. I have to be right."

"Why do you have to be right?"

"If I'm wrong, we all die."

Johnson paused for a minute. "Good reason."

We were on Fourth South heading west.

"Turn right onto State Street."

"You want me to drop you off at the North Temple entrance?"

I nodded.

The closer we got to Temple Square, the heavier traffic became, and there must have been tens of thousands of people swarming everywhere. The lights and siren didn't do much. The skyscrapers created a canyon that sucked the sound of the siren and swallowed it. When we passed the federal building, I said, "Turn off the siren."

North Temple was packed, and even though the lights were still on, we moved slowly. It wasn't really anyone's fault that they couldn't get out of the way. There just wasn't anywhere to go.

"Give me your cell phone." I had to warn Conductor. I dialed the number and waited. The line was dead. Unlike mine, this phone had a full charge; it just wasn't getting through. "Lines are jammed. Kim Song Su is here. I feel it."

We were at the Church Office Building now.

"Just let me off here. Park and go in Temple Square. You'll see where the ceremony will be. Hang in the background, and try to find some high ground. A good angle."

"Okay." Johnson knew what I was talking about.

"On second thought, use your judgment and get as close as you think safe."

"Okay. Good luck, Grant."

"You too, Johnson."

"You really protect the prophet?"

"I try to."

I jumped out, and the Mustang continued west down North Temple. There were people and Olympic-themed vendors everywhere. I ran across the street, avoiding cars as I went, then through the block where the Church Office Building stood to the Main Street Plaza in front of Temple Square.

I was inside Temple Square now, but on the wrong side. People bundled up in the cold were packed onto Temple Square. Temple Square is divided into two parts by a wall running north to south. The Temple sits in the northeastern corner. I was in the eastern side, and I had to get to the western side. There is only one way for members to gain admission to the Salt Lake Temple, and that is through the main entrance. But there are two ways out. One is through the main entrance, but the other is by an exit in the north end. Most of the wedding parties use this exit. I ran for the wedding exit.

A Church security guard is stationed there at all times when the temple is open. It was open now. It sits above ground. A short tunnel takes patrons from the temple to a very short flight of stairs. The stairs lead up and out. The security guard sits at the top of the stairs. I reached the exit and ran inside. The guard sitting there didn't know me. He looked startled and upset because I was running on temple grounds. Before he could admonish me to be more reverent, I told him to be calm.

"Be calm. My name is Grant. Conductor is in immediate danger. Get on your radio and call every law enforcement agency you can think of. If your radio won't work, use land lines. This is not a joke. Do it." I ran past him, down the flight of stairs that leads to the tunnel and the temple. At the base of the stairs patrons can go to their right and back to the temple. To the left is a door marked:

AUTHORIZED PERSONNEL ONLY

For this door I am authorized, but it needs the magnetic card key to unlock it. I used mine and pushed it open. I was beneath Temple Square now.

* * *

Conductor was in a good mood. It was a beautiful day, and the Olympics had brought an unprecedented number of visitors to Temple Square. It seemed as if Temple Square hadn't had a slow moment in over two or three weeks. He had a strong appreciation for Brigham Young. Like many members, he could trace his family back to pioneer times. His great-grandfather and grandfather both had known Brigham Young well, and they revered him for the great leader that he was. He grew up hearing countless stories about the man and his accomplishments. Conductor also thought it fitting that the Church should have a statue of President Young on Temple Square. Brigham Young was not only a great prophet and leader, but he was also the only Church leader to be recognized by the United States government in the Great Americans Hall in the Capitol building. And what better way for the Church to celebrate the opening of the second winter Olympics in Utah than by honoring the great leader who brought the Saints to Utah.

The statue was donated, but the donor had agreed to the Church's stipulations on how the statue should look. Conductor hadn't actually seen the completed piece, not with the base anyway. And it was hidden now by a large blue canvas tarp. The donor was supplying the base and had worked it all out with the artist. The donor had only insisted that he be anonymous, which really wasn't that strange a request. The Church is given dozens of things a year by anonymous donors.

Conductor was saddened deeply when the young artist had died in a terrible fire. He was planning on asking the young man to do more pieces of art for the Church. He was very talented, and Conductor felt a special bond with the young man from Springville.

Saddened as he was by the artist's death, he was grateful that somehow the statue of Brigham Young had been saved. It had been moved apparently the day before the fire, to a warehouse in Salt Lake. The only missing piece had been the base, and as promised, the donor had provided it. All was ready now for the grand unveiling and dedication.

All except for the donor's missing representative. The man was almost late. Conductor had never met the man but was given a rough physical description and his name. He was the donor's agent, and if the donor trusted him, then it was none of Conductor's business. What was his business was the ceremony to present the statue, and the man had two minutes to show up before he was officially late. And then Conductor would start without him.

It was chilly outside, and he could see his breath in the air. But Conductor wanted to do this under the February stars. He was dressed warmly. Dedicating the statue the same night as the Olympic opening ceremonies did cause some logistical headaches. But he was confident everything would work out.

The donor's man arrived, none too soon. Conductor saw the man approach the newly made temporary podium. But he wasn't sure it was him until he began to climb the steps. What did he call himself? Chang. His name was Chang, and he had a cane with him. He wasn't limping though.

* * *

The tunnel ends in the North Visitors' Center. The lower level men's bathroom has a door marked "Maintenance." There is no knob on the bathroom side, but there is from the tunnel side. I opened it and went inside. It was empty, so I thankfully didn't get someone telling me that stall number 2 needed toilet paper.

The North Visitors' Center is the largest one at Temple Square. If I was right, the dedication would happen at approximately the middle of it. Outside, of course. I knew from experience that most people would use the east entrance because it was the one nearest the north gate. So I headed for the west entrance of the visitors' center.

There were people still inside, not wanting to go out in the cold until the dedication ceremony actually began. I was hoping to see other security personnel but hadn't yet. I went through the double doors and was outside. I moved my gun from its holster to my jacket pocket. I couldn't see Johnson.

Conductor stood on a portable podium. The mayor of Salt Lake and one of Utah's senators was with him. So was Scott Bartlett, former FBI, my friend, and number two man on my team. There was someone walking to the podium and up the steps. I walked as quickly as I could without attracting attention or knocking baby strollers over. The lights focused on the podium meant that anyone on it would have a difficult time seeing the crowd, but the crowd could see them just fine. I could see who it was now: Kim Song Su. He was using a cane, but not putting any real weight or pressure on it. The mustache was gone. They were shaking hands.

* * *

Conductor welcomed Chang and shook his hand. He felt something, an odd sensation, and he didn't like it. It reminded him of an experience he'd had as a missionary. When he was in Liverpool, there had been a stranger who followed Conductor and his companion everywhere. This stranger never spoke to them, only to people that they visited, after they were gone. One such couple told the missionaries about it and how the odd man made them feel. "It's just a different feeling than when you are here. We don't like him." One afternoon, Conductor approached the man, only wanting to greet him in a friendly way and maybe teach him the gospel. They shook hands, and Conductor never forgot what he felt. It was a sense of evil. He never saw the man again, and he stopped harassing the people they taught.

Now, sixty years later, he felt this from Chang. He was evil. Conductor didn't withdraw his hand in terror or fear; he knew who had the greater power and didn't fear for his life. But there were other people here. He couldn't show his comprehension that Chang was here to do . . . do what?

Chang—he doubted now that it was the man's real name— shook the hands of the other invited dignitaries. After everyone on the podium was seated, Conductor spoke into the microphone and addressed the crowd. He had to get a message out, to the police, Church security, anyone.

"Brothers and sisters, it is my great pleasure to welcome you all here tonight, as we join in solemn dedication of this new statue of Brigham Young that will beautify and grace Temple Square for years to come. It depicts the Church's second president as a young man, full of life and strength. Wisdom is on his brow, and skill in his hands. He does not have a beard." He rubbed his chin. "I wonder how I would look with a beard." The crowd laughed politely. "As many of you know, Brigham Young didn't grow a beard until later in life, after he saw some of his associates, like William E. McLellin, become apostate."

I didn't quite believe my ears; did Conductor really say, "William E. McLellin"? McLellin was in the first Quorum of the Twelve organized by Joseph Smith. He didn't last long as an Apostle. He left the Church a few years after his ordination to the Twelve and became one of the Church's, and Joseph Smith's, bitterest critics and enemies. Use of his name, followed by "apostate," anywhere near Temple Square indicates the highest state of emergency for LDSSS. If we hear a General Authority use it, then it means he is in danger himself. We protect him then, any way we can.

Bartlett was the man nearest Conductor, and he jumped on his back, forcing him to his knees. Now, the only way to Conductor was through Bartlett. I was only fifteen feet away from the podium, but it may as well have been a mile. The crowd saw Bartlett do his job, and they erupted with a surge of fear and panic. People were running, screaming, knocking each other down. I felt like I was in the ocean, swimming against its pull, and I was going nowhere fast.

Kim Song Su reacted quickly too. Almost too quickly. Kim Song Su didn't know how, but somehow the old Conductor knew what was about to happen. Kim Song Su decided to kill him first, then destroy the city. The senator was next to him, and they stood at the same time. Song Su elbowed him in the stomach, causing the senator to double over in pain. The mayor saw what he did and jumped off the podium. Song Su grabbed the end of his cane and pulled out a long thin knife that was hidden inside. He lunged at Conductor.

Bartlett's instinct and years of training took over. He kept his head up, scanning the crowd for any possible threats. His peripheral vision caught movement behind him, and at the last moment he rolled. The blow aimed for the base of his skull instead pierced his right shoulder. He rolled the opposite way, trying to break the attacker's grip on the weapon, and it worked.

Bartlett tried to grab the weapon, but he was right-handed, and his arm wasn't working properly. He couldn't grip it. All he could do was lie on top of Conductor and shield him from other attacks. Bartlett could hear sirens above the noise and confusion. The cavalry had arrived.

Kim Song Su couldn't believe it. He saw a huge muscular man running at the podium. He recognized the man's uniform as Utah Highway Patrol. Song Su knew he was running out of time, and while he would miss the pleasure of killing Conductor with his bare hands, he could still destroy them all. He was ready to die. He reached into his jacket pocket and pulled out a small device. To anyone else, it looked like a remote control. And it was, but it wouldn't turn on a TV or open a garage door.

I had seen Kim Song Su pull something out of his pocket. I'd seen him attack Conductor and Bartlett. I didn't know if Conductor was dead or alive. I'd seen Bartlett, my friend and compatriot, go down, protecting, doing his job. But it was obvious he was hurt. That alone was enough for me. I was through the crowd now and had a clear shot. I leveled my Glock and squeezed the trigger three times.

POP! POP! POP!

People who have never been around guns think that when they are fired, they make a loud, disturbing noise. They don't. They sound like a firecracker exploding.

I ran to the podium.

Kim Song Su knew he was dying. He'd been hit three times. His heart had been pierced by a .40 slug. His motor responses were failing quickly. He couldn't use his hands and was on his knees now. Breathing was difficult; he was wheezing.

He was so close to fulfilling his ultimate dream. He was so close to repaying the U.S. for killing his father, mother, and brother. The United States, destroyer of the peaceful life he should have had in Kwang Ju, had to pay. Hurting America and her puppets was what he lived for. His entire adult life had been geared toward the ultimate goal that now was so close.

His eyes wouldn't focus. He couldn't see the tarp-covered statue.

Even with his life quickly draining away, Kim Song Su rallied his remaining strength. He concentrated and could feel his fingers grip the control in his right hand . . . Good.

Then it was gone from his hand.

I reached Kim Song Su and kicked a small black device out of his hand. It ended up a few feet away. We stared at each other, and I think he tried to spit at me.

"You lose, Skippy."

EPILOGUE

It's Thursday, March 2, in the evening, and I'm at the hospital. I went home, after leaving police headquarters in Salt Lake City following a debriefing. I slept for about seven hours. When I got up, I showered, ate, and headed south to Happy Valley. I mean, Utah County. But from now on, for me at least, it will always be Happy Valley. I've seen quite a bit of Anderson since I shot Kim Song Su; we've seen each other every day. She looks great and is doing wonderful. Dr. Crockett, minus his lavalava, predicts a full recovery. We have standing plans for a date when she gets out of the hospital. Which will hopefully be soon. Until then, I am content to walk with her around UVRMC as much as possible. She was mad at me for not keeping her fully informed, but she forgave me. After all, I did save Salt Lake City, the Olympics, thousands and thousands of lives, and Conductor. Heroes have to be forgiven, don't they? We've talked about visiting Korea together. I would like that. Maybe I can get the Johnsons' nephew to be our guide. He probably knows some good places to eat. She plans to continue her career as a police officer, and I can live with that. I'm just not sure I can live without her.

It has been almost three weeks since that night at Temple Square. Conductor was not injured in the attack. In fact, he's already back doing what he loves: visiting Church members in Asia. The statue's base was confiscated by the feds and the weapon neutralized. The statue itself is on Temple Square. It's just bolted to the ground. It doesn't have a base and never will. Millhouse is still a detective with the Utah County sheriff's office, for now. Give him some time, and he'll be a parking enforcement officer at Provo High School. Mrs. Taylor never left her home in Spanish Fork. I admire her for that; I wouldn't have left either. Scott Bartlett will be all right. His injury was painful but not life threatening. When he's able, he will take my place as team leader.

The desk sergeant at the Salt Lake City police station did call KSL before calling the FBI. It didn't really do anything. Will still ended up in federal custody, as it should be. But KSL did ask a lot of the right questions, and the FBI was forced to come up with the right answers. Will is back in Virginia now, being debriefed and interrogated. That should take three to five years. During that time the United States attorney for the district of Utah will indict and prosecute her. It will never go to trial. She will do the smart thing and cut a deal that will keep her out of a maximum-security prison. Hopefully, the buzz generated by KSL will mean the public will demand that she be given a life sentence in a maximum-security prison. That's what she deserves, and what I hope she gets.

I still haven't heard from Just Tom. I wonder how he's doing. Maybe I should call him. I'm hoping to get his e-mail. Agent Cook has been promoted and sent to Quantico, Virginia. The director of the FBI presented him with the Medal of Distinguished Service and gave him a soft pat on the head. For the next few years, Cook will be an instructor at the FBI academy. Apollo will actually instruct new agents and teach them how to be good at their job. Good for him. He's still the blond Greek-god-like brother I never wanted. I miss him. But I miss hangnails too.

As for me, I plan on retiring, again. I'm still young, and officially I haven't retired yet from anything. But I am leaving Church security. I am going to miss Conductor very much. He is more than a Church leader to me; he is my friend. I haven't told him yet that I'm leaving. But he probably already knows. I asked him how he knew Kim Song Su was evil, and he just smiled. I look forward to his counsel for years to come. Right now my plan is to devote all of my time to my consulting firm, help people with their problems, stuff like that. We'll see. Maybe I'll put an ad in the yellow pages. I doubt I'll get a sign, but you never know.

Will was wrong. I was not responsible for Dan's death. I am not a monster. I think I always knew that, and many people told me that. But I had to let go of the guilt. Sometimes that's easier than it sounds. I still dream about Dan. But now he's not dying in my arms while I desperately, in vain, try to save him. Now we go fly-fishing, and no one dies. I think he likes Anderson too. I finally forgave myself for what happened. I still miss him, and always will. I don't remember the pain anymore, just all the good times we shared.

Kim Song Su is gone. I faced the real monster and won. I didn't lose my life or who I am. I'm still Peter Grant. I'm the same man I was the minute before Agent Cook walked in my door over four weeks ago. Song Su doesn't haunt my life or my dreams. And he never will.

On the way down to visit Anderson, I stopped at a bookstore and picked up some things: a do-it-yourself book that I hope contains all of the secrets for painting a house properly and a copy of *The Fellowship of the Ring* by J. R. R. Tolkien. Maybe we'll read it together. I also picked up a picture frame. Anderson gave me a picture.

It's going on my desk.

ABOUT THE AUTHOR

Keith V. Morris was born November 30, 1970, in Honolulu, Hawaii, in a pink U.S. Army hospital. Eventually his parents settled in Marysville, California. He is the middle child of seven and the second of five boys. He graduated from Lindhurst High School in 1989 and served a mission for the Church in the Korea Seoul Mission from January 1990 to December 31, 1991. He married his best friend, Kerri J. Godbold, on June 4, 1992, in the Oakland California Temple, and they are the parents of three beautiful daughters: Miranda, Madison, and Katherine. Keith graduated from Weber State University in 1998 with a bachelor's degree in criminal justice and entered law school in 1999. He graduated from Franklin Pierce Law Center in Concord, New Hampshire, in 2002. He passed the California Bar in 2003 and is a Deputy District Attorney for Del Norte County in Crescent City, California.